# Pregnant Protector
## Anne Marie Duquette

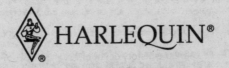

HARLEQUIN®

TORONTO • NEW YORK • LONDON
AMSTERDAM • PARIS • SYDNEY • HAMBURG
STOCKHOLM • ATHENS • TOKYO • MILAN • MADRID
PRAGUE • WARSAW • BUDAPEST • AUCKLAND

ISBN 0-373-71283-9

PREGNANT PROTECTOR

Copyright © 2005 by Anne Marie Duquette.

**Printed in U.S.A.**

To Urk.

**Books by Anne Marie Duquette**

**HARLEQUIN SUPERROMANCE**

Don't miss any of our special offers. Write to us at the following address for information on our newest releases.

Harlequin Reader Service
U.S.: 3010 Walden Ave., P.O. Box 1325, Buffalo, NY 14269
Canadian: P.O. Box 609, Fort Erie, Ont. L2A 5X3

# CHAPTER ONE

*May, Monday morning*

DETECTIVE NICK CANTELLO of the San Diego PD's homicide squad sat in shocked silence in the shift lieutenant's office, and he wasn't a man who shocked easily.

*My partner's dead? Julio's dead?*

He must have spoken the words aloud.

"Tough break," said the shift lieutenant, a big, beefy cop named Joe Lansky.

"Why the hell didn't you call me?" Nick's normally smooth baritone was hoarse and grating. His lean face was pale under his tan. "Why didn't *anyone* call me?"

"We tried, Cantello. Your cell didn't pick up and you weren't at home. Homicide rode by." Lansky's eyes were filled with compassion.

Nick was too stunned to see it. As a man who loved deep-water boating but couldn't afford a decent boat on his salary, he regularly paid for a weekend charter down to Mexican waters. Just as he had this weekend. But he always carried his cell phone charged, and he'd come straight to work Monday morning directly from the harbor, riding Julio's motorcycle.

"Someone should have called! You should have kept trying." Shock gave way to a sudden, horrible thought. "Oh, my God…his family. Does Lilia know?"

At Lansky's nod, Nick felt a painful twist in his gut. Julio and Lilia Valdez had two kids and a third on the way. In his soft, quiet way, Julio had told Nick the good news over a beer two nights ago.

"How did he die?" Nick asked.

Lansky spit out a foul expletive. Then, "It's bad…"

Nick doubted he could feel worse than he did right now. "Give it to me."

"MVA Friday night."

*Motor vehicle accident.*

"It was raining," Nick said with particular emphasis that only locals could understand. It had rained steadily all the way to the harbor, an uncomfortable event for even a man as experienced with motorcycles as he was. Southern California's desert climate made rain a rare event, something people talked about. It also provided both law enforcement and the public with a lot of grief. The freeways connecting Tijuana/San Diego/Los Angeles/Hollywood carried the densest traffic in North America. The desert climate meant no measurable rain for months. When rain did arrive, months of embedded oil floated to the surface on heavily used roads. Everything from local streets to packed interstates became almost oil slicks. For local drivers who had little practice driving in rain, vehicular accidents skyrocketed in those first wet thirty minutes. Then came the infamous California pileups, with the accompanying injured and dead.

Lansky nodded. "Yeah. His—your car—spun out. I understand you two swapped keys in the parking lot. Why'd you take his bike?"

The "bike" was a huge Harley-Davidson motorcycle, for Julio and Nick had met at a SDPD motorcycle fund-raiser and had hit it off instantly. When both were promoted and transferred to the detective unit, neither had to ask the other to be his partner.

"Julio's wife called right before the shift ended. Said the refrigerator wasn't working. The repairman couldn't get there until the next morning. She needed him to pick up some ice. So we swapped." Guilt stabbed through his pain. "If anyone should have spun out in the weather, it should have been me on the bike...not him. Hell, my tires are brand-new." An uncomfortable pause told Nick more bad news was coming. "What?"

"There's more. Someone took a shot at the car in the rain. *Your* car," Lansky said pointedly.

For a moment, Nick fought to prevent being violently ill. He took a deep breath, like a raw rookie viewing his first homicide scene.

"Julio left the office when you did. It was after rush hour, Cantello. Traffic was moving, but not that fast, with the rain. Julio spun out right after the shot was fired. We got cell phone reports from other drivers on the scene and we've been interviewing them all weekend."

Traffic on Southern California freeways was congested day and night, Sundays and holidays included. Beach exits were standstills in the summer. Tempers flared. Drive-by shootings in slow, crawling congestion were no novelty. Like earthquakes and wildfires, road rage was a price to be paid for living in the Sunbelt's beach paradise and driving its massive freeway system.

Nick swallowed hard. "Did…did Julio take a hit, or just the car?"

"We don't know yet. The divers are still trying to recover the vehicle, but it's been all weekend, and still nothing. That shot sent Julio straight into the ocean. We had a chopper on-site, but by the time rescue got there…" Even the gruff veteran couldn't finish.

*Julio drowned, and I was off on a pleasure cruise with a damn cell phone that didn't pick up in Mexican waters. It's my fault.* Nick's heart seemed to stop as he realized, *That should have been me. I had his bike. He had my car.*

Nick echoed the words of all loved ones during tragedy. "I can't believe it. Are you sure?"

"We interviewed more than twenty callers over the weekend."

"Did they find the shooter? Description of vehicle?" He didn't ask the question he usually asked, *What about motive?* He desperately tried, but for the life of him he couldn't get the words out.

"Nothing. The captain contacted the local gang specialists, but initiations usually involve members of another gang. Never cops. We'll be checking out more after the autopsy. In the meantime—" Lansky drew in a deep breath "—the department's handling the funeral arrangements. Julio's wife and kids have left to stay with family in Mexico until then. She said she'd call you in a few. You need to check in with the captain and take some time off."

Nick issued an earthy expletive, which miraculously loosened the constriction of his throat. "I switched vehicles with my partner, he ends up dead, I might be tied to the real motive and you want me to go home?" Nick swore again.

Lansky's reaction was mild. He even shrugged.

"I didn't say home. You'll probably get desk duty. Take it up with the captain after roll call."

Nick said nothing as his lieutenant rose from his chair. Sorrow had largely replaced shock now, but the guilt was still there when Lansky called the roll and started the fifteen-minute morning briefing. Nick ignored the other members of the squad—the lucky ones who still had their partners—and listened to Lansky skip Julio's name on the roster. It hurt, almost as much hearing the news the first time.

Lansky reviewed what new information SDPD had gathered from the cell phone callers over the weekend—which wasn't much. "Funeral details will be posted later on. As always, full dress," Lansky ordered.

The silence in the downtown San Diego squad room was broken by a whispered, "I knew that rain meant bad luck."

During funerals held for Southern California cops,

it always seemed to rain. This, in water-rationed San Diego. Always. Half the shaken cops in the room would probably repeat the old superstition—cops who rarely cried on the job, but waited until they were home with their lovers or spouses or six-packs of beer.

"Any other comments?" Lansky asked. "No? We're still investigating the possibility that the killer was targeting Cantello."

Nick felt the eyes in the room turn toward him.

"So far, we have no motive. The captain himself will be coordinating with Homeland Security. If anyone has any leads, come to us. As I told you before, expect overtime. This is one of our own."

Nick's lips tightened into a thin line. *I should be in charge of this. He was my partner.*

"Keep your eyes open," Lansky continued as he picked up his uniform hat. "The same goes for your wallets, boys and girls. For those of you who missed seeing me over the weekend, I'm collecting for Valdez's wife and kids. Contribute on your way out."

"Baby showers, birthdays, retirement parties—now this," someone mumbled. "Any more collections and I'll need a second job."

Nick recognized the bleak attempt at humor, and wished it had been from anyone other than that particular guy. Nick didn't particularly like Homicide's T. J. Knox. In fact, he found him just as irritating as his father, Sergeant Richard Knox. Nick tended to avoid both men. Still, he couldn't fault the son's generosity. The bill in T.J.'s hand was a large one.

Nick didn't bother with his wallet. He quickly scribbled out a check, instead, then ripped it out with a vicious yank that tore a tiny chunk off the corner.

"Here, Joe." He folded it and dropped it into Lansky's hat.

Lansky unfolded the check and deliberately eyed the first digit and subsequent three zeros before the decimal point.

Nick snatched the check out of Lansky's beefy fingers and stuffed it back into the hat. "Mind your own damn business."

"You cops *are* my business. The captain's still waiting to see you."

"I said I'm not going home," Nick ground out.

"So tell Girard, not me. I'm just passing on the message." Lansky's eyes were already on the next contributor. "Is that all you can give? Now Cantello here, there's a man who knows how to donate. Look at *his* check."

Nick's face burned as Lansky retrieved his check and waved it in the offender's face.

*Damn that Lansky. Damn dress uniforms and funerals. And damn Julio's killer to hell.*

CAPTAIN EMIL GIRARD WAS waiting as Nick stepped into his office. Seated at his desk, his boss looked thin and faded, almost to the point of frailty. But the correct impression of an elderly man soon to retire vanished when you noticed his eyes—alert and intelligent. Girard's body might be past its peak, but his mind still functioned in high gear.

"Sorry about Valdez. We tried to track you down," Girard said quietly, gesturing toward a chair. "You don't have a house phone, do you?"

Nick shook his head and sat. He thought having an economical cell phone voice-mail system was enough. Sunbelt house phones were expensive, and like many practical residents, he did without one, using his cell exclusively for his personal calls; he had a police cell for work. Unfortunately, California's cell towers couldn't always handle heavy traffic or Mexican waters.

"How are you holding up?" Girard asked.

Nick's response was clipped. "A hell of a lot better than his family. I didn't even get to talk to them! I want to work this case, Captain. I've got a high percentage of solves, and—"

"I'm familiar with your record, Detective," Girard interrupted softly. "Just as I'm sure you're familiar with policy. It's against procedure for you to investigate your partner's death."

Nick was prepared. "Then I'll quit and investigate this case myself. I *am* this case. Julio died, when it should've been me. And with or without my badge, I'll do whatever it takes to bring the man in, procedure be damned. Take your pick—it's your call."

Girard looked away. Nick rose and reached for his police-issue 9 mm. "Fine. You have my resignation—effective immediately."

"Sit down, Detective. You can stay."

"I can?" Nick couldn't believe it. "No refusal, lecture or a trip to the police psychologist before forced desk duty or a leave of absence?"

"Later. Your co-workers warned me you'd pull a stunt like this. We need your help now. That *is* what you want, isn't it?" Girard asked.

"Yes. What's the catch?"

"You need a partner to watch your back."

"I already have…" For the first time, the full impact of his loss sunk in. He didn't have a partner. He *had* a partner. Julio was dead.

Nick's hazel eyes narrowed. "I don't need a babysitter."

"Until we know more, you get one. She's a cop, it's her job and you have to sleep sometime." Girard handed Nick a file from across the desktop. "Consider yourself joined at the hip until this case is solved."

Nick read the name on the file. "Lara Nelson? Doesn't ring a bell."

"She's never worked San Diego Downtown. She works Pacific Beach and La Jolla."

If he hadn't been so grief-stricken, Nick would have felt envious. The seaside section of San Diego called Pacific Beach sprawled north from Mission Bay and Sea World. P.B., as locals called it, teemed with bronzed surfers, college students, bars, nightclubs and comedy clubs. P.B. ran smack into La Jolla's multimillion-dollar cliffside homes of the rich and famous—San Diego's version of Los Angeles' Malibu Beach. And it definitely lacked the crime other parts of San Diego had.

Grief didn't quite suppress his curiosity. "How'd she manage that beat?"

"She's just come off compassionate leave. We're easing her back in."

Nick avoided the too-sensitive subject of compassionate leave.

"Besides, the Nelsons breed and train canines for us. We want them to keep providing those dogs. Nelson Kennels are the best, Cantello. The best."

"She's not a detective?"

"No, K-9."

"That's no help!"

"Doesn't matter. She and her dog also do private bodyguard work. She'll keep you in one piece. And she'll understand your feelings. She just buried her fiancé—I understand he flew choppers for the hospital up near Yosemite." The captain paused. "Anyway, she passed her psych evaluations. I want her to keep an eye on you. Emotional men with guns shouldn't be working the streets alone—or at all, for that matter. If Lara Nelson tells me you've slipped up, you go on desk duty."

Nick swallowed hard at the thought of his new partner. He couldn't work up resentment against anyone who felt the pain of loss he now experienced.

"Or," Girard continued, "straight to the seventh floor."

Nick didn't want a trip to the police psychology unit.

Profilers and counselors worked on the seventh floor. The only therapist he'd ever seen had been years ago during mandatory testing interviews for all rookies in the academy. A private person, he hadn't enjoyed the experience, though he'd been classified as normal. His innate honesty would compel him to admit that he wasn't feeling normal now.

At present, he barely kept a lid on his emotions. And that inner whisper, the one saying he should have kept his own car in the rain, received the original phone call, come in and gone straight to "the scene," had to be kept quiet. Because of a pleasure trip, others had supported his friend's wife and two young sons. He hadn't even seen them after the death and before they'd left for Mexico! What kind of cop wasn't there for his partner's family? He had to call them as soon as possible.

Nick realized Girard was still talking. "…inter-agency cooperation. We've got the feds looking into this one. And Lara Nelson's objectivity could be a plus. Lansky agrees."

Nick's eyebrows rose. "Lieutenant Lansky?"

"Yes. He and I both knew Lara's mother—she was a cop—when she worked K-9," Girard explained. "The Nelsons aren't outsiders. I trust them. So does he."

"But the lieutenant's—" Nick broke off. He'd been about to say: *As close to retirement as you.*

A pause. "We won't let Julio's death go unsolved. Your job is to provide information. Nelson's is to keep you alive."

"Get someone from Homicide. She'll hold me back."

"Not as much as if you tried to do this as a civilian."

Nick backed off, knowing he'd pushed his luck as far as he could. He reached for the file and reopened it, scanning the photo. Lara Nelson, white, late twenties. She looked somewhat nondescript, as did most subjects in the small official photos. Her record showed brains and nerve. The blue eyes beneath blond bangs in the photograph spoke of determination, not foolishness. But then, determination hadn't kept his partner alive. Nick took a deep breath.

"When do I meet her?"

"She's waiting down the hall. For now, we've given her an office here instead of at K-9. You go where she says. And Cantello, no driving. Give yourself some time to get your feet back under you."

The meeting was over. Nick headed for the door, immediately using his cell to call the family in Mexico. There was no answer, nor did any answering machine pick up. He called again, with the same result.

Sympathetic looks followed him as he headed for the office. Nick ignored them all. He wasn't ready for sympathy. Sympathy never eased the pain of a death. He'd seen the families of too many victims to believe it did. Justice helped a little—sometimes. Nick's heart ached anew for Julio's widow and children. Even a marriage that included kids didn't always make for happily ever after. Not if one parent was a cop.

Nick knocked at the closed door of the spare office and stepped back as a woman with a big German shepherd at her side opened the door. He found himself meeting the eyes of a woman who didn't hide her emotions. She might be a stranger who never knew Julio, but he knew that sympathetic look of pain couldn't be faked. It hit him hard. He felt a powerful urge to reach out and pull her close.

"Officer Nelson?" he said instead.

She nodded, her eyes unblinking, her tanned face framed by head-hugging short blond curls. The simplicity of it suited her, Nick noticed objectively. He also noticed she wasn't very tall, small even for a female cop. But he knew that brains often made up for brawn. With her dog, he suspected she had all the brawn she needed.

"Detective Cantello." She reached for his hand and held it tightly. "Sorry to meet under these circumstances." Only after releasing his hand did she turn briskly to the door to close it behind him and gesture toward the chair.

She ordered her dog to sit in German, the language the animals were traditionally trained to follow. Before 9-11, most police dogs were obtained in Germany, and though they weren't now, law enforcement continued to use German commands. This prevented the dog from responding to a criminal's English-language commands.

Nick watched her dog sit strategically at the side of the desk where it could watch both partner and newcomer. Lara Nelson moved with strength and grace, and so did her dog, a large female, mostly tan, with black markings on the face, ears and legs.

Lara introduced Nick to Sadie, then asked outright,

"You have any problems with me, now's the time to say so."

He appreciated her bluntness, and suddenly the words spilled out. "I don't want a bodyguard. I only agreed to this to keep from getting a desk job during the case. I refuse to stay sidelined or holed up someplace, and I intend to find Julio's killer with or without your help." The words came out more harshly than he'd intended. "Or your company." He defiantly stood.

She didn't. Her hand dropped from her dog's head, and her soft, feminine look was replaced by a surprising toughness.

"I'm in charge of your safety," she said. "My partner and I are now your shield. If I have to use my training and my dog to make you follow my orders, I will. Sadie comes from my parents' kennels. They train only the best dogs, and they gave me the best of the best. Would you like a demonstration of our ability to keep you in line?"

She didn't even move from her chair. "Sadie, *Zur Wache!*" Immediately the shepherd changed from adoring pet to dangerous guard dog. Nick realized Lara's hostess act had nothing on her dedication to duty.

"No need," he said, annoyed yet respecting her stand. "I'll take your word for it."

"Wise move. My mother was a K-9 handler. One of my older sisters works K-9 with the bomb squad. The other works K-9 Search-and-Rescue. Our dogs will do anything for us. If you deliberately work against me and anything happens to the public, to Sadie or to me as a result…" She left the words unfinished.

"I won't do anything to risk anyone else. You have my word." *There's been enough death already to go around.*

"Then we understand each other." With a single command, Sadie relaxed. Lara leaned forward on the desk, the hint of restrained power remaining in both woman and canine. "That being said, I am not in charge of your emotions, Detective. Nor am I your superior when it comes to law enforcement. As you *are* an officer of the law, I don't think restricting your movements and hiding is needed at this time."

Nick's head jerked up. "No safe house?"

"No official safe house, but my house. Definitely safe," she emphasized. "With the Valdez family in Mexico, we'll need you to cover ground only they would know."

Nick found himself quite speechless for the second time that day. There was something in the way she held her head, a quiet dignity about her, that spoke volumes.

"So I'll be able to investigate Julio's murder unhampered?" he managed to ask.

"As long as you let me protect you. You'll follow my orders for your safety. To do that, I remain at your side until this case is solved." She brushed away a speck of dust from the desk and met his gaze straight on. "If your...activities interfere with that, then and only then will I feel the need to curtail your actions by any means necessary. That includes reporting to your superior and mine—that's Captain Girard." There was steel in the voice coming from that delicately boned face. "Until I get back to K-9."

"Got it," he said, his voice grating like gravel. "Appreciate your understanding, Officer Nelson."

"Hey. He was your *partner*." Her businesslike manner slipped more than a little as she smiled. "My car's outside. Let's roll. And please, call me Lara."

THE K-9 SQUAD CAR computer display and communication unit kept track of messages as Lara and Nick rode in silence. Sadie sat alertly in the back, Nick's bag of clothes from the weekend on the floor beneath. Nick felt strange sitting next to her, instead of Julio, during the drive toward the pricey homes perched on the cliffs of the La Jolla shoreline. As the squad car approached her home, he took in everything with a trained observer's eye: the white stucco front, the riot of flowers, the carefully manicured lawn. His gaze skipped over the expensive foreign cars to the frothing shoreline far below. As the Pacific sparkled and crashed green-blue in the sun, he thought of his own small apartment in an older blue-collar neighborhood of San Diego.

Nick couldn't help but be curious about Lara Nelson's circumstances. Girard had said Lara worked in La Jolla; he didn't say she *lived* there. Homes in La Jolla went for three million dollars and up. Only movie stars, hi-tech industrialists and old-money types lived on these cliffs. Space and the world-famous view were at a premium. Those looking for an opportunity to buy had to wait a long time for a property to go on the market.

Nick breathed in the salt air as Lara parked the car on the pristine, oil-free driveway. He'd always appreciated beauty and begrudged no one his or her fair share. He wondered if Julio's fatherless children would ever find their own place in the sun. Then, because a man in his kind of life accepted harsh realities, he shoved aside such thoughts and exited the car, stepping onto the fancy tiled sidewalk.

As man, woman and dog entered the pink-tiled foyer, Nick slipped and stumbled slightly. Lara grabbed at his waist, alarmed.

"You okay?"

"Fine. Just slipped on the tile."

"Carrara marble. My dog and I slip on it, too." Surprisingly, her arm remained firmly around his waist as she steered him to the couch in the large foyer.

"Sit down. I'll get you some coffee, if you'd like."

"I don't want any damn coffee," he said harshly. Then he backpedaled, realizing she didn't deserve rudeness. "I'm sorry. No, thanks."

"Okay, but how about a beer? Or a scotch. You're not on duty."

Nick thought for a moment. "Scotch sounds good."

"Ice?"

"Neat."

"Sit down and put your feet up. I'll be right back. Sadie, stay."

He felt the dog's eyes on him as he studied the room. A concert grand stood as the room's focal point, its lacquered finish gleaming despite the curtains being drawn over the huge bay windows. The floor was highly waxed parquet hardwood, while the obviously expensive leather couch and matching hassock were the only pieces of furniture evident. There was no television and no stereo. The only things in profusion were voluminous collections of sheet music on the shelves and a few scattered pieces on the piano.

Lara returned with an iced tea for herself and the scotch for him. Her dog rose to its feet expectantly and trotted to her side. Lara shook her head, but remained standing. "Relax, Sadie. I'm not going anywhere," she said with a smile of affection for the animal. Sadie lay down again and stretched.

The smile transformed the woman's face. She was breathtakingly lovely. So lovely that it took him a moment to realize she was still holding out his glass.

"Thanks." He tested the scotch with a small sip, then a bigger one.

"Feeling better?" she asked.

"Yeah," he said. "Thanks." The scotch, smooth as silk, burned a path to his midsection, replacing some of the icy coldness with heat.

"There's more if you want," Lara offered. "Just say the word. You wanna get drunk, I don't have a problem with it. God forbid if anything happened to *my* partner." Her hand dropped to rest on the molded head of her four-legged companion.

Getting drunk—something he hadn't done since his college days—appealed, but only for a moment. If he were drunk, he couldn't work. He'd take a quick shower, not for hygiene but to shock his body into alertness, and he'd exchange the constricting work clothes for jeans. He'd shove his grief down where it couldn't hamper him, and then, only then, would he start to work on finding Julio's killer.

# CHAPTER TWO

*Monday afternoon*

"DAMN!" Lara swore as she hit yet another wrong note on the piano keyboard, the third in the past five minutes. Julio's body was now in the hands of the medical examiner, and she hadn't yet told Nick. At present he was showering. She planned for them to visit the police station to check on new developments, but first she needed to eat. She'd missed her breakfast, and it was already past noon. Lara suspected Nick hadn't eaten since hearing of his partner's death. Okay, she decided, she'd tell him about the phone call from Girard *after* they'd eaten. There was no harm in stalling. No sense ruining his shower, as well.

She'd sat down to practice at the piano while waiting, one of her passions but unfortunately not one of her skills. She pushed away from the Steinway, the legs of the piano bench scraping the waxed parquet floor. Might as well take a break. Her mind wasn't on her music, anyway. It was on Nick Cantello.

Lara crossed to the big bay window overlooking the

Pacific, parted the drawn curtains slightly and took in the view. In many ways, she thought, Nick was exactly the way a law enforcement officer should be. Strong, both in his hard, lean body, and in his personality. But there was something else about him she found disturbing—his loneliness. He tried to hide it, she knew, but having reviewed his file on Girard's orders, Lara sensed it. Nick considered Julio's family more his than his own, distant one; his parents, siblings and grandparents lived in Italy. Now, sadly, the Valdezes were back in Mexico. Despite Nick's brusque, almost rude manner, she'd instantly warmed to him, both emotionally and physically, utterly surprising feelings for her to have toward a stranger suddenly thrust into her life.

Circumstances such as murder and a grieving, angry man didn't bode well for romantic attraction. Nick wanted justice for his partner, with or without her, and Lara knew a brick wall when she met one. Her dog's ears swiveled suddenly, alerting her to Nick's passage down the stairs from the guest room on the upper level. She swung around and greeted him with a smile.

"Giving up on the ivories?" Nick asked.

"I should have given up years ago. I'm terrible. Still, I love music." She shrugged. "I try not to inflict too much suffering on others. Thank heavens Sadie doesn't mind."

"Your dog's tone deaf?"

Lara noted it was the first time she'd seen him smile. "Yep. So is Lexi—that's my oldest sister Kate's dog. Kate's the real musician. We share this house. But she's out of town on business," she said, anticipating his question. "It's just us."

Lara sat back down on the bench and dropped her hand, feeling for the furry head never far from her side. "Hungry? We can leave whenever you're ready. I thought we'd stop at a place I know near the beach. Or wherever you prefer."

"In a bit." Nick sat down on the couch, his expression one people close to him would recognize as alert. "Tell me about your…house."

"Two stories, seven bedrooms, five bathrooms, kitchen and bar, formal dining room, four-car garage, pool and spa, tennis courts, plus a beautiful ocean view," she said. "Actually quite modest for La Jolla."

His eyes traveled around the room, sparsely yet elegantly—and expensively—furnished. "You win the lottery?" he asked.

"In a way." Lara grinned. "Wanna know the story?"

"Please."

Lara noticed his *please* was more an order than a question, a characteristic of most law enforcement officers who set up and controlled interviews. She did it herself, but today being treated as "business" was irritating. She'd never had a problem maintaining her emotional distance from co-workers before. But Nick had somehow skipped right past her "official" mode, and suddenly she wished the reverse were true.

Lara lifted her foot to the bench and tucked her knee under her chin. "My mother used to be a K-9 officer, and Dad worked with explosives canines. Dad runs the kennels. Both Mom and Dad train. We all help out on our off time."

"We? Your siblings?" he asked.

"Kate and I, now. My other sister, Lindsey, is married and works up at Yosemite with her husband. Kate and I occasionally do bodyguard work for friends or friends of friends."

Nick jerked his head in the dog's direction. "You freelance with the dog?" Law enforcement officers were allowed to moonlight, such as working parking control at sports events, but dogs rarely were.

"Sorta kinda. I don't charge my friends. And legally, Sadie's my personal property. I wasn't assigned her. I came to the job with leash in hand."

"Unusual."

"Not since 9-11. Increased numbers of law-enforcement dogs are becoming a normal part of life in this country. And as our kennels provide many of the working law-enforcement dogs in this area…" Lara shrugged. "Sadie passed her certifications."

"Go on," he ordered. Lara lifted one eyebrow, and was rewarded with another "Please."

"Kate and I worked a charity event for children's cancer a few years ago. A rock concert," she specified. "My father's a friend of the lead singer. The rock star's girlfriend and their young daughter were there. The daughter has cancer."

"Damn."

"Yeah. Anyway, Kate and I foiled a kidnapping attempt on the daughter. We caught the perps and kept the family safe. The rock star was *very* grateful."

"So, this?" he gestured around the expensive room.

"We don't take pay, of course. But Kate had her arm broken. I had a couple of broken ribs. Our dogs were okay, thank God. They got a good workout on the kidnappers." She grinned. "And despite their zeal, neither dog damaged a tooth."

"Good girl, Sadie," Nick said. In acknowledgment of the praise, Sadie graced him with a single, minute twitch of her tail.

"The rock star paid Kate's medical bills, and mine. When I got out of the hospital—"

"You were hospitalized?" he interrupted.

"I needed a few stitches," she said. "No biggie. So when I got out, the rock star presented the house as a fait accompli to our kennels, complete with gardener, pool man, stocked bar and paid utilities. Plus a Mercedes in the garage. Like I said, we don't charge friends, but we couldn't refuse or sell the place without taking a heavy tax hit to our business. The client must have paid his lawyer big time to set it up that way. He and his girlfriend really love their daughter. Happy ending for all parties concerned."

Nick nodded. "So you and your sister moved in?"

"We did. Mom and Dad still live on the kennel property, of course."

"Where's your sister now?" Nick asked.

"Kate and her dog are at a FBI convention—new bombs, new antiterrorist methods, new canine training.

Kate works for the Port of San Diego—coastal cities need harbor security just as tight as airports. She gets to do the occasional cruise ship. They always request her when in port."

Nick noticed the pride in Lara's voice when speaking of her sister. He found himself asking, "So you're both single?"

"We are."

Her tone said, *Back off,* but Nick suddenly remembered Captain Girard's words. "You up to this? Girard told me you've just come off compassionate leave yourself."

"That's right. Jim was a pilot. We were to get married last year. His chopper crashed. End of story." She lifted her chin. "But don't worry, I won't hold you—or the investigation—back. The shrinks said I'm good to go."

"Sorry. Damn." He started to reach for her, to give a consoling hug, then stopped. An awkward pause filled the room. He filled it with the lame "Well, with your sister not here, at least I won't have to share the shower."

Lara eagerly seized the opportunity to change the subject. "With Kate gone, it's quiet, but secure. I don't think you need a 'safe house' yet. For the present I'd rather Sadie and I stayed on our own turf to protect you."

"Makes sense," Nick admitted. The security measures in his older apartment building couldn't match those in La Jolla's rich district. Nor did his apartment have the hi-tech central monitoring system he'd noticed throughout the house.

"And we'll be using my Mercedes. It'll draw less attention than my squad unit."

"You're very lucky."

"Yep. Sadie even has her own pool."

"I didn't mean the house. I mean, you lived to fight another day. The rock star and his family remain intact. The bad guys are behind bars—where I intend to put Julio's killer."

Lara blinked, and her chest tightened with surprise. Most people envied her free home and raved about her "luck." Obviously that wasn't true with Nick. She noted he hadn't asked for the name of the rock star. Nick had his own priorities.

"Let's crank up that fancy car of yours, grab a bite and head over to the police station," Nick said. "Time to find out what's going on."

A COUPLE OF HOURS LATER, Nick sat in Lieutenant Joe Lansky's empty office waiting for him to return with coffee. Lara had placed badges around both her neck and Sadie's, where they were visible for all to see. When she wasn't in her special K-9 squad car, she didn't wear her uniform.

"I'm gonna roam, if you don't mind. You'll be safe enough in here," she'd said before leaving. "We got news this morning when you were in the shower."

"What news?"

"Lansky will fill you in. You've got my police cell

number and my personal cell number. Don't even think about leaving the building without me. Got it?"

"Got it." Her posture and tone said it all. It reminded Nick of Lara's story of foiling a kidnapping. The hairs on the back of his neck rose as he remembered her saying dismissively, "A few stitches." Clients—even wealthy ones—didn't usually compensate "a few stitches" with La Jolla mansions.

Nick took the liberty of logging onto Lansky's computer. First he tried to access any information on his partner's death, but found only a flashing, coded "pending."

Annoyed, but still logged on, he pulled up the police details of the rock star case. Four men had attempted to kidnap the rock star's daughter; Lara and her sister with their dogs had won the battle, but not without a price. Lara had been knifed in the ribs by one of the men. The knife was polymer, just as hard and sharp-edged as metal, and had escaped detection by concert security in the metal detectors. Three of Lara's ribs had been slashed right through, and the knife-wielding kidnapper had died by two bullets, one from each sister; either hit would have been fatal. Lara needed emergency surgery, according to the police reports. The three remaining kidnappers were in prison, the ringleader on death row due to "special circumstances," stalking, the attempted kidnapping of a minor, the attempted murder of law-enforcement officers and assault upon said officers.

Nick logged off the computer and returned to Lansky's visitor chair, his face thoughtful, his suspicions confirmed. Lara had courage when it came to law enforcement. Terrible thing, her fiancé dying…

Lansky entered the office, two cups of coffee in hand, and Nick gave himself a mental shake. He lifted his gaze to Lansky's ruddy face. "What's new with the investigation?"

Lansky set both coffees down and sat behind his desk. "Nothing on the shooter. The divers recovered Julio's body around ten this morning. We contacted Nelson, and—"

"Ten this morning?" She could have told him. She hadn't. Nick remembered the cheery breakfast they'd had, and his lips thinned. He needed information, not a babysitter.

"Yes. Julio's driver's-door window was destroyed by a single round, which continued into his body. What with the slow traffic speed during the rain, it's conclusive, Cantello. We're talking murder."

Nick blinked. A bullet. Shot at his partner.

"What caliber?"

"Dunno yet."

"Anything else?"

"The burial arrangements are pending. When the body is released from the coroner's office, the family will return. Have you talked to them?"

"I haven't been able to get through. I've tried more than once."

"We've reached them. They know."

"That's all?"

"You know, you're just as impatient as your aunt."

"You knew Magda?" Nick's late aunt, Magda Palmer, hadn't been a law enforcement officer—women didn't hold such jobs in her day—but she had worked as a clerk-typist in the old paper-records department. She'd also raised him.

Lansky shrugged. "Professionally. She used to type up some of my cases. So tell me. What's up with your new bodyguard, Lara Nelson?"

"She's a pro with dogs, obviously."

"Where's she gonna stash you?"

"She's not."

Lansky's forehead furrowed. "No? I hope this lady knows what she's doing."

Nick jumped to Lara's defense. "Captain Girard said you agreed to her assisting."

"Only because we didn't want you quitting and going vigilante," Lansky said pointedly.

A muscle worked in Nick's jaw. "Point taken. What else?"

"Valdez's wife called him at work, she said, right before the shift ended and you two walked to the parking lot. We replayed our phone logs from Friday this morning…something about a broken refrigerator and needing ice. Julio agreed, but he'd be a few minutes late."

"I know that. That's why we swapped vehicles," Nick said with impatience. "What else?"

"Julio'd discovered information on a fellow officer he needed to check out. Even wished you were around to give him a hand—but you'd already left for the weekend. On the phone, he told Lilia he'd catch you when you got back Monday. He died before he made it home."

Nick felt a twist of pain in his gut. "What are you saying? This *fellow officer* killed Julio. Shot him with a heavy round of ammo and watched him skid into the ocean?" He didn't think anything could have made him feel worse. But he was wrong.

"Maybe you weren't the target," Lansky said. "Maybe Julio was. Cantello, didn't Julio say *anything* about that information?"

"No," Nick said bleakly. "He knew I was in a hurry to catch my charter. The boat doesn't wait."

"Go see Girard," Lansky said next. "He has more info for you."

Nick rose.

"Cantello…" Lansky said.

Nick looked at him. "What?"

Lansky's eyes were soft, kind. "I hear you and Valdez used to grab a beer after work now and then."

Nick didn't answer. Memories of Julio laughing, Julio dragging him to their favorite sports bar for a cold one flooded him. Nick could almost hear him now, see his twinkling brown eyes warm with friendship.

"My kids are crazy about you, Cantello," Julio had often told him. "So's my wife. No accounting for taste, but she'd have my hide if you ate alone. After this beer, you come home for dinner."

Nick had always let himself be persuaded. Lilia Valdez would welcome him with a big smile, while

Julio's two boys greeted him with hugs and excited chatter....

*I hear you and Valdez used to grab a beer after work now and then.* Those days were gone now, never to return.

"What about it?" Nick said to Lansky. He didn't want to travel down memory lane. He didn't want to grieve for Julio yet. There would be time for that later.

Lansky clapped a beefy hand on Nick's shoulder. "If you ever need a drinking buddy, look me up. I'll even buy the first round."

"I'll buy—after we find our killer."

NICK KNOCKED on the door to Captain Girard's office and went in. Lara and Sadie were there with the older man.

"The gang's all here," Nick observed.

"We've been waiting for you," Lara said.

"Ballistics confirmed the bullet caliber—25 mm," Girard said. "Antitank, military issue, high velocity. Deadly—and unusual."

High velocity was favored by the military. The police used lower velocity bullets, greatly lessening the chance of one passing through a criminal and hitting an innocent bystander. The military considered that a plus, not a minus.

"Whoever was gunning for you or Valdez didn't want to take chances," Lara said softly.

"At least we'll be able to trace the weapon through the military," Nick stated. Among civilians, handgun registration was only recently mandatory in California. Rifles and shotguns did not have to be registered.

"It's a starting point," Girard agreed. "We're running a cross-check on employed veterans and those still serving in the reserves."

"You think it's one of us?" Nick asked.

"Well, our own staff is the place to start. All we have to go on is Julio's conversation with his wife. My thinking is, computer files are a dead end."

Nick caught the expression on Girard's face at the word *dead*. It came and went so quickly that only a trained observer could have seen it. Like himself. *I'm not the only one torn up about this,* he thought. *Maybe an outsider's a good idea.*

He glanced at Lara, and for a moment she didn't feel like such an outsider, after all, until Girard said, "There's one more thing. As I told Lara earlier this morning on the phone, we've recovered your car and your partner."

"You knew this morning and didn't tell me, Lara?" Nick flew to his feet. "I'm going to see Julio."

"No," Girard said. Lara quickly blocked the door, dog at her side, and placed her hand on Nick's arm.

"Your partner took an antitank round, Detective," Girard said. "The M.E. says he died on impact of the round, long before the car submerged. Officer Nelson just came from the morgue."

"You should have told me!" he said angrily, shaking off her grasp.

"Trust me, Detective, you *don't* want to see his body. I wish *I* hadn't," Lara said bluntly.

An uneasy silence filled the office until Girard said, "You've got work to do. Best get going."

Lara stayed in front of the door, still shadowed by her dog. "Captain, if you could have your assistant e-mail those ballistics reports to me? Here's my card."

Nick was grateful for the interruption as Lara passed his boss the business card with her official cell phone and office number, e-mail address, title and K-9 Department unit number. It wasn't until they were outside in the parking lot that she spoke again.

"Well, we've made some progress today," she said matter-of-factly.

"I still would have liked finding out earlier. Next time you get a call from the station, let me know. I want information about Julio when it comes in, got it?"

She didn't argue nor make excuses. "Agreed."

Using the remote on her key chain, Lara unlocked the Mercedes door as they approached. Sadie shoved her nose under the back door handle, lifted it and opened the door, standard training for police dogs. Next she grabbed the rubber ring attached to the inside door handle and closed it herself, just as she did in Lara's squad car. Lara took the driver's seat like before, and Nick climbed in. He couldn't drop the subject.

"You should have told me they'd recovered the body. And that the autopsy had been performed. I had every right to know. Every right to see Julio's body."

Lara faced his accusation head-on. "If I were you, I'd be furious."

"I'm *way* past furious. It was *my* call, *my* partner."

"Not today, Detective." She closed her eyes, then opened them. "For God's sake, don't let his wife and kids see what I saw." Her voice was calm, but it took her two tries to get the key into the ignition. Nick didn't miss it.

"You okay?" he asked, his anger gone.

She actually smiled. "I should be asking you that."

"Want me to drive?"

"Nope. I'm fine." Lara took a breath and turned the key. "Besides, I've taken the bodyguard-driving course. I can drive like a Hollywood stunt driver. Sadie might get bored with you at the wheel." She attempted a lighter mood that failed, but impressed him just the same. "Which reminds me, I arranged to have Julio's motorcycle temporarily stored in Impound. As your bodyguard, I don't want you exposed. I could have told you that earlier, too."

"Oh, the bike. I need to take care of it. I have a storage unit near Julio's place. I was always there…" His voice trailed off.

"Later. For now, let's head for your apartment so you can pick up your things." They fastened their seat belts and Lara automatically locked all the doors. "Hope you're not a fresh-air fiend like Sadie," she said, turning the air-conditioning on high. "She likes to hang out the window. It's bad for eyes and ears."

"No problem," he said, appreciating the comfort of the leather seats.

Lara pulled through the parking lot and to the stop-light-regulated exit onto the main drag. She stopped at the red light. "What's the quickest way to your place?"

"I'd take—"

He never finished his sentence. Gunfire slammed into the driver's-side door of the Mercedes. The door collapsed, glass cracked, then a second and third shot hit the back of the car as Lara cut the steering wheel hard and jammed the car into reverse, gunning it backward and away from the source of gunfire. Nick drew his gun and frantically searched for the shooter, but could see nothing through the mottled glass of his section of the car.

In seconds the attack was over. Police officials ran to the Mercedes, Sadie barking furiously at them. As Lara brought the car to a complete stop, Nick slowly reholstered his gun to stare at the windows—cracked but still in one piece. His gaze met Lara's.

"Whoever this rock star is…I have *got* to start buying his albums."

## CHAPTER THREE

"I'LL HAVE TO REPLACE two windows. And the armored body. My insurance better cover this," Lara stated as the Mercedes was towed to the police impound yard to join Julio's motorcycle. Sadie sat behind them in Lara's squad car, which a fellow officer had retrieved for her, her nose pointed toward Lara, ears perked and alert for any command. A crowd of police officers, including Captain Girard, buzzed about.

"Insurance?" Nick said. "Someone fired three shots at us, no suspect is found and all you worry about is insurance?"

"Do you know how much bulletproof glass costs?"

"Done venting?"

"Yeah, I guess." Lara sighed. "I don't care about the car, anyway. I'm just upset. We were shot at with rounds that would stop a dinosaur!"

Captain Girard interjected. "Lara, calm down. We'll get him."

"Him? Her? We didn't see a thing!"

Nick laid a casual hand on her shoulder as Girard spoke, his voice confident. "I'm going with a man. Statistically, most women kill in self-defense on domestic turf. Men are much more liable to kill in public, and this—" he gestured toward the expansive downtown police parking lot "—is about as public as it gets."

Lara nodded.

"Cantello," Girard ordered, "you and Nelson get out of here—and out of your houses. Nelson, call for a safe house. It's moving day for both of you. We'll touch base later."

"I've sent a squad car ahead with a couple of my buddies," Nick said to Lara.

"When did you do that?"

"A few minutes ago. We'll meet them at my place first, then yours."

"I'm in charge of your safety. You shouldn't be giving the orders," Lara immediately said.

"You shouldn't be in morgues or doing detective work," Girard insisted. "You're as white as a ghost."

Lara didn't like the tone of the older man's voice. "Hey, I've been shot at. I'm entitled to a little adrenaline. And I've got questions! Are we dealing with Julio's murderer or something totally different? My window took the shots, not yours. What if we have a serial cop killer on our hands?"

"Don't get hysterical, Officer."

Lara's mouth opened, but before she could honestly protest, someone called out Girard's name and he turned away. Nick gently pushed her toward her squad car.

"Drop it, Nelson. And get in." He jerked a thumb at the passenger side. "This time, I'm driving."

LARA SHIFTED in her seat during the drive, her nerves still raw—and aware that both her dog and the man driving had picked up on it. Nick kept flicking her quick glances, while Sadie, in back, kept her long nose near Lara's neck, past the open grill that, when locked, separated a prisoner from the officers in front. The remote control could pop open the back door, as well, when a quick exit was needed.

"Are we almost there?" she asked.

The corners of Nick's lips twitched. "You sound like Julio's kids. Next you'll be wanting ice cream."

"Ha, ha," she replied, feeling more of her courage flow back into her spine. "Still, it's better than being accused of being hysterical. Talk about old school." Girard's comment still stung.

"Girard *is* old school." Nick glanced at her. "You ever been shot at before?"

"Never."

"First time for me, too. Guess we're not virgins anymore."

Lara deliberately made her voice light. "Another milestone in a cop's life."

"Well, you handled yourself well. Drove us out of the line of fire. Plus that fishtail spin so the shooter had a smaller area of car to hit. Excellent work, lady."

"You, too, Detective," Lara admitted. "I saw you draw your weapon and check for our shooter. All out of the corner of my hysterical little right eye."

"I'll take your hysterical over others' calm any day." Nick flicked on his signal light. "We're here," he announced, then gestured at the other squad car waiting for them. "And there're my guys." Nick pulled up into an oil-stained driveway in front of a faded apartment complex. It was definitely older, but maintained well.

"You live *here*?" Lara asked, surprised. She took in the old trees, their roots making cracks in the sidewalk. They were just a part of the many concrete areas, including the driveways and carports, where children played in lieu of yards or parks. Water in San Diego was expensive, as was irrigation. Grass refused to grow on just air and sunlight. Landlords knew that—and children tore it up, anyway. Better to mount swing sets in cement and let the parents deal with skinned knees.

"Not La Jolla, but it's home," Nick said casually.

"I'm no snob. I meant that this place looks more like it's for families. Pets, kids, picnic tables. Swing sets and slides."

"Julio and his wife used to live here until they found a bigger place. I moved in. My last place was bulldozed for condos and the management company takes good care of this place." He shrugged, then reached for the mike as the car's radio crackled with confirmation from the other two officers that they'd searched his apartment, courtesy of the landlord's key, and the premises were secure.

"Would you mind leaving Sadie in the car?" Nick asked.

"Actually, I would. Sadie's like my badge and gun— they rarely leave my side."

"I wouldn't ask, but I've got a cat, and he's not too good with dogs," Nick said.

"Oh. Well, since we already have men here."

In German, Lara ordered Sadie to stay in and guard the car, which was parked in the shade with open windows. Nick and Lara went through the open courtyard filled with dead leaves, gum wrappers, bikes, toys and the accompanying children. Some shouted out his name and waved. He smiled, caught and returned a tossed football.

Lara actually jumped as an aged cat emerged from behind the potted cactus near his door. As it hissed and arched its gray back, Nick met her gaze.

"Calm down, Nelson. It's only my cat."

"I'm calm, and is *that* what this is?"

"Yep." To her surprise, Nick bent over and scooped the wild-looking thing up into one hand, while with the other reached for his mailbox on the stucco outer wall. "I don't have the wife or kids yet, but I do have the pet. Someday…"

Lara blinked, thinking of Jim and the family they'd planned. Only, she'd wanted a family *dog* for the children, not a scarred feline with defiantly unsheathed claws. The animal had obviously been through some rough times, had probably tangled with San Diego's coyotes, which shared the heavy areas of population due to habitat destruction; their only source of water was automatic city sprinklers. Adult coyotes learned the hours they went on and off, females taught their pups. Generations of coyotes who'd lost their fear of man trekked through the streets like so many stray dogs. Trouble was, these animals lived off fruit from the local citrus trees and mammals, including small domestic pets. Even fenced yards weren't protection.

"You picked out this cat?" she asked.

"He picked out me…used to live next door. The last tenants left him behind. The new ones couldn't take him in. Their youngest is allergic."

"Poor thing."

"The cat or the child?"

"Both." Lara couldn't imagine a life without animals, but she didn't venture closer to pet the feline. Smelling of dog, she wasn't about to socialize with this set of claws.

"The child is happy, and this cat is old and doesn't like kids, anyway. He's been fixed, I get him his shots, and he's content to hang here."

"That's good. I doubt the shelter would consider a war-torn veteran like him adoptable," Lara observed.

He stroked the gray head once, then set the cat down and opened his door.

"What's his name?"

"The old tenants just called him 'the cat.'" Nick unlocked the door. "It's all he'll answer to. Come on in."

The gray tiger streaked by her as she stepped inside. It immediately made its way to the kitchen at the other end of the living room. After a quick shuffle, Nick tossed his mail on the coffee table.

"They've already searched the place, so make yourself at home. I'll grab my things," Nick said.

Lara felt tempted by the comfortable, padded recliner. Murder, the morgue and a bullet-riddled Mercedes had made for a rough day, she thought, as she studied the room. The inside of Nick's place was a pleasant contrast to the shabbier courtyard outside. She took in the neat surroundings, freshly painted walls, clean carpet and the dust-free furniture. As she waited, she realized the room held few touches of its owner. There were no magazines or newspapers carelessly scattered, no photographs on the wall, no personal mementos anywhere.

If it weren't for a single boating magazine and mail on the coffee table, she could have been in a nice hotel and never known the difference. Lara's gaze wandered about, her eyes troubled. There had to be *something* that spoke of the man who lived there. She saw nothing except a cat without a name.

"Everything meet with your approval?" Nick asked suddenly.

Lara turned to see him watching her, a nylon gym bag and plastic suit carrier slung over his arm.

"I was trying to learn more about you," she admitted.

"Any success?"

"Nope. You don't even have a television. A room like this—" she gestured with one hand, and met his gaze "—seems so sterile."

"My cleaning lady lives in the complex. She's a neat freak—even for her profession. I lent my TV to the tenant across the complex. He's home alone on worker's comp with a broken leg." Nick looked around his place with new eyes. "Besides, I'm not here much. Julio's wife keeps a spare room for me at her place and gave me a key. Most of my personal stuff's there."

She nodded.

"I've got to feed the cat."

He set his two bags by the door and walked to the kitchen visible from the living area. The feline immediately jumped off the counter to rub against his legs, purring all the while. Lara watched from the living room.

Quietly she asked, "Tell me about your partner."

Nick opened a cabinet and removed a can of tuna. He opened the can, then set it on the floor. It wasn't until he threw away the lid and leaned against the counter that he replied, "What's to say?" Nick's expression was as sterile as the home he lived in. "We were close. Now he's dead. I haven't talked to the family yet. His wife may or may not kick me out of their home. I don't know."

"I meant professionally—regarding this case," Lara explained. "Like enemies, money problems... I'm sorry, I should have specified."

"It's been a wild morning," he said, his law-enforcement manner back to normal.

Lara did the same. Obviously Nick wasn't the one incapacitated by emotions now. He'd assumed control, as she had earlier in the day. It was time for her to get her own emotions back in control. But if she hadn't owned an armored Mercedes...

"Hell, yes. I wish we could find a motive for two attacks. Any ideas?" she asked in a brisk voice, moving to stand at the breakfast bar separating the rooms.

"No. Julio and I worked the day shift. Our last case involved some small-time drug hustlers—no major players—until one of them shot another over money."

"Seems pretty cut and dried. Was it?"

"Yes. Julio and I had enemies, but there are only two or three I'd consider dangerous, and at present they're behind bars. Julio was a good cop, a faithful husband and a great father. He didn't touch dirty money, nor did I. I was positive either he or I was the target until *you* were shot at. Now I don't know what to think."

They were both silent. Nick waited a few more minutes until the cat had finished eating, then rinsed out the can—San Diego was home to ants, as well as coyotes and sunshine—and tossed the empty tin in the recycle bin. He retrieved the suit carrier and bag, then let Lara and the cat out of the apartment.

"What will happen to the cat when you're away?"

"The bathroom window's open for him and I took out the screen," he said, gesturing toward the high, hinged pane of glass. "He can come and go as he pleases. The cleaning lady feeds him if I'm not home. She has a key."

Lara exhaled a slow sigh at the sight of the old, battered animal. For a moment—just a moment—she felt like hell over the unfairness of the cat's life—of a cop's life. Then she shook it off. The cat was a survivor. She'd do better to use her energies for those who weren't, like Julio Valdez.

She followed Nick to the squad car. The backup officers took off first, to check out her home premises, leaving the two of them to follow.

"Keys, please. This is my squad car," she reminded him.

"True. But where do we go now?"

"My place. I need to get some clothes, too."

"I won't stay at any safe house out of the area," Nick warned. "I want to stay local. And you should think of yourself. You're a target as long as you're with me."

"We're not going to a safe house."

"But Girard said—"

"Girard said I was in charge of your safety. We're going to my parents' home—Nelson Kennels. It's in a good neighborhood, the food's free and the beds are clean. We have to sleep sometime. And it's pretty damn safe."

"You sure?" Nick asked.

Lara grinned with satisfaction at the security measures and the many trained dogs on the compound. "Oh, yeah. I don't even need to ask."

"I do," Nick insisted. "Better sound out your parents. I don't want to drag them into this."

"I know what they'll say. Now give me the keys to my unit. I'm driving."

# CHAPTER FOUR

*Monday evening, east of Escondido*

"WE TAKE A RIGHT at the stop sign, then we're just five minutes from Nelson Kennels," Lara said to Nick. Then, "Sadie, calm down!" Sadie was standing in back, ears perked and tail thumping against the window. "Yes, we're going to my parents'."

Sadie's tail thumped even harder and she whined with excitement.

"She's certainly excited," Nick said, flicking the dog a glance as Lara concentrated again on her driving. The city of Escondido wasn't beach, but rather a transition area of inland valleys and foothills. Next came the mountains and after that, the desert, but even these foothills were full of hairpin curves and sharp inclines.

"She knows the way. Hard to mistake this route, even for a dog."

He nodded. The rugged driving took them around another sharp turn on the narrow two-way road. Pin oaks hung determinedly onto the sides of rocky inclines, while olive trees flourished in the heat and sandy soil. "Nice country, though."

"It is beautiful, isn't it? Great place to raise kids and dogs. Too bad it's getting so settled," Lara said.

"The casinos?" Nick guessed. Ever since the Native American gaming laws had passed, they'd been popping up all over California. San Diego County was no exception, with a dozen operating and even more planned.

"Yeah. Harrah's, Valley View, Pala—you name 'em. They're smack dab in the middle of what used to be livestock dairy and poultry country. All this land is a seller's market." Lara sighed. Always an animal fan, she hated that the thousands of Jersey cows from her youth were gone. Others, like fruit farmers, horse ranchers and vineyard owners, couldn't resist swapping hard labor for the money they'd get for the land, which developers would turn into spas and golf courses.

"Your parents aren't selling?"

"No way. It's home. Besides, where would they go? There's no beachfront property left—and even if there was, it's wall-to-wall people and not zoned for animals. The mountains are too far away from where we do business, and as for the deserts—" Lara shrugged "—too hot for working dogs."

"There's plenty of open space left, especially the citrus groves," Nick observed. They'd finished climbing and were now descending into a valley area. "Looks like some people have kept their land."

"True. The tourmaline mine's remained. And the chicken, llama and horse ranches are still operating—

the thoroughbred ranches, especially. But so many of the flower growers have moved on—especially with the drought."

"Progress is a mixed blessing."

"Tell me about it. Still, if it wasn't for the booming population, trained security dogs wouldn't be needed, and my parents wouldn't be in business. Okay, there's our sign. We follow this road to the end and we're there in ten minutes."

As soon as Lara flicked on her blinker and turned, Sadie, already excited, went into overdrive, squeaking, whining, then full-fledged barking.

"Sorry about that," Lara sang out. "In case you haven't guessed, Sadie was born here. Just roll down your window for the noise. That's what I do."

Nick rolled down his window, his ears ringing. "Don't you have a command for quiet?"

"Sure, but let her bark. It's good for the lungs, and she'll calm down when we get there."

Sadie proved Lara right. As soon as Lara pulled up into the private drive opposite the business parking area and unlocked Sadie's door, the dog stopped whining. However, she ran straight to the double-gated entrance of the chain-link fence where the four family housedogs ran free in the many-acred landscaped family yard.

"Stay outside the gate," Lara warned Nick. An older German shepherd bitch, Mrs. Nelson's current pet and Sadie's dam, along with three other dogs, rushed barking to the fence. Their aggressiveness abated some at seeing Lara, hearing her voice, smelling her scent. The red dachshund and the shepherd bitch continued to growl suspiciously at Nick through the fence, while the more sociable graying black Lab and young white terrier pranced outside the second, pad-key gate separating Lara and Sadie from them on one side, and Nick on the other.

Lara took off Sadie's special collar/chest shield with her badge on it and hooked it to her own belt. That meant Sadie was officially off duty. Lara opened the gate. "There you go, girl. Break time!"

Sadie bounded inside to eagerly exchange licks and sniffs with her canine family. The other dogs gathered around the police pair, but Nick saw that Lara didn't take the time for a long hello or enter the open yard. Much to the pack's disappointment, she closed the gate to the main yard, locked it, then exited again.

"Let's find my parents," she said. "The office is this way."

They didn't have to look for long. Before they'd even stepped into the building, a couple came out to greet them. Though he'd never seen Lara's parents, Nick easily recognized Lara's mother—she was simply an older, taller version of Lara. Sandra was in her mid-sixties and her facial features were lined, but mother and daughter both wore expressions of alertness and intelligence. Character, even more than similar coloring, marked them as related.

The older man was introduced as Lara's father, Edward Nelson, "Call me Ed." He had to be at least a decade older than his wife, Nick estimated, but the handshake Lara's father gave him showed no hint of weakness. He noted Lara had inherited her father's more angular, stubborn chin.

"We always know when you're coming. I could hear Sadie whining a mile away!" Mr. Nelson said, hugging his daughter, then noticed her lack of uniform. "Saw your squad car. On duty?"

"Actually, I'm on special duty."

"Then what brings you here?" Mrs. Nelson asked. The older couple had begun leading the younger couple to the kennel office.

"Trouble," Lara said.

"Damn," Ed said at the same time that Sandra lifted her eyebrows, accompanied by a curious, "Really? Brief me."

"You're retired," Ed warned his wife—to no avail.

"I think I'll let the staff handle the rest of my day," Sandra said. "I wouldn't want to miss a visit with my youngest. Ed, please tell the others," she ordered with the easy authority of a woman used to command. "We'll all meet at the house."

A SHORT WHILE LATER the four sat in the comfortable living room—informal save for the many photographs, awards, ribbons and official commendations on the shelves and fireplace mantel. At Ed's invitation, Nick studied the photographs while waiting for mother and daughter to emerge from the kitchen.

"You've got quite a family here," Nick said.

"That I do. Here's my first dog." Ed pointed.

A much younger Edward Nelson in military uniform stood proudly beside a military bomb-sniffing dog in a jungle setting.

"Vietnam?" Nick guessed.

"Yes. I smuggled my partner back here," Ed said. "They destroyed canines in the old days, but I had a buddy who owed me. My dog and I came home together. I've been working with dogs since." He gestured to another photo. "Here's my wife."

Sandra Nelson's photo showed her in her younger days, as well, in police uniform with her first K-9 officer, yet another German shepherd.

"And Kate, the eldest." Ed indicated a photo with a woman in uniform with her explosives canine. Then, "Lindsey, my middle daughter." Her picture showed her standing in a ranger's search-and-rescue uniform, her newest shepherd posed beside her new husband and his own dog. "And here's Lara."

Lara's photo also showed her in uniform, with Sadie beside her.

"Impressive," Nick said. "The world needs more families like this."

"I understand you come from a law-enforcement family yourself."

"More administrative, and only my aunt Magda. She worked as a clerk typist back in the days before computers. That was a long time ago."

Nick felt a sudden surge of loneliness. Julio was gone, his wife and children were in Mexico. The aunt who'd raised Nick—she'd left Italy with Nick for "a better life" in California and even changed her surname Palameri to Palmer once she'd settled—was dead.

Nick's grandparents and parents still lived in Italy, along with his three older siblings. His mother, Mara, had been ill after Nick was born and had asked her younger sister to care for Nick. Magda had never married. Although he and Magda had kept in touch with their Italian relatives, Nick had never been close to any of them.

Even as a boy, there was an emotional gulf and a stretch of ocean between them and him. Obviously the Nelson children didn't have that problem with their elders. The many photos on the wall showed the daughters' respect for family and pride in their work. They also showed a great deal of courage. The older couple had dedicated their lives to the public. Now the three daughters were doing likewise.

His thoughts were interrupted by the women's reentrance with drinks—coffee and soda—trailed by the family pack and Sadie. Dogs and people found places in the living room, and Lara and Nick in turn related the events of Julio's case, ending with the attack on the Mercedes. The expressions on the faces of Lara's parents were solemn when Lara said, "We need a safe base of operations. Can we stay here?"

Sandra flicked her husband a quick look and received an affirming nod. "We'll do all we can to help," she said. "You'll need your sleep. Gotta keep those reflexes sharp."

"And you'll have separate rooms," Ed added, his gaze on Nick. "Even the Secret Service doesn't sleep in the president's bed."

Lara flushed pink. "Dad!"

Sandra rose to her feet. "Ed, why don't you go back

to the office while I get some sheets for the guest room?" she suggested with a hard stare at her husband. Various dogs followed the couple either to the back door leading outside or down the hall to the linen closet.

Lara didn't say anything until they were out of earshot. "Forgive my father. He's a very traditional man."

"It's his house, and I wasn't offended."

Lara excused her father's behavior, anyway. "Dad was shocked when I moved in with my boyfriend—we didn't get engaged until later. I don't casually hop into bed with anyone, and certainly not under my father's roof," she said with a frankness Nick appreciated.

His gaze swung again to the photos on the walls. "Perhaps he'd have accepted sons in high-risk jobs more easily than daughters."

Lara ran her hand through her short blond curls. "I doubt it. Dad always wanted his children, no matter the sex, to have safe jobs. He keeps reminding me how lucky he and Mom were to make it to retirement unscathed. He didn't scare any of us off, though. In fact, just the opposite. That's why Jim—my fiancé—and I didn't wait. No long courtship, no waiting until after the marriage to move in together."

Nick tactfully said nothing.

"Anyway, don't worry about my father. He knows I'm here to protect you. That's enough." She rose, followed by Sadie and the dachshund. "Come on, I'll show you the guest room. You can freshen up. Take your time."

"I will," Nick replied. "I need to make a few calls."

"Don't plan on using the house line," Lara said immediately.

"But—"

"They're much easier to trace than cell phones."

"Right." Nick shook himself mentally, embarrassed. He'd planned on trying Mexico again from a conventional line, hoping he'd have better luck than earlier.

"Who did you want to call? Your partner's wife?"

"I haven't been able to reach Lilia," he admitted. "And I want to check in with headquarters, too."

"Ah. Use your cell," she repeated.

"Got it." If he didn't connect on the first call, he knew he'd have no trouble with the second. That call would be to Internal Affairs.

LARA LET NICK UNPACK and settle in as she placed the fresh sheets on the bed. When she finished, she took a chair in the room and absently scratched the ears of the dachshund she now held in her lap. Sadie wandered in, followed by her dam, Shady Lady—aptly named, as she was mostly black as opposed to Sadie's dominant tan. Nick hung his suit bag in the closet. He was finished, as well.

"You hungry? We missed lunch, thanks to our shooter."

"I don't want to put your parents out."

Lara grinned. "You won't. I make a mean sandwich." She set the dachshund back on the floor. "Kitchen's this way."

In the kitchen she seated Nick at the small wooden table and opened the bread box. "You want rye or white br—"

Nick's cell rang.

"I don't know who that is, but don't tell anyone where we are," Lara warned. "It's an easy guess, but there's no need to confirm."

Nick's sideways glance showed he didn't need the warning. "Rye." The phone call took him completely by surprise, and Lara intently listened to the one-sided conversation.

"Well?" she asked when he clicked off his cell.

"That was Homeland Security."

"And?"

"It's confirmed. The bullets used against your car were 25 mm. They would have penetrated an ordinary car."

"But we know my car isn't ordinary. You want sliced ham or roast…what?"

"Homeland Security says the bullets that hit Julio came from the same gun, but they weren't light rounds."

"We knew that, too. Ham or roast beef?" she repeated.

"Julio's slug was made with DU."

Lara's lips actually parted in shock. "Not…depleted uranium?"

Depleted uranium was a by-product of leftover natural uranium after U-235 was extracted to fuel nuclear weapons and power plants. Common in the United States, the leftover uranium was weakly radioactive, but still had its uses. It remained a deadly tank-piercing heavy metal that made guns loaded with lead bullets look like popguns. Any "heavy" ammunition or artillery was strictly regulated and controlled by the Federal government. "Light" ammunition, such as that used by police or civilians, remained under local control.

"Why didn't Girard tell us before?" Lara demanded.

"Because everyone at the station assumed the extensive damage to the car body resulted from the crash and the rocky bottom. Hell, I've never seen a DU bullet hole in person. Homeland Security has, and they checked for radioactivity."

"My God! That stuff's military only. Hasn't the United Nations classified it as a Weapon of Mass Destruction?" Lara asked, horrified. "The radioactivity and heavy-metal toxicity threatens the environment!"

"True, but a single DU bullet could take out a whole armored personnel carrier filled with enemy troops. That's why we still use them."

"No wonder I…" No wonder she nearly lost her breakfast after viewing the skimpy remains of Julio Valdez. "Nothing. Go on."

"So does Great Britain," Nick said. "Homeland Security said our military prefers 25, 105, and 120 mm rounds."

"And now someone's shooting them here in San Diego?"

"So they say. Homeland Security also said they'll be handling further ballistics investigation and other aspects, as well."

Lara rubbed her forehead "But…I'm confused. I thought another law-enforcement member targeted Julio. He went to buy groceries, you said. Is our shooter a cop or terrorist? *We* weren't shot at with DU. *Julio* was."

"Homeland Security will handle it. They're better equipped. Even if they weren't, I'm not leaning toward the terrorist angle," Nick said. "Internal Affairs finished checking out Julio's computer."

"Internal Affairs?"

"Yes, I just talked to them. I know Julio was writing a speech for the next department retirement dinner. IA said there was no file on the hard drive. I doubt a terrorist would delete a retirement speech, DU ammo or not."

"A speech?" Lara echoed. "Why *your* partner?"

Nick's lips thinned into a hard line. "English or Spanish, Julio wrote the best damn reports in the department. He was always writing something for the bosses."

"If he had to write a testimonial, he would have had to research the subjects. If he did—he might have found something he shouldn't. Who's retiring?"

Nick frowned. "Girard, Lansky and Knox. All from Homicide."

"Girard and Lansky I know. Who's Knox?"

"Sergeant Richard Knox. His son, T.J., works in Homicide, too. But the sergeant isn't the one I want to talk to right now." Nick pulled out his cell phone. The dachshund and Sadie watched from their spots on the cool tile as Nick dialed Girard's direct number.

"Girard here."

"Hey, Captain. It's Cantello."

"What's up, Nick?"

"Thought I'd check in with you. Any news?"

"Nothing yet at this end, though I did get a call from Homeland Security ballistics."

"Same here." A beat, then Nick asked in a bland voice, "Did Julio finish his retirement speech?"

Silence. "If he did, he didn't keep it on the computer."

"I know for a fact he did. Someone wiped it."

"I'll tell Internal Affairs."

"I already did."

"How's your new bodyguard doing?" Girard asked.

Nick couldn't help but notice the abrupt change of subject. "She's kept me alive so far. Do me a favor, Captain. Have ballistics call me when they're done picking apart Nelson's Mercedes."

"Planned on it. So, you think she's gonna be any help in solving this murder?"

A chill streaked down Nick's spine. It was his warning system, and had saved his life more than once. "She's a good worker," he said in a deliberately casual voice. "But she's not a detective."

Girard sounded reassured. "Where are you staying?"

"Wherever Ms. Nelson stashes me. After this morning, she and I will be keeping a close eye on each other." Nick smiled, but it wasn't from pleasure. "Pass the word around, would you?"

"Of course. Keep in touch."

"Of course," he echoed. Nick set down the cell.

"What are you smiling about?" Lara asked.

"Looks like we may have a starting point, after all. Three retiring men. First thing in the morning, we'll see if any of them served in the military." Nick pushed aside his cell phone. "Make it a ham on rye. Please."

# CHAPTER FIVE

*Tuesday morning*

AFTER A GOOD NIGHT'S SLEEP at her parents' home, Lara met Nick in the kitchen for coffee. There, she'd suggested that civilian clothes and no cruiser would make them less of a target. But using any personal car, including her parents', could make them easier to spot.

"I don't need a red bull's-eye on our backs. We're getting a rental and I'm not wearing a uniform as long as I'm your bodyguard."

In keeping with a low profile, she dressed in jeans, a navy tank top with the yellow words SD Police on the front and back, and a navy windbreaker that would effectively hide both the top and her gun. She attached her badge to her holster, where it wouldn't be seen. Sadie, as always, had her official collar badge on. Lara could simply discard her windbreaker for an official presence.

After some breakfast, Lara drove Nick to the rental agency, then they both drove back to the kennels. Lara led the way, Nick right behind. Once home, she parked and waited outside for Nick. His rental was only a few lengths behind. Her mother spotted her from the office and walked over, the old black Lab at her side. The women exchanged good-mornings as Nick approached and parked his car. Lara watched him key in numbers.

"Rental car, huh?" Sandra observed. "How's he doing?"

"Besides being sleep-deprived? And unable to reach his partner's wife? Not bad—but he's got to stop and sleep sometime."

"Poor guy," Sandra said. "You two come up with anything?"

"We're already targeting three men." Lara quickly filled her in on what Nick had related about the retiring men and Julio's missing written testimonial. She concluded, "Ballistics says the military ammunition used on Julio Valdez came from the same weapon used to fire at us." Lara deliberately avoided the topic of depleted-uranium bullets. Her mother worried too much as it was, and Nick still needed to learn if the three suspects were military veterans.

"That seems a bit thin for a motive," Sandra said. "But if you intend to run with it…" She hesitated.

"What?"

"Ordinarily I wouldn't bring up old gossip, but those three men… You and Nick check out Magda Palmer."

Lara immediately whipped out her notebook. "Who's she?"

"Nick's aunt. She raised him. He came to California with her when she left Italy. You didn't know that?"

"No."

"Magda Palmer—used to be Palameri—worked at the police station with Girard, Lansky and Knox."

"The three men retiring."

"Yes. Knox Sr., Girard and Lansky were all close friends—until Magda came along. The official story was that they wanted Magda for their own private secretary."

Lara didn't like what her mother's expression was saying. "The unofficial story?"

"Palmer's typing skills weren't what they were fighting over, despite the three men being married. Nick's aunt was an alleged adulteress, to use the lingo of the times, and had more than one man fighting over her."

"Who was the man?"

"I don't know."

Lara put away her notebook. "No proof, huh?"

"No, but office affairs are nothing new, and no one ever defended her innocence, either. Back then, even today, she would have been fired. On the other hand, Magda Palmer could have given any glamorous movie star serious competition. She was blond, buxom and brainy."

"A buxom adulteress?" Lara smiled. "Really, Mom. You sound like Dad."

"You heard me, and that was before implants became commonplace. Most men noticed her body first, her brains second. Magda made men breathless with both—perhaps not the wisest idea in a man's world a few generations ago. They found her body in the ocean beneath the La Jolla Cliffs."

Lara blinked. "No one swims in those waters. You're suggesting it wasn't an accident?"

"It was never proved, but rumors persisted. Let Internal Affairs and Girard investigate Julio's background. Let Homeland Security handle ballistics and would-be terrorists. But *you*—you investigate Nick's family. And Nick himself."

"Do you think Nick knows this?"

Sandra shrugged. "Find out. Girard, Lansky and Knox were good friends with Magda. Use that as your springboard." Sandra's blue eyes glittered in the way of an experienced cop. "Complacency kills. Your father's right. Watch Nick's back, but watch your own, too."

The two women looked up as the dogs started barking as Nick exited the rental car.

"You be very careful, baby, or I'll kick your ass." The blunt warning came with a maternal hug. Sandra kissed her daughter's hair, then headed back into her office as Nick closed the car door. Lara took in a deep breath. She hurried over to the nondescript sedan, Sadie at her side. They'd chosen a four-door with latches Sadie could open.

"Do you want to take that rubber ring out of your squad car now?" Nick asked without preamble.

"No." Lara studied the U-shaped inner latch and removed her jean belt. "This'll work." She threaded it through the latch and rebuckled the leather, then tucked the metal end close to the latch, leaving the leather free for Sadie, the metal safely away from teeth. "Don't suppose they provided us any bulletproof rental glass."

"Afraid not. But we purchased the extra insurance."

"Then I guess we're all set," Lara said lightly. "You drive."

Nick climbed back into the driver's side, leaving her to "ride shotgun," the Old West term for the armed protector.

"And try to stay away from any rifles with 25 mm bullets," she added.

"No kidding," Nick replied. "You may as well know I called Internal Affairs on the way back and named three senior officers as murder suspects."

"With no evidence?"

"And I told IA, I intend to interview them, as well. That's our plan for the next couple of days, if that's all right."

"It's more than all right."

"Why?"

Lara took in a deep breath. "According to my mother and some old gossip, these three men have more in common than retiring. They were all involved with your aunt. I doubt it means anything, but—"

"Define 'involved.'"

"That's for us to find out. You didn't know about this?"

"Hell, no."

"Get in, Sadie." The dog lifted the outside latch, bounded into the back seat and easily closed the door using Lara's leather belt. "Good girl."

"That was English," Nick said.

"Sure. Police dogs can tell from body language

what's expected of them and whatever language the handler wants to teach them. Sadie was raised at our kennels, remember? I only use German for certain work-related tasks. So…who's first on the list?" Lara asked Nick as they started off.

"Captain Girard. He's working swing shift today. He's still at home."

"You know the way?"

"I have directions. He's expecting us."

"THIS IS IT," Nick announced a half hour later. He parked at the curb in the hilly residential area of Claire-mont.

They both unfastened their seat belts and climbed out of the car to look around. "What a great view," Lara sighed. The upper-middle-class community was sprawled across the hills overlooking Mission Bay, San Diego's huge recreational inlet.

"High praise, lady from La Jolla. Come on."

Lara called her dog to heel. Sadie bounded through the window. Lara attached the leash, then started up the inclined driveway to Captain Girard's place.

"Wait," Nick said.

She paused. "What?"

"It wouldn't hurt for you to be low-key around Gi-rard."

Lara used Nick's expression from earlier. "Define low-key."

"Play bodyguard, not detective. I don't want anyone thinking you're a threat. Threats are targets."

"Since I'm protecting you, I'm certainly a target," she agreed. "More importantly I *am* a threat, Detective. That's what's keeping you safe."

"Listen, Lara—" she noted it was the first time he'd used her first name "—I've named three high-ranking officials as murder suspects—with no hard evidence. Working with me isn't a good way to advance your career."

"Thanks, but I'll worry about my *own* career."

Lara determinedly rang the doorbell. Captain Girard immediately answered. Lara wondered how long he'd known they'd been there. They were shown in, seated and offered hot or cold drinks after being told Mrs. Girard was out. They exchanged small talk, delaying the official questions as a courtesy.

"Beautiful dog," Girard said, directing his attention toward Sadie, who had earlier obeyed Lara's "Down" command. "A female, right? I'm surprised. I thought males were the rule—larger and more aggressive. And the females were saved for search-and-rescue or contraband work."

"That's the rule of thumb," Lara agreed. "But Sadie's enthusiastic about police work and she's a big girl, just like her mother. Bloodlines can be important."

"Can't argue there. Why don't I go get her some water?"

"All right, thanks," Lara said.

"You watered the dog just before we left," Nick said in an undertone as Girard left the room.

"I know. But look at the captain! Talk about being a gracious host. He hasn't so much as broken a sweat."

"Girard does have a refined, genteel air."

Thinking about what her mother had told her, she lowered her voice even more. "I'd never peg him for a murderer."

"Profiling isn't an exact science," Nick reminded her.

"True. Still, I'm glad Mrs. Girard isn't here. He might not be very cooperative if we questioned him in front of his wife."

"Here you are, Officer Nelson." Girard returned, water in a plastic bowl, to the small living room, and gave it to Lara.

"Thank you, Captain."

Lara put the bowl near the dog, but didn't order her to *Nimm,* or take it. For safety reasons, both canine and human, she never let strangers feed or water her dog. Following Lara's lead, Sadie ignored the water.

"Cantello, I heard from Internal Affairs this morning about your…theory," Girard said. "They didn't even bother to advise me of my rights, or suspend me, Lansky or Knox. I can't say I approve. However, I asked them to let you follow this up."

"In other words, you're humoring me."

*Nick gets points for honesty, I'll say that for him,* Lara thought.

"We want the killer found," Girard said, "and as the saying goes, no stone will be left unturned." He took a seat in a chair. "However, this…idea of yours won't hold up. I refuse to upset my wife with your accusations. I expect everything to be cleared up before Nell gets back for my retirement."

"She's out of town?" Nick asked.

"Yes, home in Ohio. Her sister has leukemia."

"I'm sorry."

"So am I, but that's not the point. We both know that just because Julio Valdez mentioned me in a speech doesn't make me guilty. It doesn't mean I erased Julio's file, or killed him, either."

"What else did you have in common with Knox and Lansky?" Nick pressed.

Girard shrugged. "We're from the same generation. We worked at the same station, but our promotions took us in different directions. I made captain, Lansky made lieutenant, and Knox made sergeant."

"You three worked with Detective Cantello's aunt," Lara said.

"That was years ago. We knew—still know—many of the same people."

"You all wanted Magda Palmer for your secretary. Or clerk. Or whatever they called her job back then," Nick said.

The accusation hung in the air. "Who told you this? Ah, I can guess." Girard's gaze swung to Lara. "Your mother. She always did love a good gossip."

Lara felt the change in the room; like when she was out on the street and a suspect would lie or run, fight or surrender. Unconsciously she clenched the leash she held in her hand.

"But you have to admit it sounds suspicious," Nick continued. "Valdez does research for three men and ends up dead in a car in the ocean. My aunt used to do research for the same three men and drowns in the ocean in her own car. I know the facts."

"Only as you remember them."

"I was in college then. And my memory is good. Plus, as next of kin, I have the police paperwork."

"That part's true. As for the rest…" Girard's lips lifted in a condescending smile. "Nelson's mother was an excellent K-9 officer, Nick. But her detective skills left much to be desired."

"Did you have an affair with my aunt?" Nick asked.

"Of course not. I was newly married when I met Magda Palmer. Our relationship was strictly professional."

"Did you help her career?" Lara couldn't help asking.

"Some," Girard admitted. "Magda was basically a single parent. She had no family in the area. She needed an income back in the day when few women worked in law enforcement. But make no mistake. She didn't use her looks to get a job."

"What about Lansky or Knox? Did they think she did?" Nick asked.

Girard shrugged. "It's no secret that Magda was drop-dead gorgeous."

"That's some description, sir," Nick said.

Girard said nothing. Nick had no uncertainties as how to proceed. "If there's more, now's the time to tell us, Captain."

The man paused only a moment. "You might as well know. Your aunt and I were a team. She wasn't my lover, but she was more than just a typist. She was my partner—like Julio was yours."

"Why the big secret?" Nick asked.

"Call it…discretion. I was married, but Magda and I both needed to earn a living. Magda had a brilliant mind. She was an excellent detective, but when we first met, it was a different time, a different age. She could infer things—just from typing up reports, mind you—that others couldn't. The first time she ventured her opinion, she was laughed at, then when she persisted, officially reprimanded. No one would follow up on her lead."

"Except you?" Nick qualified.

"Yes. My instincts about her were right. I believed in Magda when no one else did. I even urged her to try to get into the academy."

"This is news to me," Nick said.

"Of course, there weren't that many female detectives back then. The department didn't think women could be anything more than meter maids. And Magda had you to consider, Nick. So she didn't fight the system. I had no problem using Magda as a crime-solving tool, and I have the captain's bars to prove it."

"But you never gave Magda any credit?" Lara asked.

"Not publicly. I told you, those were different times."

Lara couldn't help herself. "Alice Wells, the first policewoman ever in this country, was appointed in Los Angeles. That was 1910. You and Magda aren't that old. And my mother worked patrol, then K-9."

Girard looked down on her like a sergeant would a rookie. "If you knew your history, Officer, you'd also know that women were never issued a uniform or allowed to patrol before 1969. Wells worked only with women and children. Magda excelled in detective work. If anyone discovered that I routinely consulted Magda on my cases, we'd both have been stopped from doing the good work we did. My silence ensured she kept her typist job."

"Sounds like…forgive me, sir…that her silence ensured *your* job," Lara said softly.

Nick immediately jumped in. "Captain, is your wife aware of all this?"

"I don't know. I refused to discuss the subject with anyone, and after Magda died…Nell let matters drop."

*How convenient,* Lara thought, but her expression must have conveyed her cynicism, for Girard's eyes narrowed.

"Are you here to ask me about Julio's death?" he said. "See if I have an alibi? I was here with my wife." He passed them a sheet of paper with writing and a phone number on it. "Here's where she is. You can confirm it yourself, not that it matters."

"Thank you," Nick replied.

"Investigating Magda Palmer isn't going to help you find Julio's killer," Girard said.

"I understand you were in the army, Captain Girard."

"Infantry, Cantello. Not the tank corps. And Homeland Security can verify that fact, too. And that there are no antitank weapons in my house." Silence filled the room. "I have to get ready for work." Girard determinedly rose to his feet and walked to the door, leaving the others no choice but to do the same.

"Thanks for your time, Captain," Nick said. "We'll get in touch with Mrs. Girard." Lara knew the interview was over.

Girard showed them both out, Sadie at Lara's side. Behind them, they heard the *snick* of the dead bolt engaging. Lara welcomed the brightness of the California sun.

"Whew. I'm glad that's over. Actually, I'm surprised he put up with us as long as he did."

"I don't care if Girard's humoring me. I want to follow through on this," Nick said.

"Yeah. Funny how he had his sister-in-law's address and phone number ready for you. No one's that organized."

"I find it strange that he didn't mind talking about my aunt, but as soon as I brought up his military service, he showed us the door. But not before letting us know his house had been searched for antitank munitions." Nick unlocked the car door.

"Sadie, get in." Lara watched as Sadie let herself in back, closing the door from inside. "What do you know about your aunt's work history?"

Lara opened the front passenger door and climbed in, Sadie alert and panting again. Nick started the car and the air conditioner, but remained parked.

"I know Magda worked for Girard. I never thought past that—never saw him at the house or anywhere in my life," Nick said thoughtfully. "As for Knox or Lansky, their names didn't come up until I was a detective myself."

"There must have been *something* to the rumors if my mother remembered it. Despite Girard's cheap shot, my mother was never into gossip. If the three of them fought over your aunt, either professionally or personally, there's something there. You have another aunt, I understand. Perhaps Magda confided in her?"

"I planned on calling her," Nick said. "And I want to talk to your mother."

"How did Magda die?"

"She drowned. Her car went off the road."

"The same way Julio died?"

"Not the same," Nick replied. "Julio was shot. My aunt lost control of her car while driving along the coast."

"So you think it was just a motor-vehicle accident? But what if your aunt's accident wasn't an accident at all?" Lara suggested. "I mean, think about it. This is California. People here rarely drive into the ocean. It's so...so..."

"What?"

"Hollywood! Like some fifties black-and-white movie. The old Coast Highway is mostly freeway now. There aren't that many places left with a clear shot into the water." Eager for the car to move, Sadie leaned forward, nosing Lara in the ear. Lara scratched the black ears, but her attention remained focused on Nick. "You know about Julio. But who knows about you and your past? Your background? Who's checking on you?"

"No one's interviewed me yet," Nick said slowly. He put the car in drive and hit the gas.

"Doesn't it seem strange no one's interviewed you?" Lara asked a couple of minutes later. "This is a murder—a cop murder."

Nick stopped at a red light, tapping his thumbs on the steering wheel. "Maybe you've got a point."

"I'm confused. I'm no detective, but I know procedure. Save for Homeland Security, no one's contacting us or freely sharing information. We're always going to them, instead of the other way around."

"You're right about procedure." Nick edged forward as the light changed to green and the line of cars before them began to move. "They haven't scheduled me for grief counseling yet, either—as far as I'm concerned, that's to my advantage."

"I keep thinking about your aunt. Could Julio have discovered evidence of a crime of passion?" Lara wondered. "What if Magda had an affair, and Julio found out about it? The proverbial skeleton in the closet wouldn't sit too well at a retirement dinner."

"Now you're reaching. Magda was a traditional woman. She wouldn't sleep with one married man, let alone three."

"Well, I suppose you would know." Lara shook her head and changed tack. "Why do you call her Magda?"

"She asked me to. Said *Aunt* made her feel old."

Lara frowned. "You just said she was a traditional woman. That doesn't fit."

Nick gave her a sharp glance, then turned his attention back to the road, but didn't argue. His expression was troubled as they headed toward the beach and the freeway that snaked up the California coast.

"We need to know more about Magda's personal and professional life," Lara said. "Especially in connection with Girard, Lansky and Knox."

"Perhaps. But Magda couldn't have killed Julio, and the military didn't use depleted uranium when she was alive. Enough guessing. Right now I want to swing by Julio's house and see what I can find."

"I don't have a problem with that. You've got a key?"

"And permission. Anything else?"

"I do need to let Sadie stretch her legs first. Let's hit Mission Bay and get some burgers. I'm buying."

Nick met her eyes briefly. "*I'll* buy," he said. "Includes one for Sadie, too."

Her lips curved upward in a smile. "You're on."

MISSION BAY WAS no tranquil ocean park. From his shaded spot on the tree-dotted higher shore grass, Nick could see hundreds of people sailing, jetskiing in the bay, jogging on the sand, children laughing and playing. Beside him Lara and Sadie finished their burgers.

"I'm really not supposed to feed her fried food," Lara said, giving Sadie a ketchup-smeared fry. "But she loves them."

"You're a good officer," Nick said out of the blue.

Lara glanced at him in surprise. "Well, K-9 officer," she corrected. She finished her last bite of hamburger, and wiped her fingers on the paper napkin.

"If you weren't K-9, what would you be?"

"I'll always be K-9. But if I weren't, I don't think I have the mind-set for detective work."

"Explain."

Lara thought about it for a moment. "I'm best dealing with the here and now. You detectives start with a body and work backwards and forwards. Your cases could drag on for years, might never be solved. That's not for me. Sadie and I find the drugs, find the bad guy, or we don't. Case closed. Plus…well, it seems—to me, at least—that detectives don't enjoy their jobs like K-9 teams do."

"That's not true," Nick argued. "There's nothing like that satisfaction of arresting a killer and taking him off the streets."

"Yes, but I look forward to my job. I love being on the street with Sadie each and every day. I see *everything,* from motivated citizens who stop at an accident scene to help strangers to people killing over a parking spot at the mall. I take everything in, and then have to come up with a realistic view of any situation and act— in conjunction with my dog—in very little time. That's the strong point of any K-9 officer. We're all good at it."

"Once with K-9, always with K-9?" Nick asked.

"As long as our instincts hold out, yes. Then we, or should I say I, can always go into training new teams. Until that day arrives, I can't afford to make a mistake—things can go sour in seconds."

"Like the kidnapping attempt on the rock star's daughter? Where you ended up in the hospital?"

Lara tilted her head. "Why, Detective Cantello," she drawled. "Have you been checking me out?"

"Yes."

"Next you'll be following me around on my doughnut runs."

They both smiled at the old joke. "So what's your favorite pastry?" Nick asked.

"Raised sugar twists. Nothing for Sadie, of course."

"I never had a dog. Julio talked about getting one for the kids this Christmas, but he never got around to it."

Suddenly the lighthearted mood faded, and Lara sensed it was time to get back to business. Lara quickly walked Sadie, watered her and soon the three of them were back in the car, driving the route Nick had taken so many times before to Julio's home. They weren't expecting to see anyone there. To Lara's surprise, a stranger waited outside the house.

"Who's that?" Lara said, instantly reaching for her gun.

"Relax, he's one of us. T. J. Knox, son of Sergeant Knox."

"Thought you could use some reinforcements," the man said as the three exited the rental. "Hey, Nicky. Who's your friend?"

*Nicky?* Lara blinked and studied T. J. Knox, her voice and body language automatically calming Sadie, who'd instantly gone on alert. He looked about Nick's age and carried his civilian-clothes-clad body nicely. Lara, always alert for details, noticed no trace of grief on his face, just professionalism. Despite the friendly-sounding *Nicky,* the two men didn't seem close. And since Nick had just named the guy's father as a murder suspect, she didn't expect any sudden camaraderie, either.

Nick did curt introductions. "Officer, this is Detective Knox. Knox, Officer Lara Nelson."

"Pleased to meet you, Lara."

"Detective Knox. I prefer Officer Nelson when I'm on duty."

"Sorry, Officer. Didn't mean to step on any toes."

"What are you doing here, Knox?" Nick asked. "I didn't request your presence."

"I'm out here on my own time. Whether I like it or not—and I don't—you're the only one who's come up with any kind of working theory. It's all over town. No one wants to believe one of our own killed your partner. You may not have evidence and my father hasn't been suspended, but I *know* he didn't do it. Why do you think I'm here?" T.J. said impatiently. "You want to find Julio's killer. I want to clear Dad's name."

"Sounds like a conflict of interest."

"Same with your presence, and it isn't bothering anyone downtown. You want to hear what I have to say or not?"

"Speak your piece," Nick said.

"Okay. I think someone's using the old scandal to draw attention away from Julio's killer."

Nick drew in a breath. "Now why would you think that?"

T.J. shrugged. "Come on, I've heard the rumors.

And I know my father knew Magda. He told me he met her through Girard years ago when they were working together."

"You're sure?"

"Hell, yes. Dad let it slip once after a couple of beers." T.J. shook his head. "Poor guy. He found out that Magda Palmer had already teamed up with the captain to solve cases. That Girard beat Dad hands down for promotions, thanks to Magda."

"You're not telling us anything we haven't heard."

"Dad told me Lansky's involved in this, too. Someone was sleeping with Juliet, and Lansky was blackmailing the Romeo—Girard."

"Any proof? Can't your father be more specific?" Nick asked.

"No. Dad wants to let it drop. The statute of limitations on the blackmail ran out years ago, when Magda died—or so he says. Even if my father did have knowledge of any crimes, that doesn't make him a killer."

"There's no statute of limitations on murder," Nick reminded him.

"I'm well aware of that, but Dad won't talk to me. Maybe he'll talk to you. I want him to retire with his head held proud."

"I'd planned on talking to him. Tell him we'll be stopping by the house tomorrow to question him," Nick said.

"The sooner the better. You have my phone number," T.J. said, heading for his car. "And Dad's."

"The official funeral's tomorrow," Lara reminded Nick. "We need to get through that first."

"God. I hate funerals."

Lara stared into the outside sunshine, and thought, So do I. They're so sad. So tragic and predictable.

She couldn't have been more wrong.

# CHAPTER SIX

*Wednesday morning*

A GENTLE KNOCK on her bedroom door roused Lara.

"It's me," her mother said. "Can I come in?"

She opened her eyes, then sat up. "Umm, yeah," she said fuzzily, noting her alarm hadn't yet gone off.

Sandra opened the door, and something white streaked into the room to launch itself onto her bed, much to Sadie's dismay. It was a terrier.

"What time is it?" Lara asked.

"Six. The funeral is at nine, but Nick wanted me to wake you early so he could visit with the family before the funeral."

Lara blinked and petted the terrier on her lap. Jealous, Sadie softly growled a halfhearted protest, but the terrier ignored her. Sadie gave up and left the bed to head for the dog door off the kitchen and let herself out. The terrier promptly took Sadie's warm spot and curled up at Lara's feet. Lara affectionately rubbed the scruffy head.

"Breakfast is ready. Nick's already at the table with

his coffee." Sandra paused. "Dad and I thought about going to the funeral, unless you object."

"I'd rather you didn't. If you're present and someone's looking for Nick, they'll know for certain we're staying with you—if they haven't guessed already. Besides, I'll concentrate better without you there."

"That's what your father said." Sandra sighed. "Shall I feed Sadie for you? It'll keep hair off your dress uniform."

"Thanks, Mom."

"Come on, silly," Sandra called to the terrier. "You too. I—"

Lara's cell beeped. She picked it up from the bedside table. "Officer Nelson."

"Lara, this is Captain Girard."

"Yes, Captain."

"Sorry to call so early, but there's been…a development. Mrs. Valdez says the family doesn't want Nick in the funeral procession. She doesn't even want him at the church."

*"What?"*

"You heard me. You'll have to tell Cantello."

"But why? What's the reason?"

"It's the widow's wish. Nelson, I have to go. You understand."

"I…yes. Yes," she repeated. "Family only. Okay."

"Goodbye." Girard clicked off.

"Who was it?" Sandra asked.

"The captain. I can't believe it! They don't want Nick in the funeral procession."

"The police?"

"No, Mom, the *family* doesn't want Nick at the funeral." Lara rubbed her temple in agitation. "What if Jim's parents had banned me from his funeral? Said I wasn't blood kin? Girard wants me to tell Nick! How can I?"

"Follow orders. Be a good cop."

Lara lifted her chin. "It's not right. I know it's not right."

"Lara, if there's anything I can do…"

"Just don't say a word to Nick. I have to get dressed. He and I are going to that funeral, anyway."

THE DRIVE TO St. Paul's in San Diego was a good forty minutes from North San Diego County on the interstate. It was rush hour, so traffic was congested. But Lara, who was now driving her squad car, Nick riding shotgun, Sadie in back, took advantage of her official vehicle. The route from Escondido was a straight shot south. They would hook up with other police cars for an official funeral procession.

The car's air-conditioning, the low static of the muted police radio and the gentle panting of Sadie filled the car. Nick sat rigidly, pressed and formally dressed, hat in his lap. The vegetation along the sides of the freeway was brown and burnt from the usual summer drought. The soil, long since baked to dust, hung in the air, and slowly mixed with the traffic's exhaust fumes.

"Lord, it's dry out," she murmured. It had been six months without rain until the day Julio had died. Ocean notwithstanding, desert conditions were desert conditions.

"It'll rain again." Nick gave her a quick glance. "Look at the beach."

She did. The coastal sky was a thick gray, but that could easily be the thick morning marine layer before it burned off.

"It'll rain," he repeated. "Hope Lilia and the boys don't get wet. The rest of the family will be here, too." Nick flicked at a piece of lint on his dress hat.

"You're family, too."

"Not anymore. Whether Lilia moves back to Mexico or stays in San Diego, I'm out. I'm sure they blame me for Julio's death. If he hadn't been driving my car…"

"They won't close ranks forever."

"Lilia hasn't taken or returned one of my calls since Julio was killed. Who can blame her?"

Lara reached for him then, her fingers curling around his arm. He made no comment, but neither did he shake her off. She ended the touch only when she approached a tricky interchange. She smoothly navigated the looping turns, the congested ramps, and merged into a new lane with both hands on the steering wheel. It wasn't until after that he spoke again.

"I thought we were close." He sighed. "I've been here before. After Magda died, my parents were too far away to fill the gap she left, except for the money they sent me to finish college."

"Don't you keep in touch?"

"Holidays. Birthdays." Nick readjusted the hat on his lap. "When are we hooking up with the motorcade?" he asked. A pause, then, "We're not, are we?"

"No."

"For safety reasons, or because the family…? Come on, I'm not stupid."

She hesitated. It would be too cruel to keep up the facade any longer. "Nick, the family doesn't want you at the funeral."

He blanched.

"I'm sorry. Headquarters called me this morning. I was told to keep you away." Lara reached for his arm, squeezed it. "I didn't agree to keep you away. That's why we didn't drive in with the motorcade procession, though. And that's why we're going to stand in the back. It's the only way you can be at your partner's funeral."

"Are…are you sure?"

"I didn't talk with Julio's wife, only Girard. But apparently she made the decision. And it's her right to choose who sits with her. But it's *your* right to pay your last respects. We're not leaving. No one will eject us if we keep a low profile and stay in the back." Lara checked her watch. "The ceremony starts any minute. We go in quietly and stay at the back, then be the first to leave. So if we go, that's the only way we do it. Your choice."

Lara fell silent…and found herself remembering Jim's funeral. The mourners and the prayers did little to comfort her; Jim was gone and nothing would bring him back. But she realized that many people *did* derive comfort from funerals. Funerals were important rites of passage for the living, not the dead. And Nick was very much alive.

"I do want to go," Nick said at last.

"No one will make a scene," she promised him, and she meant it.

Seconds later she turned on the windshield wipers. The weather had proved Nick right. It was raining. Within minutes Lara stopped the car at the barricade detouring normal traffic around and away from the church. She rolled down her window as the officer directing traffic motioned her to stop.

"We're out of parking. Lot's been full for hours," the officer said, flicking a glance at a wary Sadie in the back seat. "You'll have to hike in. What perimeter are you working?"

"I'm not working. I'm escorting Julio Valdez's partner—Detective Cantello—to the ceremony."

"But why so late?"

"Traffic," Lara said. "Detective Cantello, let this officer see your ID."

Nick did as she asked, his face grim. The officer inspected it, rain running down the edges of his broad hat, as Lara continued speaking.

"Radio ahead and find us a parking spot. Tell them K-9 Officer Lara Nelson and dog will accompany the detective to the church. We'll stand in the back."

The wet officer returned Nick's identification. "Sorry about your partner."

Parking arrangements were quickly made and occupied. As Lara shut off the engine, Nick turned toward her.

"I wish I could sit with the family," he said, his voice harsh with emotion.

"So do I. Remember, we leave if there's any trouble."

Nick took off his hat. "Got it."

Lara gathered up her dog's leash. "Heel, Sadie."

The trio entered the church, police monitoring their entrance. Lara and Nick both stood as seated mourners followed the sitting, standing and kneeling motions of the Catholic service. The funeral Mass was confusing to Lara, the sermon heartbreaking and lengthy. The huge church, filled with police, family and friends, the mayor and other city officials, couldn't accommodate all the uniformed and government officials. The overflow spilled outside. Wet mourners huddled outside, listening to the service over a loudspeaker.

Lara kept her attention on the man beside her. He stood stoically, his face serious, eyes dry. Those in law enforcement who recognized him must have marveled at his composure, for even veterans had tears in their eyes during the ceremony. Suddenly Lara knew that his dry eyes were an act of courage. Lara's own eyes filled with tears, but for Nick himself. He had no family to support him in his grief as she'd had at Jim's funeral.

He kept his stoic pose, in no manner drawing attention to himself or alarming the family. When many of the attendees rose to their feet and lined up for communion, Lara flicked him a quick glance. His Italian roots probably meant he was Catholic, but she had no idea if he still practiced that faith. Did he plan on getting in the line? But then the family would see him. Sadie felt Lara's confusion and looked up at her. The dog's movement caught Nick's attention. Somehow he knew, it seemed, what she was thinking. He didn't speak, but jerked his chin toward the exit, then began to head there, Lara and Sadie following.

As they made their way through the standing crowd, Nick turned and looked over his shoulder at the Valdez family in the front—the family that would eventually set off for the ride to the airport and a Mexican cemetery…without him. He finally gave in to his emotions.

"Is there anything I can do?" she asked quietly as they reached their K-9 vehicle.

"Just get me out of here."

Nick climbed into the shotgun seat. Suddenly Sadie, all eighty-five pounds of her, jumped onto Nick's lap with muddy paws and rain-beaded fur, and laid her nose on Nick's shoulder.

"Sadie!" Lara exclaimed. "Sorry. She's never…" She was so shocked at the damage to his dress uniform, words failed her.

"Let her stay," Nick said gruffly, his arms around the dog to stabilize them both.

Lara didn't bother with procedure. She climbed into her seat, started the car and carefully snaked her way through and out of the packed parking lot.

"I'm gonna stop at my house," she said, mentally gauging the long ride from the church to her parents' kennels compared to the much closer home in La Jolla. "We can change. My father has clothes there you can use." She drove by the waiting hearse, seeing its muddied black lines between sweeps of her windshield wipers. "I'm not driving in this damn rain."

THE RAIN STILL FELL as they pulled into Lara's driveway. The midday sun remained hidden beneath clouds of gray, its dim light coloring the ocean the same dull gray. Only when Lara was parked did Sadie finally stir, jerking Nick out of his silence.

"We'd better search the grounds," he heard Lara say. The three did a thorough search of the grounds and house before Lara grabbed some of her father's clothes.

"Here, Nick, you take this bedroom. It has its own bath," Lara suggested as water from their rain-soaked uniforms dripped onto the tile floor. "I'll use the one in my bedroom. Let me towel down my dog real quick, then I'll grab you some fresh towels, okay?"

NICK NODDED. From a far-off place in his mind, he noticed the water dripping from his clothing onto the floor. In the bedroom there was no place for him to sit without ruining comforters or upholstered chairs. So he sat on the edge of the tub, his wet tie crumpled in his hands. One black dress shoe was off and the soggy suit coat was unbuttoned. That was as far as he could get. The anguish of Julio's death had been compounded by Lilia's rejection of him as a family friend. His pain nearly overwhelmed him. In another moment he'd start sobbing, and if he did, he wasn't sure he'd be able to stop.

He heard Lara's knock on the half-closed bedroom door, then, "Nick? I have your towels."

He couldn't answer.

"Shall I leave them on the bed?" She opened the door just a crack more. "Nick? Can I come in?"

Still no answer. Lara opened the door all the way.

His anguish clogged his throat. He shouldn't have had to stand in the back of the church. But he shouldn't have gone boating. He shouldn't have loaned Julio his car. And most of all, Julio shouldn't be dead.

"Oh, Nick…"

He jerked his head up. Lara was looking at him from the bedroom door, towels in her arm.

He stood. "Thanks for the towels. And thanks for taking me to the church. I needed to be there." The last of his control vanished when she dropped the towels on the floor and stepped toward him.

"I know you did." Lara placed one hand on his cheek, he placed his lips on her cheek, and they moved together for a hug of comfort. Then it happened. Shared tragedies, grief and death, make you crazy. The only cure is passion and life. Each knew of the other's loss, the other's pain. They shed their dress blues, the unhappy reminder of the funerals. Neither thought of being sensible. They ended on the bed, holding each other, comforting each other, and finally ridding themselves of wet undergarments. As passion mounted, Nick couldn't tell where he ended and she began. He only knew she had offered herself as a lifeline, and he'd taken it.

It wasn't until much later, when she was asleep in his arms, that Nick realized he hadn't used protection. And he forced himself to slowly start rebuilding the control he'd set aside in Lara's arms—control that would enable him to search for Julio's killer. Hopefully Lara would remain at his side. He prayed she would remain at his side.

# CHAPTER SEVEN

*Thursday morning*

THE MORNING SUN SHONE bright and hot over the Pacific. Nick awoke to the sound of the piano and the smell of fresh coffee. He reached to the other side of the bed—empty—although the night before he could touch Lara's smooth skin, taste her mouth, feel the silkiness of her soft blond hair. He frowned, then rose to shower. He'd crossed the line last night, and hadn't even remembered her leaving his bed. He felt disoriented, yet rested. A check of the alarm clock in the room showed a whole afternoon and night had passed—most of the former in passion, the latter in healing sleep.

Lara was still playing the piano when he entered the studio, coffee in hand. To his relief, she didn't stop when she saw him. This "morning after," the day after Julio's funeral, would be especially awkward. What could he say to her? "Yesterday should never have happened"? Or, "Last night was incredible"? Both statements were true, but what he'd *have* to say was, "We can no longer work together."

LARA ATTACKED a difficult crescendo sequence and fumbled on the fingering. The wrong notes crashed discordantly, then mingled with her soft curse. She heard Nick clear his throat behind her.

"Hell," she said with a rueful look his way. "I'll never get this. Hope I didn't wake you."

"No." Nick noted the gun in its shoulder case, the dog at her side. She'd slept with him last night with gun and dog in the room, as well. Obviously she hadn't forgotten reality, as he had.

Lara sighed. "I wish Kate were here. She's the expert. This fingering is a real killer."

Nick's erotic memories of the night before faded slightly. His face must have shown something, because Lara said, "Maybe 'killer' was the wrong word to use. You sleep well?" she abruptly asked, which threw him even more.

"About last night… I was completely unprofessional. We shouldn't… I can give you a copy of my latest blood test from my police physical," he offered.

"Same here," she said.

"I didn't use a condom. Are you on any birth control?"

Lara blinked as reality sank in. She hadn't taken the pill since Jim's death. He'd been her fiancé, almost her husband. She hadn't planned on dating anyone, let alone having sex. She hadn't thought she'd be ready for a long, long time. That surprised her more than anything. Nick took her silence as embarrassment.

"Sorry," he said. "I know it's personal."

In her head, Lara counted the days back, trying to

pinpoint her last fertile period. Women who routinely endured rigorous physical stress and possessed little body fat commonly suffered from irregular menstrual cycles. She was one of them—and irregular cycles meant irregular ovulation. She should be safe, she hoped, as long as she didn't buck the odds and share a bed with Nick Cantello again. A shame, she thought. Being with him had been more than just mutual comfort. She and Nick had connected far more than on a physical level. Last night, she'd welcomed him with no rational thought; she'd been willing and ready….

"Before we get into that subject," she said slowly, "I apologize for not getting you back to the kennels. It would have been safer."

"Don't beat yourself up. I notice you slept with your gun and dog."

"Still—"

"We messed up."

"I messed up more." Lara touched Sadie's head for reassurance, fingering the delicate fur behind the ears. "I'm not using any method of birth control. I haven't since my fiancé died."

"God." He sat down on the couch, coffee splashing onto his hand. "Lara, we can't work together anymore."

"Oh, for heaven's sake! I'm not looking for a wedding, if that's what you're worried about."

"Dammit, Lara! If you're pregnant, you shouldn't be working as a bodyguard, let alone as a bodyguard on a murder case."

"Who says? I shouldn't have done a lot of things!"

Lara threw back. "Like taking you to the funeral. Or spending the night with you. It's just that…well…at the time…what I did seemed right." She waited for his response and was disappointed in his answer.

"You know, your file said you were a model officer."

"I'm a damn good officer. Just as good as you are."

To her relief, Nick smiled. "I believe that."

"Then let's go to work. You wanted to interview Knox."

"And Lansky. I want to find Julio's killer and lock him up, and soon. Especially if…" He hesitated.

"What?"

"You end up pregnant. It wasn't just one time yesterday, you should remember."

"Oh, I remember, all right. But for now, let's sideline the topic of pregnancy."

And so neither remarked on it as Lara drove to Knox's house in the K-9 unit they'd used to attend the funeral. Lara would exchange it for the rental car later, but for now, the police vehicle would help her remember who and what she was, especially while working with a man she admired so much.

And who she'd let make love to her again and again and again…

IN DISMAY, Lara looked out the car window. "Sergeant Knox lives here?"

"It's a beat-up neighborhood, that's for sure."

"Why would Sergeant Knox live here?" Lara asked. "Even a rookie could afford a better area."

"Something else for us to find out." Nick gave her a

glance she recognized as his characteristic determination. "He knows we're coming. Interview time."

Lara parked the car. From within the comfortable interior of the air-conditioned vehicle, she saw that the neighborhood screamed of neglect. Adults with spiritless faces watched still-spirited children kick a dirty soccer ball among parked cars. Lara's home above the beautiful Pacific seemed light-years away.

They were met outside immediately by Sergeant Richard Knox, who was blatantly hostile about their arrival. The invitation he issued for them to come inside was reluctant, and unlike Girard during his interview, he didn't ask them to sit down or offer them a drink.

"I'm supposed to retire this week, Cantello. I wasn't planning to spend my last days before retirement being suspended and charged."

"Neither of those has happened yet," Nick said.

"No, but I'm on desk duty and had to turn in my gun. Just like Girard and Lansky."

"I wasn't planning on burying my partner, either," Nick returned. "The sooner we find who killed him, the sooner you can start enjoying…the fruits of your labor." Nick looked around the dingy, littered room. "Gonna offer us a seat?"

The older man flushed. "Help yourself," he said abruptly. "But I want my son here for any questioning. He's out back. He told me he's already talked to you, the idiot. I'll go get him."

Lara moved to follow him with Sadie, standard procedure, but Nick shook his head.

"I doubt he'll run, not with his retirement waiting," Nick said. "Besides, Internal Affairs took his gun."

"That doesn't mean he doesn't have another," Lara said. But she remained where she was.

Suddenly Sadie's ears twitched and a low warning growl rumbled in her throat. Lara and Nick observed the father return with his son. Lara was struck by the difference between the two men. Even in jeans and work shirt, T.J.'s carefully put-together appearance and clean-shaven face contrasted sharply with his father's scruffy appearance. While the son's expression was carefully arranged into lines of polite welcome, Richard's was still lined with hostility.

"Officer Nelson," T.J. greeted her, while acknowledging Nick's presence with a short, "Nicky," and nod of the head.

Richard said matter-of-factly, "I'll save you some time, Cantello. I didn't kill your partner. I was in bed with a six-pack the night he died."

"Can anyone provide an alibi?" Nick asked. "Family or friend?"

"Dad doesn't have a lady friend," T.J. drawled. "And Mom died a long time ago. But I was here, my car was here, the neighbors can confirm," Knox said.

Lara watched T.J. carefully. He didn't seem the dutiful-son type, and Lara uneasily wondered if T.J. shouldn't be added to the list of suspects. The best she could do now was listen and remain alert as Nick continued his questioning.

"What do you know about Magda Palmer, Sergeant?"

"What does she have to do with Julio's death?" the elder Knox countered. He glanced at his son as if *he* could provide the answer.

Nick shrugged. "You tell me. Her name always seems to pop up. Makes me curious."

Richard swore. T.J. threw a restraining arm around his father's shoulders. Again, Lara was struck by the contrast between the two faces.

"Come on, Dad, don't make this difficult. Sorry," T.J. apologized for his father. "Dad's been cranky ever since mandatory retirement proceedings were started."

"I still have a few good years yet. I could use the money."

"Tell them the rest, Dad."

The elder Knox lifted his chin. "I gamble."

"Legally?" Nick asked.

Richard didn't answer, so T.J. did. "Yes, at the casinos. And quite heavily, as you can see." T.J. made a sweeping gesture of the shabby room.

"Not as fancy as Lansky playing the stock market," Richard said maliciously, "But I have more fun."

"Keep going, Dad," T.J. quietly urged.

There was silence in the room. Then Richard said, "About Magda… Girard liked pretty women to get promotions, and Lansky liked to bed them. I never used women, especially Magda. And I'm not a killer. So save the arrest and the questions for the right guy."

Nick rose to his feet. "There's no warrant sworn out for any arrests yet, Sergeant Knox."

"I still want you to find him. Cop killers shouldn't be allowed to live."

Nick neither agreed nor disagreed. "We're done here, Officer," Nick said.

BACK OUTSIDE at the car, Lara said, "Lovely family, aren't they?"

"Hold on," he said, checking his phone. "I've got a message." He dialed his voice mail, listened and hung up.

"Homeland Security says all three of our suspects were military veterans and skilled in arms. Certainly any one of them could have fired antitank weapons. Damn. I was hoping we could narrow the field."

"Maybe we can," Lara said. "How come we don't have more detailed financial files or background checks on Lansky, Girard and Knox? At least rule out money as a motive. If Girard's still in charge of the investigation—"

"He's not. Internal Affairs is," Nick corrected.

"Still, I'd think he'd order them to clear himself, if for no other reason. And none of the three has been suspended, either."

"What are you saying?"

"I'm saying maybe we need a more objective resource than our superiors. Why don't you call Homeland Security and ask *them* to do the checks for us? Financial, background, everything. See if it tallies up with Girard's information. That is, what he even bothers to give us. Communication on this case sucks."

"I agree," Nick said thoughtfully. "Let's remedy that, and see Lansky next."

"I'm game."

AFTER A MERCIFULLY SMOOTH drive on California's wreck-prone freeways, man, woman and canine left their car and stood in San Diego's noon sun. Lieutenant Lansky's home was located in a much nicer neighborhood than Knox's. The lieutenant's well-maintained condo rose above the green minilawns thriving amidst the California drought. In the distance splashes and laughs could be heard as adults enjoyed the pool.

"Now *this* is a nice place," Lara murmured.

"Sure beats mine," Nick admitted.

As usual, Lara studied the surroundings, looking for possible ambush spots, and found nothing to concern her.

Nick put on his working-detective persona. "Come on. Lansky and his wife are expecting us. Oh, to give you a heads-up, Lansky's wife is in a wheelchair. She was permanently injured in the same crash that killed Magda. She was a passenger in Magda's car."

"You could have told me this a little earlier!" Lara protested.

"When—last night?"

Lara refused to blush. "Point taken. Come on, then."

The lieutenant and his wife were sitting outside on a spacious porch that overlooked a riot of lush plants and desert blooms. The couple noticed their arrival by spotting Sadie, boldly trotting past the No Pets sign. Lansky, with a smile on his rugged face, raised a beefy hand in greeting as they approached.

Lara already knew Lansky, but she'd never met his wife. She found herself smiling as introductions were

made. Helen Lansky's pleasant welcoming manner be-
lied the lines of pain on her face and the wheelchair in
which she sat. Lieutenant Lansky's welcome was just
as warm. With Nick, the man was positively jovial; so
much so that Lara had to comment after taking a seat.

"You seem awfully cheerful for a man who attended
a fellow officer's funeral only yesterday."

"Can't cry forever. Especially when I'm spending
time with my favorite gal." Lansky reached for his
wife's hand and held it tight. The couple seemed to gen-
uinely care for one another, which made Lara wonder
about Knox's saying that Lansky liked to bed women—
plural.

Nick threw Helen Lansky a quick glance: "Maybe
you and I can go inside and talk, Lieutenant?"

Lansky immediately turned toward his wife, her
hand still in his. "Sweetheart?"

"I'd like to hear this," she replied softly. "Anything
that concerns my husband concerns me."

"She may be in a wheelchair, Detective, but she's one
tough lady. Besides, she'll just grill me later on, anyway."

Helen gave her husband's arm a loving swat. "You'll
give these people the wrong impression."

The two smiled at one another, and Lara still wasn't
certain the affection was real or put on for company.
Cops had more than their fair share of divorces. Lara
found herself wondering if Lansky had considered
Magda a temptation long before his wife became an in-

valid. And Nick's bombshell that both women had been in the car hadn't helped compose her thoughts.

Nick asked his questions, including verification of Lansky's wife-supported alibi. Lara made herself a mental note to study the financial printouts of the couple herself, then realized Helen had addressed her.

"I'm sorry," she said. "Could you repeat that?"

"I said I was noticing how much Nick resembles Magda."

Lara asked, "You knew her well?"

"Of course," Helen said. "The police department was much smaller fifty years ago, and Magda was one of the few women working there. In fact, your aunt and I were friends for years."

"It's true," Lansky confirmed. "Helen was the one who introduced Magda to Captain Girard."

"Did you know they were working together—under the table—on the force?" Nick asked.

"Oh, yes," Lansky said. "But they were a good team and got the job done, so I kept quiet. Later on, when Girard's marriage was on shaky ground because of Magda, I still kept quiet."

Nick lifted his chin. "Do you have any proof Girard and my aunt were lovers?"

"For a court of law? No, but they were," Lansky asserted. "Forgive my bluntness, Cantello, but your aunt was lonely, and Girard was only too happy to help her out. She and Girard may have started off with a professional relationship, but it didn't stay that way."

"What made it worse was that Knox was interested

in her, too," Helen added. "He didn't get married until *after* Magda took up exclusively with Girard. I understand he's divorced now. His ex is in Florida."

Nick came to Magda's defense. "I'd prefer to think men were more interested in my aunt's crime-solving abilities than her looks."

Lansky shook his head. "Wrong. She turned the heads of even happily married men like me when she walked by. She was that kind of woman."

"I'm sorry, Detective," Helen said. "I'm sure my husband didn't mean to be rude. But we knew Magda well, and she had something…" Helen shook her head. "Her physical looks were nothing compared to the sheer sensuality she exuded. And she wasn't even trying."

"Sensual women can be loving, even maternal, and still have strong morals. I know," Nick stiffly insisted. "She raised me."

"And your loyalty is commendable," Lansky added. "But we knew her, too. When men saw Magda, they wanted her."

*Bad enough to kill her?* Lara wanted to ask. But Nick had his own question.

"Was Magda obvious about her feelings—if this is true—for Girard?"

Lansky and Helen exchanged glances. Then Helen spoke. "No. She was discreet."

"She wasn't intentionally a home-wrecker," Helen said quickly. "She didn't flaunt herself, but men still coveted her. Few understood how much better she was at police work than the men. Magda hated having to stand aside and let others blunder through the case-work she'd spent all day typing up. She was a single woman taking care of a nephew. I wouldn't blame her for seeking—" Helen searched for a tactful word "—a little comfort."

Lara winced. Was that what she, Lara, had done with Nick? Sought a comforting port in a storm? Her innate honesty forced her to consider the question, then answer it. No, she wasn't afraid to be alone. She suddenly realized that with Nick, she didn't feel lonely, even when she was physically alone. It was a breath-catching revelation.

"Your aunt had beauty and brains. Girard's friendship, whatever it entailed, was good for her. His wife never found out how much a part of his life Magda was. Girard still misses her. I know I do," Helen said.

"The three of us were good friends," Lansky said.

"So you hold nothing against Magda?" Nick asked.

"No," Lansky said.

"Not even the crash?" Lara pressed.

"What do you want me to say? I'm happy about it?" Lansky stubbornly refused to elaborate any more, but Helen did.

"I wish Magda's car hadn't crashed. She'd still be alive and I wouldn't be in this chair," Helen seconded. "It was an accident. You know that, Nick. That's what you were told when she died."

Nick's eyes narrowed. "I believed it then. I don't know if I believe it now."

# CHAPTER EIGHT

"HELEN, WOULD YOU review the events of Magda's death?" Nick asked. "You were a witness."

"Not much of a witness," Helen said quietly. "I was unconscious. But later I told the police Magda's brakes weren't working. She tried to slow down, skidded around a curve and flipped the car. It went over the edge into the ocean."

"Despite her seat belt," Lansky said, "Helen was thrown from the car. Both her hips were broken, and she had spinal trauma. As you can see, she never fully recovered."

"I don't seem to remember an autopsy," Nick said.

"No," Lansky said. "Magda died because of her injuries. It was an accident."

"Was it? Could the crash have been an attempt to kill Magda—or even you, Helen?" Nick said. "Julio found out and was killed to keep quiet?"

"Lord, no. Not Helen." Lansky suddenly seemed quite shaken. "But Magda…"

"Nick, you've got to find out." Helen took her husband's hand.

"None of you know any other reason that Julio could have been killed?"

Both answered in the negative.

"I understand you're a military veteran," Nick said. "Army?"

"Yes."

"Any experience with 25 mm antitank weapons?"

"Sorry, I was in intelligence."

"That's right," Helen confirmed.

"Check it out," Lansky suggested. "Any other questions?"

Lara looked at Nick, who shook his head. Farewells were made, then Lansky rose to his feet and wheeled his wife inside.

"THIS GETS MORE and more confusing," Lara said when they were back at the car. "If Julio was murdered because he found out that Magda had been murdered, then we're still short a motive. Why was *she* killed? Certainly not just because she was working with Girard. Or had some alleged affair with him or one of the other two…"

"Everyone wants to talk about Magda instead of Julio."

"You think it's a smoke screen?"

"Or there is a connection. Let's talk to your mother."

"I'll call her," Lara agreed.

She grabbed her cell and punched in Sandra's number. After a few minutes, she disconnected and said to Nick, "Mom's out working a new dog at Belmont Park. You know it?"

Nick nodded. "Yes."

"We can meet her there on the boardwalk just past the Big Dipper," she said, referring to the vintage roller coaster.

BELMONT PARK WAS thronged with people attracted by the arcades, rides, the indoor pool, ocean surf and food vendors. The sight it presented hadn't changed much in the past sixty years. It was a good place to accustom a new dog to a lot of people, for Nelson Kennels never had anything close to a crowd.

Lara, however, despite all the fun and excitement around her, the happy adults and the laughing, squealing children, felt distant and apart from it all. Her badge and gun, canine and squad car separated her.

As she walked with Sadie and Nick toward the wall dividing the beach from the midway, Lara realized how alone she'd been since Jim's death. But for once, thinking about Jim didn't leave her close to tears.

"Isn't that her?" Nick asked, gesturing toward a woman with her dog.

It was indeed Sandra Nelson. Dressed in jeans and a denim shirt, she was leading a male shepherd, so young that his ears were only partially upright, the puppyish cartilage unable to support the full weight of the big ears.

Lara waved, but Sandra had seen them and was already heading their way. In no time the two dogs were sniffing each other.

"Hi, Mom," Lara said. After a few remarks about the performance of the new dog, they moved from the boardwalk crowd onto the beach for more privacy.

In Southern California only service animals for the handicapped were allowed on most public beaches, but an exception was made for Sadie and the puppy—Lara had removed her windbreaker to display a K-9 Police T-shirt. So the lifeguards and curious bathers watched but said nothing as the group of three adults and two canines walked toward a kelp-strewn area of the beach, devoid of castle-building children and sun-worshippers.

"You didn't come home last night," Sandra said without preamble. "And you didn't call. Why?"

"It's my fault," Nick said.

"We spent the night at my place," Lara added.

"Was that wise?"

Lara lifted her chin. "We'll be at the kennels tonight."

Sandra waited unsuccessfully, but Lara wasn't more forthcoming.

"We talked with the last of the suspects today," Nick said, changing the subject. "I'm getting the impression my aunt was more than just water-cooler gossip. Did she actually have an affair with Lansky, Girard or Knox?"

"I think so. I didn't bring this up before, but perhaps I should," Sandra said. "It was rumored she was pregnant."

"Pregnant?" Nick echoed.

"Yes. With you."

The sounds of gulls screeching above the waves pierced the air.

"With Nick? Mom, that's ridiculous!"

"No one had any proof, of course," Sandra said, her face pensive. "But Magda suddenly took an extended leave of absence and went back to Italy. She explained her absence by telling everyone that her sister Mara had had a difficult childbirth, and she'd left to help out. I was a rookie then, but I remembered the old gossip about 'a bun in the oven.' She came back with you and told everyone her sister was too ill to take care of you."

"If that were true, my mother is really Magda." Nick hesitated. "And my father?"

"I don't know," Sandra said frankly. "But the rumor was that Magda and one of the three men suspected of killing Julio had a child."

"It could fit the facts," Nick said slowly. "I came to California as an infant and my aunt raised me."

"And your biological father, if he was one of the three, would have been able to see you—and probably help support you," Lara said.

"Hard to believe."

Sandra shrugged. "Those were different times, Detective. A single, pregnant girl couldn't survive the stigma, let alone keep her job."

"So she just pretended to be Nick's aunt, but wasn't?" Lara asked. "She wouldn't have been able to live such a lie for long, would she?"

"Well, she did, and why not?" Sandra said. "Her family lived and worked in Italy. This was before satellite phones and the Internet and instant information.

No one questioned her or her use of the last name Palmer. No one took the time to verify her story."

"Especially if my parents backed her up," Nick said.

Silence. Sandra's dog moved closer to Lara, and Sadie growled a warning. The two women stepped farther apart.

"Mom, why didn't you tell us this earlier?" Lara asked.

"I told you some of what I remembered. I made a few calls around and planned to share the rest, but you didn't come home last night. Obviously you aren't taking this case seriously enough. Neither of you. Your father and I spent the night imagining the worst, and debating whether you knew what you were doing, or if we should call Girard or the funeral home. You didn't even answer your phone!" Sandra's voice broke.

Lara flushed with remorse. "I'm *so* sorry, Mom. I had my reasons."

"I can only think of one thing that would cause you to forget your training," Sandra said sharply. "Nick, I know you've been through some shocks, but this discussion isn't over. Lara, I'll talk to you later."

"I apologize," Nick said. "I should have given you my cell number."

"We just—" Lara felt like a teenager caught out after curfew.

Sandra interrupted her daughter. "You know better, because I taught you better. You two do your jobs and watch your backs, or I swear, Lara, I'll get you removed from Detective Cantello's case myself."

At that Sandra gathered up her dog's leash. "I've got work to do. So do you." Then she heeled her dog for a quick trot back to the crowds of the midway. Lara and Nick continued to stand on the sand.

"Your mother probably worried all night."

"Yeah. Dad, too, I'm sure. Damn." There didn't seem to be anything else to say.

"You hungry?" Lara asked after an awkward pause.

"Starving. I could use a late lunch."

Lara smiled at the polite lie. She led them across the beach to a hot dog and ice cream stand. They carried cardboard boats with hot dogs and French fries that smelled greasy and tasted even greasier. The two made a halfhearted attempt to eat. Lara gave up first.

"Regarding this case... Perhaps you should call your relatives in Italy again."

"I intend to. And I'll request a formal autopsy of Magda's remains and DNA testing for maternity. She was buried locally."

"Nick, are you sure you want to do this?"

"Yes. My parents and I have never been close. Even if I talk to them, that doesn't guarantee they'll tell the truth. This way I'll know. If Magda really is my mother, not my aunt, I'll have enough evidence to warrant DNA paternity testing on our suspects."

Lara couldn't believe how calm Nick sounded. "But...all this is just hearsay! You shouldn't have to—" she searched for the polite words "—exhume Magda's remains. Maybe it's just a diversion—the old red herring."

Nick cut through her hesitation. "I've got no other choice. We have three suspects with only circumstantial motives. Girard wanted to keep his professional life—maybe an affair, too—with Magda secret. In the past, Knox was a compulsive gambler in need of money, and Lansky had his sick wife's medical bills to pay. Julio's research would have threatened their pensions. They're too old to go into any other line of work after retirement."

"Knox said Lansky played the stock market. He could have been into more of a sure thing—something illegal."

"Maybe one of them decided to blackmail Magda and got carried away."

Lara had a sudden thought and reached for Nick's arm. "One of the three could have been on the take. Magda typed crime reports. Magda could have discovered it. She was a detective at heart."

"I need to order that autopsy," Nick said. "Our leads are nebulous at best. The only solid lead we have is that Julio was killed with 25 mm military ammunition. Homeland Security hasn't tracked down the ammo source yet. Or the weapon. And they're the only people cooperating. There hasn't been any real police procedure on this case. The three men I suspect were placed on desk duty, not suspended, and Girard is still in charge of the investigation."

"Don't forget the fact that I was assigned as your sidekick instead of another detective."

Nick smiled. "Dog or not, you're nobody's sidekick, Nelson."

The sea breeze caught a strand of his black hair and blew it across his forehead. Lara had a surprising impulse to brush it away from his face. Instead, she said, "Are you ready to beat rush hour and get back to the kennels?" Rush hour started at three, and it was already past two.

"Not until we stop at the county coroner's office. I need to sign those autopsy papers, and my signature has to be notarized."

Lara studied the circles under his eyes. "Then we definitely call it a day."

LARA AND NICK ARRIVED at Nelson Kennels before dark. Nick spent most of the time in the guest room on the phone with the police station and with his relatives. Despite the time difference between California and Italy, he left voice mail at both his grandparents' and parents' homes. He hoped they'd return his call almost as much as he hoped they wouldn't. Sandra Nelson's comments about Magda being pregnant had shaken him to the core.

Somehow, it all made sense. Nick had always considered himself closer to Magda than anyone. His family had been geographically and emotionally distant. Magda's much older sister, Mara Palameri Cantello, had married a widower and become stepmother to his three children. Only Magda Palameri had remained single, deciding to Anglicize her name to Palmer and moving to California for "a better future," then later "taking in"—or was it giving birth to?—Nick "Cantello."

Magda had told him that his mother was too sickly after his birth to raise him, let alone her three other children. Nick wondered if his parents were Magda and one of the three retiring cops. If so, his grandparents, the single Magda and the married older sister, Mara, had lied to him his whole life. He felt confused, hurt and angry—when he needed his wits about him.

Worse, instead of acting in a mature fashion, he'd been needy and hurting after the funeral. He'd slept with Lara, and he still remembered the warmth of her soft skin. He also remembered the break in Sandra's voice when speaking of the phone call her daughter hadn't made. He'd have to make it up to Sandra—even though deep inside he couldn't regret his actions with Lara. Julio's funeral, and the rejection of Julio's family, had blindsided him. He'd been so grateful to Lara for taking him to the church—despite the orders she'd been given. Hell, she'd probably hear about that from IA or Girard, or whoever was in charge of the investigation, at least on paper. He prayed like hell that Lara would still be in good shape professionally when the smoke cleared.

Not a single woman suddenly pregnant…

*Friday morning*

"LARA?" A soft knock came on her door. "Can I come in?"

Lara recognized her mother's voice. Time to face the music. "Of course. I'm dressed."

"I'm going for a walk," Sandra said. "Come with me?"

"Sure."

The house dogs quickly gathered around Sandra as she led the way outside. They started down a well-worn path that followed the perimeter of the yard area.

"I'm worried about you," Sandra said without preamble. "You and Nick together is a big mistake. Spending the night in an unguarded house goes far beyond the bounds of sense or luck. I kept quiet when you took Nick to a funeral where his presence wasn't desired, but I won't keep quiet about this. Not when my family is involved."

"I appreciate what you and Dad are doing for Nick," Lara said. "Letting him stay here."

The two continued to walk, the little dachshund and terrier trotting to keep up, the big shepherd and Labrador retriever wandering with bigger strides off and on the path to sniff out bushes and check for rabbits. Sadie kept pace with Lara.

"You're the only reason I've involved myself, Lara," Sandra went on. "You could have learned of Magda's past by asking others. I volunteered the information because I have your best interests at heart. Unlike Nick."

"You're wrong," Lara argued. "In fact, he wanted me off this case. I refused."

"Why? You should be doing what you're trained to do. He'd be better off with a detective as a bodyguard."

"I know that!"

"So you're staying because you're a good officer who wants to help, or because you have the hots for Nick Cantello?"

Lara actually stopped walking so abruptly that Sadie,

heeling, had to backtrack. "That question is none of your business."

"Yes, it is. Lara, you buried Jim only last year! You're emotionally vulnerable. I want you safe."

"As long as I'm in law enforcement, safety isn't a guarantee," Lara said. "You know that. As for me being vulnerable, that's not your call."

"As your mother, I'm allowed my say! Nick has a dead partner and possibly a murdered aunt—or mother—whichever it is, tied to that death. Add to that the Valdez family's rejection, and…well…how much stress can one man take?"

"He's handling himself. You might as well know the rest, Mom. Nick signed the papers yesterday to exhume Magda Palmer's body. That should happen today. We hope to get the autopsy results late tomorrow."

"Oh, my God. Nick's already on the edge without exhuming relatives! I don't trust him to watch your back," Sandra wailed.

"Mom, please! Listen to yourself! You taught me policewomen have to be twice as tough as policemen and criminals. Now you want me to walk away? I can't do that! I appreciate your concern, but I have to handle this myself."

"Lara, if anything happens to you…"

"Mom, don't. Please."

Sandra seemed to pull herself together. "If you don't mind, I'd like to finish walking the dogs. Why don't you take Sadie back to the house? I'm sure Nick is waiting." At that curt dismissal, Sandra walked briskly away, the house dogs circling her and leaving Lara and Sadie behind.

Back in the house, Lara found Nick in the kitchen.

"I wondered where you'd been. Your father's left for his office. I don't know where your mother is."

Lara poured him a cup of coffee and freshened hers as Sadie sprawled contentedly underneath the table. "She just read me the riot act."

Nick glanced up. "Because of me." It was a statement, not a question.

"No, because I'm her daughter and she's a good mother," Lara said.

"Sorry about the fallout when you took me to your house…and Julio's funeral."

Lara sipped her coffee again, thoughtful. "Girard never said a word about me taking you to the church. You'd think headquarters would say something. You get any flack from them?"

"No, not a word. Strange. Really strange." Nick set down his half-full cup.

"What should we do about it?"

"Talk to Girard again. He should be in the office. And then Internal Affairs."

"In that order?"

"No. First stop is the morgue. I need to leave cheek cell and hair samples for DNA testing. We'll go from there. This whole case hasn't been handled following procedure, starting with Girard and right on down."

"I know I handled us at the funeral—and after—all wrong," Lara admitted.

"That I'm not worried about. In the grand scheme of things, breaking a few rules won't hurt us."

She had no idea how wrong Nick could be.

REAL-LIFE INVESTIGATIVE SCENES rarely match the public's television-fed image, Lara thought, but the morgue was one place that did. It was hidden away, quiet and definitely eerie.

She and Nick and Sadie took the elevator to the basement and turned left. They walked along the corridor, pipes overhead, walls bare of soothing photos or police awards, Sadie's toenails clicking and echoing down the hall. Lara wrinkled her nose. She couldn't help but notice the sickly odor of chemicals.

"You okay?" Nick asked.

"I've been here before, but I really hate this place."

"The dead can't hurt you. It's the living you need to worry about. You wanna wait out here? It'd be easier on you."

Lara remembered Julio's pitiful remains. "If you don't mind…"

"I'm just going to give samples. Magda's remains won't be there."

Nick was gone for a mercifully brief time. She and Sadie looked up eagerly as the electronic double doors hummed open. They both stood, then headed with Nick back down the long corridor to the elevators.

"How long will it take for the results?"

"Usually a week or more for criminal cases."

"That long?"

"They've agreed to rush it through for me, if their caseload isn't too bad. They won't have to do as many backup tests, since it isn't for court, so maybe in a few days… But there *was* something. The coroner pulled my aunt's original autopsy and medical records in anticipation of the new autopsy. Magda's paperwork has no mention of the name Palameri."

"If Magda was your real mother, that makes sense. She'd want to cover her tracks as your aunt. DNA will tell us who she really was, and if Girard, Lansky or Knox is your biological father."

"That father wouldn't want the information about my parentage—whatever it is—to get out."

"Secret babies aren't a motive for murder, though," Lara said. "At least not here in California."

Nick lifted a skeptical eyebrow. "You're wrong. I can imagine your mother's reaction if you end up pregnant. I think she'd seriously consider murdering yours truly."

Lara was aghast. "You didn't tell her, did you?"

"No. But we need to talk about more than just this case. We need to talk about what to do if you *are* pregnant."

## CHAPTER NINE

THE MIDMORNING SKY WAS a stark blue without a trace of clouds. Instead of a caressing sea breeze, the Santa Ana wind blew out of the desert, its harshness tearing at the wings of all but the strongest gulls. Even the surfers were sparse in number, but Lara and Nick were both up and in the rental car, Nick driving, Lara beside him in plain clothes with badge and gun like Nick, Sadie in the back seat. They avoided the freeways and drove the coastal route, heading for the rough cliff paths. Creeping, heat-wilted red apple vine and ice-plant clung tenaciously to the crumbling incline at spots.

"You sure you wanna do this?" Lara asked. Nick planned to visit the scene where his partner had plunged into the ocean.

"Yes, and revisit the place my aunt died."

"But, Nick, you've been here before. We've seen the reports. The two areas aren't even close. We won't discover anything new from an investigative stand-point."

"I want to go there for personal reasons, not professional. Besides, we still need to talk, and I didn't want to do it at your parents'."

Lara didn't argue. She kept a close eye to make certain they weren't being followed, taking in the scenery at the same time. Southern California wasn't simply flat golden beaches and sunshine. Rocky outcroppings that extended down the Mexican coast had claimed many a ship of old, and in more recent times, too. The jagged, broken edges marked death to all but the strongest mammals or sharks. Only the sea lions, with their heavy, muscular bulk, could survive the currents and rocks, and during storms, sometimes not even them. This was the place of Magda's death.

Nick pulled off the road and parked. He and Lara exited, leaving Sadie in the car, and climbed to a higher level. The wind and treacherous rocky footing were obstacles Sadie could handle if need be. But now was not the time to risk her dog's feet. She wanted her full attention on her new partner, not her four-legged one.

There were no people fishing, swimming or sunbathing at this part of the coast. Lara looked down the cliffs to the spindrift below, and settled for standing on a rare somewhat level area with Nick.

"Magda's car went over there." Nick pointed to the sharpest curve in the road. Lara could see how little protection the guardrail offered.

"What a lonely place," she observed. "And dangerous."

"Places can't be lonely. Only people can."

Nick's statement stuck deep within Lara. She followed Nick's lead as he sat down on the sparse vegetation to watch the sea.

"Who do you think is your father?" Lara asked after a while.

"Girard seems to be running ahead of the pack at present. Why?" Nick asked.

"Because you'll have gained a parent at the expense of your friend. It seems too ironic."

"I suppose, on the surface. But I had a father and mother—even if they weren't biological. And Magda was a loving parent. Personally, I don't feel the need for any more parents in my life."

"Your reality seems confusing to me," Lara said, thinking of her own loving family.

"It could be clearer, I'll admit," Nick said. He turned to face Lara. "What would you do with a child? *Our* child?"

"That possibility doesn't seem real to me," Lara said.

"Humor me. Would you have it?"

"Oh, yes. Definitely." Her voice carried the ring of truth.

"That's good to know. I'd do my part," he promised. "Child support, parental duties. Whatever you need or want. Including marriage."

Lara's face settled into serious lines. "Last year, I'd found Mr. Right, planned for my marriage and children down the line. I hadn't planned to repeat the experience this year…."

To her relief, Nick didn't seem offended. "If you go the single-parent route, what then?"

"I'd end up with a desk job for a while during the pregnancy, and I hate paperwork. Sadie and I would be sidelined. Afterward…well, it'll be tough being a single parent in law enforcement and leaving the baby. I'd need day care. My hours aren't regular. I can't expect my parents to raise my child while I worked, or worse yet, if something happened to me. I don't want strangers raising my child, either. I'd want my sister Kate to adopt the baby—that's something she and I never discussed, of course."

"You wouldn't consider taking a hiatus or a job change? Are you that into police work?"

"I used to think so. I believe in the job, especially K-9 work. It's a proven statistic that suspects surrender without gunfire more easily to K-9 units than to human units. But lately, what with Julio's death, and knowing one of our own might have killed him…I guess the badge seems kind of tarnished."

"I don't feel that way," Nick said decisively. "People are people, and there are rotten apples in any job, from teachers to cashiers."

"You don't expect perfection?"

"No, but I do expect justice, at least due process. This case, I'm worried about. I've never worked a cold case before, and procedure has gone right out the door. I didn't expect my first cold case—Magda's death—to be hinged to Julio's murder. All I have to go on is hearsay and old gossip and Homeland Security, whose job is terrorist-centered. And three men who may or may not know how to fire 25 mm weapons. If I don't solve this, I'll never be able to face Julio's wife and children."

"We," Lara corrected. "If *we* don't solve the case. And we will."

"What makes you so certain?"

"Because," Lara said, "too much effort is going into covering up the past. Internal Affairs might have taken Girard's gun, but they're still letting him remain in charge of the investigation. And the computer's central calendar still lists the retirement ceremony for him and the two others. Doesn't that strike you as odd?"

"Almost as much T. J. Knox trying to help us out. He must have as little confidence in Girard's investigation as I do."

"That's right. Sooner or later, something's got to break free, especially after the exhumation and the DNA results on her and you come back. Of course, if Magda wasn't murdered, we still need a firm motive in Julio's murder. Adultery—if it's true," Lara quickly added, "isn't enough."

"T.J. might have had something when he brought up blackmail. Girard used Magda as a detective instead of a clerk and wanted that kept quiet. Knox Sr. had gambling debts. Then Magda died suspiciously, more fertile ground for blackmail. Lansky could have been the blackmailer. He could be covering up for himself. Lansky's wife racked up the medical bills. He needed money. Or he needed it because he was the victim of blackmail instead of the other way around."

"I say Lansky blames Magda for his wife's accident. I definitely sensed some resentment."

"I agree," Nick said. "But IA is still doing financial checks on our three. Even if blackmail *is* a possibility, that doesn't mean they kept their money in a U.S. bank—if they even used a bank at all."

"You know," Lara said, "this connection between Magda Palmer and Helen Lansky…do you think Helen knew more than she told us?"

"I think everyone knows more gossip than facts, and it's not helping us find Julio's killer," Nick said. "If this was a love triangle, it ended after Magda's death, accidental or not. I don't know if Julio found out about it when he had to write the retirement speeches. But retracing his steps and interviewing all concerned hasn't gotten us very far."

"Maybe we're going about this all wrong," Lara said.

"Explain."

"Julio didn't do *his* research with interviews. Maybe he found his information from other sources. We need to find out how Julio researched his speech."

"I told you, he did everything via computer, and Julio's work computer was wiped, according to Internal Affairs. He didn't own a laptop, I know. Homeland Security hasn't come up with much, either."

"Yes, but we have something neither IA or Homeland Security has. Julio's wife. Maybe she can tell us something. Maybe her family in Mexico has a computer or a disk or something. Have you checked?"

Nick sat up straighter with excitement. "No, I haven't, but that's a good idea."

"We need to find out. You need to talk to her in person, Nick. What if she went back to Mexico for safety? Or to protect whatever personal effects or evidence Julio had?"

"She would have talked to me, sent me a message," Nick insisted.

"I think she did. By not inviting you to the funeral."

Nick breathed in sharply. "My God...have I been that stupid?"

"You're not stupid, you've taken a hit. Julio's only been dead a few days. We need to go to Mexico," Lara said. "In the meantime, ask all three suspects to voluntarily undergo paternity tests. That ought to keep them guessing while we cross the border."

"While *I* cross the border."

"I'm coming."

"You're not. We can't cross with our weapons or your official vehicle unless we clear it with Mexican authorities through our office. I don't want to notify anyone, and I don't want you without a gun. Or your dog."

"I go where you go, and all I need for Sadie is a regular collar and her vaccination papers for customs. I know that for a fact. We'll take the rental car, and we'll simply be a couple with their pet visiting friends across the border. You know exactly where Lilia's staying, do you?"

"She's at her brother's. It isn't more than an hour's drive from the border."

"From my parents' with crossing time, that's about two. Let's switch cars and get a quick bite to eat. There shouldn't be any problems," Lara said firmly.

"Famous last words," Nick said.

# CHAPTER TEN

*Friday noon*

"YOU'RE GOING WHERE?" Ed Nelson asked his daughter.

"Mexico—Nick, Sadie and I. Would you mind lending me your car?" Lara asked. It was easier and less costly to get foreign insurance at the border for a privately owned vehicle than a rental car. Nick was in his room checking his voice mail.

"When?"

"Right now. Nick wants to see Julio's family—check on them. He didn't get a chance to speak to them at the funeral. He hasn't been able to reach them yet by phone."

"Is that all this is?" Ed asked. "Just a social visit?"

"I'm sure Nick will want to ask a few questions, as well, Dad." Lara placed her gun and belt in the family room's small safe—because she couldn't transport her weapon across the border, though she'd take Sadie's badge and her own in her purse—before closing it and scrambling the keypad. "I can't let him go alone. Nick doesn't trust anyone but me."

"So that's why you slept with him after the funeral?"

"I never said that."

"I'm not blind, Lara. I've seen the way you look at him—like you're in an R-rated movie."

Lara stiffened, but forced herself to speak calmly. "That's out of line, Dad. Either way, it's none of your business."

"Dammit, Lara, I thought you had your act together since Jim's death."

"I do." She realized with sudden clarity that when it came to Nick, she did, both professionally and personally. "So let me handle it."

Ed scowled. "How can I? You're dragging your latest lover into my guest room and borrowing my car for him."

"Skip the sarcasm, Dad." Lara lifted her chin as she faced her father. "I've behaved as a professional under your roof. A fellow police officer has been murdered. Someone shot at Nick, my dog and me. You don't want us here or me using the car, say so. I'll make other arrangements when we get back from Mexico."

"I didn't approve of you moving in with Jim after what—a few weeks?"

"I loved him, and you didn't approve of me moving in with Jim at all," Lara corrected. "My morals are not your concern. I'm at peace with them, even if you're not."

"I taught you better."

"You didn't teach tolerance, Dad," Lara shot back. "I remember what you called Jim—and *me*. You didn't even apologize after we became engaged, either. It's hard to forget how you acted."

"I had every right. I'm your father!"

"I'm a grown woman with my own conscience."

"Your conscience isn't going to keep you from getting AIDS."

Lara sighed. "I have to go, Dad. I'll see if Mom will let me use *her* car." She headed for the kennel office.

NICK, LARA AND SADIE cleared customs easily, and were south of Tijuana in the neighborhood where Lilia's family resided. Lara drove Sandra's car slowly while Nick gave her directions, for the street signs and house numbers were deliberately vague or missing in Mexico's wealthier neighborhoods. Carjackings and kidnappings were a sad reality of life in a country with a lot of poverty and an almost nonexistent middle class.

"We're here," Nick said. "That's Lilia's car on the right."

Lara parked in the shade. After walking Sadie, she left her in the car with water from the jug she always carried, and she and Nick walked up the front pathway to the sound of barking dogs in other courtyards. Nick pulled the string and rang the bell—cast iron in the old Spanish style complete with clapper—and waited. In seconds the double doors from the house to the courtyard opened, then Lilia herself was unlocking the courtyard gate and throwing herself into Nick's arms.

"Oh, Nicky, I knew you'd come!" she cried.

Lara stepped back to give Lilia and Nick privacy. Both adults had tears in their eyes. In a moment a male member of the family showed them all inside. He was introduced as Lilia's older brother, Orlando.

"Where are the boys?" Nick asked.

"With their aunt, but they'll be back later. They'll be so happy to see you," Lilia said. "Please, sit down."

They sat in a pleasant formal room with large ceramic floor vases, an iron-grated fireplace, leather furniture and two rich woven rugs on the adobe-tiled floor. A ceiling fan provided a pleasant breeze, and the inside air was kept cool by the thick outer walls of the house and the numerous shade trees in the courtyard. After Lilia's brother left the room, the three were left to talk.

Nick sat on the couch next to the woman whose brown eyes were dark with grief. He took her hands in his and held them tightly.

"Were you so afraid to call me?" Nick asked, his voice kind and without accusation.

"I don't trust the phones—not after I heard that Julio was killed in your car. That awful night, when the refrigerator broke and I called him at work… I was afraid to talk to you with others around, even at the funeral. That's why I didn't want you there." Lilia broke down in sobs, and for a moment there were only the soft sounds of her pain.

"I understand," Nick said. "But we went, anyway."

"Oh, Nicky, you did? I thought I heard someone mention it, but I wasn't sure."

"We came late, stayed in the back and left early," Lara confirmed, glossing over details. "Nick wanted to pay his last respects to your husband, Mrs. Valdez, as did I. I'm very sorry for your loss. And he knew you didn't blame him for your husband's passing."

Lilia wiped at her tears. "How could I ever blame you, Nicky?"

Nick swallowed hard, but kept his composure. "How are the boys?" he asked, his voice low with gentle concern.

"Not good. Your being here will help. Have you discovered anything new? Anything at all?" Lilia begged.

"We have, but the more we learn, the more confusing it gets." Nick sketched a portrait of the investigation, concluding with the discovery of Magda's possible biological relationship to him.

"Your family lied to you? But family should be everything," Lilia said, shocked.

"Homeland Security's still working on tracing the weapon. And if we can find out what Julio discovered about Magda and the three men involved with her… But there was nothing found in your home, and Julio's computer at work was wiped clean."

Lilia lips upturned in a small smile. "But not my laptop. Julio often used it, and his research on the three men's retirement background is in it."

"You brought it here?" Nick gasped.

"I did and the police don't know about it. That's what I didn't want to say over the phone. I know Julio would have wanted you to see it first, Nicky. And you can later, after we've all eaten," Lilia promised.

LILIA WAS AS GOOD as her word. After the meal, which included the boys' aunt and uncle and their three children, the five cousins went outside under the uncle's watchful eye, while the aunt did the dishes. Orlando showed Lara the previous owner's dog kennel. Set close to the house, Sadie could stretch her legs, safely away from family members. Then Lilia took Lara and Nick to the room she and Julio used whenever they stayed at her brother's.

"My sister-in-law uses this as an office when there's no company. My laptop is on the desk. There are some of Julio's papers that I brought from home, too, before the police searched. I've been meaning to go through them…but I thought you'd do it for me…" Her voice trailed off.

"Of course I will," Nick offered.

"Thank you. I know Julio wouldn't mind. If you don't need me," she moved nervously toward the door, "I need to go check on the children."

"Are you sure? Some of these things could be personal," Nick said, but Julio's wife left, anyway.

"Let her go, Nick," Lara said. "It's hard to go through a loved one's things. I know."

"Your fiancé's?"

"Yeah. Everything of Jim's, every piece of clothing or paper—even his car keys—held so many memories, it was overwhelming. I ended up letting my sisters go through most of it while I sat in the bathroom and bawled my eyes out."

"Yes, you're right. It'll be easier for me than Lilia," Nick said. "I just hope we find something we can use." He gestured toward the two piles of paperwork on the desk. "Grab one for yourself. We'll do this first—there isn't much—then the computer."

Silently they started going through the paperwork that marked the daily transactions of an adult's life. The photos, bills and receipts sorted on the bed prompted Lara to say, "They must be a close family to feel comfortable enough to leave their things here. And to feel at home in two countries."

"There's a lot to be said for extended-family living." Nick completed his pile. "No red flags here." He put his batch back on the desk. "Thanks for earlier."

"For what?"

"For letting Lilia think everything was under control. For telling her I understood why she didn't want me at the funeral, that I was there, anyway."

"No need for thanks. The woman's had enough hard truths this week. Besides, what else could I say? The important thing is you've hooked up again."

"Thank you," he repeated. Nick leaned over and kissed Lara on the cheek.

Embarrassed, Lara toyed with the corner of a manila envelope. "Yeah, well, I understand some of what you're going through. I thought Jim's parents and I would be friends for life. Jim had a sister, too. We got along so well. But after he died, things between his family and me died, as well. They stayed in the Yosemite area, I came back home and the phone calls and e-mails between us dwindled down to nothing."

"That won't happen with me and Lilia."

"I'm glad." Lara dropped the envelope and lifted her head. "I think that would be as bad as the funeral. In my case, I didn't just lose Jim. I lost people I thought would be part of my family for the rest of my life."

Nick drew her close, despite the desk drawer and stacks of papers on the bed. She let herself be held, drawing strength and comfort from the embrace.

"We need to watch out for those hugs," Lara said with a shaky smile. "Remember what happened the last time."

"There are worse things in life. Like two children growing up without a father." Nonetheless, Nick released her. "I want more than memories for them. I want justice. Enough stalling. Time for the computer." Nick reached for the laptop and sat at the desk.

"My fingers are crossed," Lara said as Nick started checking Julio's files. She perched on the edge of the bed and looked over his shoulder, seeing, but not understanding, the Spanish files. Once more she went out to check on Sadie, then returned. Nick continued to read every word of every text file.

"Anything of interest?" Lara asked an hour or so later. "I'm afraid my high school Spanish isn't up to translating."

"Nothing in the text files. I just have the JPEGS left." Nick referred to the computer format used to store pictures. Nick scanned the laptop's monitor and picked at the keyboard. "Just a minute. I'm not familiar with this software," he said.

"I am. We use it at the kennels all the time to document photos of sires, dams and litters," Lara said with excitement as they traded places. She keyed up the software for saving and editing scanned photos and material, then began opening files.

"Look at this!" Lara said after a moment. "It's a picture of you, Nick, and he's scanned his boys' artwork." Lara kept scrolling through the individual entries. "Some of these are pretty good," she marveled. "I wish I had a niece or nephew. Lindsey's the only one of us who's married, but no little ones yet. Not that you need marriage to have chil—" Lara broke off. The artwork suddenly changed to scans of newspaper clippings and old photos meticulously labeled. "What are these?"

"How many do we have?" he asked.

"Looks like about a half-dozen newspaper scans, and a page of his keyed notations," she said.

"Magnify," Nick ordered, leaning over her shoulder. "Damn, I wish we had a printer."

"Got it magnified. Nick, these are scans of old police files, too, not just press clippings."

"With Girard, Lansky, Knox and Magda listed in each of them," Nick said. He studied them as Lara pulled up the last page of Julio's notes in Spanish. Lara slowly translated.

"These words are in bold. *Adulterio*…adultery. *Homicidio*…homicide. *Chantaje*—um, threats?"

"Blackmail," Nick said.

"I don't know this last one." Lara gestured at the

screen; her finger pointed to the word, *embarazada.*
"Embarrassed?"

"No. It's also known as *encinta.*"

That word Lara knew. "Oh. Pregnant." As in Magda
Palmer. Or possibly, Lara Nelson. "What else?"

The two leaned close to the screen, Lara in the desk
chair, Nick on his feet and leaning over her. His hand
was braced on the wooden chair back, gently resting
next to her shoulder as they studied the screen. Lara
found it hard to wait for him to translate as he silently
read more of Julio's Spanish police notes. Finally she
could wait no longer.

"What does it say?"

"I can translate them—something about old weap-
onry—but I can't put his brief notes in context. Pull up
the clippings."

Lara nodded. "Here's the first. It's from the *San
Diego Sentinel.*" She scanned the photo, easily recognizing it as Captain Girard. A woman stood next to
him, smiling at the camera. "It's a write-up on Girard's
promotion to captain. Is that his wife?"

"Yup. That's her," Nick verified. "Nothing exciting
here. Next," he ordered, no polite niceties, all business.
Lara recognized it as such.

She clicked the keyboard, and pulled up the next
short, similar article. "Another promotion notice. Lansky this time, no wife. Here's another for Knox," she
said. "Nothing revealing, no photo."

"Keep going," Nick said.

Lara clicked to the fourth JPEG, a fuzzy, smaller

image that showed a different newspaper typeface. Unlike the other articles, they couldn't pick out any words except the bigger, blurred headline, ARMS DEPOT CLOSES and the shadowy figures in the photo.

"I can't read it," Nick said, squinting.

"Hang on." Lara accessed the filters and clicked on "sharpen edges." Then words started to form. She clicked "sharpen more." The words weren't chiseled in marble, but at least they were recognizable. She magnified once again, and suddenly the figures of Girard, Lansky and Knox appeared in front of a stockpile of wooden boxes.

Nick stared at the screen. "My God..."

"What?"

He pointed, his forefinger pressed against the glass of the monitor. "Right here...toward the back, near the boxes."

"A woman?"

"Not just any woman. Magda." Lara didn't see Nick's lips draw into a thin line. "Somehow, Julio made a connection between these four and armaments."

"You don't mean..."

"I do. Depleted uranium—adultery, blackmail and murder."

# CHAPTER ELEVEN

*Friday evening*

THE NELSON HOUSE LIGHTS were on and the dogs fed and kenneled for the night when Nick, Lara and Sadie finally returned from Mexico. Earlier they'd made their farewells to the Valdezes and crossed back over the border with a copy of the files on a CD. Lilia wanted the laptop itself to remain with her, and Nick didn't insist on taking it back as evidence. Nick had made prints at a nearby Mexican copy shop for their own reference and taken the CD with him. The drive back across the border was slow, with traffic backed up for miles behind Customs. Fortunately Lara had filled the gas tank before they left.

Now they were finally back at the kennels. It was after ten at night, yet the house dogs and some of the working dogs, as well, roused themselves at the sound of the familiar car engine.

As they let themselves through the double gate to the family yard, Sadie gamboling ahead of them, happily stretching her legs after the long drive, Lara said, "Whoever our blackmailer is, he sure made a career of it—from secret work alliances to affairs and depleted uranium. But we still don't know who our killer is."

"We know more than we did when we started."

"I'm still worried," Lara groaned. "What if our killer has friends covering up for him in the department?"

"Do you believe that?"

"Lilia does, and so do you. You let her keep the laptop and gave her a set of copies for safekeeping. I didn't see you printing out a set for Girard."

"You're right, I didn't. He shouldn't be in charge of this investigation, and I'm beginning to question the lack of resources assigned to this case. I'll give Internal Affairs a copy of the clippings—at least we should be able to get our three suspects, including Girard, off desk duty and suspended."

"This is depressing. A murder by a crooked cop." Lara sighed, and looked at Sadie. "At least police dogs don't turn dishonest. I'm staying in K-9."

"I'm glad." Nick slung his arm around Lara's shoulders as they continued to walk toward the house. "You've been a big help, especially with that software."

"I had no idea detective jobs were so exhausting," she said as they reached the back porch door with dog door, both always left unlocked. "I get physically tired on patrol with Sadie, but murder investigation is emotionally draining. How did you ever get used to it?"

"You never get used to it."

"I certainly wouldn't." Lara reached for the door, and Nick's hand dropped from her shoulder. She looked at him and said, "We're off duty. I don't mind a little physical contact, and I'm not embarrassed in front of my parents."

"Discretion is the better part of valor," Nick said.

"I don't need valor. I need a bed and a warm shoulder, and if this wasn't my parents' house…"

Nick lifted an eyebrow as they stepped inside, Sadie coming through with them. The other house dogs barked a few times, than calmed down when they recognized the visitors.

"Lara? Is that you?" Sandra called out from her bedroom. "I heard the dogs."

"It's us, Mom," Lara called back.

"See you in the morning. Night, sweetheart."

Lara sighed.

"Staying at your place definitely had its advantages," Nick said quietly.

"Yeah, well, I'll stay professional. Between the dogs and my parents, at least we won't have to worry about the printouts being destroyed. I should put them in the safe, anyway, until morning."

"We'll start fresh then."

"I'll be ready." Lara stifled a yawn. She put her mother's car keys on the kitchen table, grabbed a dog treat out of the dog's "cookie jar" for Sadie and said, "Good night, Nick."

He nodded. "See you in the morning."

NICK WATCHED woman and dog go down the hall. Not until she was out of sight did Nick head for the living room. He sat on the love seat positioned conveniently near the phone. Using his charge card, he dialed Italy, and the home number of the people he had always thought were his parents.

Despite the difference in time zones, his "father" picked up the phone on the other end. Nick began a conversation he never imagined he would have.

"Dad, I have an order in for a maternal DNA profile on Magda. Is she my biological mother?"

He concluded the conversation with, "Thanks for being honest. Give my love to everyone." Nick hung up and sat quietly on the love seat, thinking.

Lara's soft voice startled him. "Nick? I thought you'd gone to bed."

"I'm headed there. Hope I didn't keep you awake," he said.

"You didn't. I still have to turn out the lights." She paused a moment, then asked, "Are you okay?"

"It's been a long day." He ran a hand through his hair. "I was on the phone with the man I used to think was my father."

Lara joined him on the small couch, Sadie sprawling on the carpet against Lara's feet. "You wanna talk about it?" she asked.

"My parents are really my aunt and uncle." He shook his head in wonderment. "Magda's my mother."

"So they admitted it."

"Yes. Magda always wanted to move here, even as a child. Seems living in California appealed more to her than Italy. Dad said…" Nick broke off. "I mean…"

"I know who you mean," Lara said kindly.

"My uncle said Magda never told them who the father was—she left for California as a single woman and one summer came back pregnant. I was born there. My grandparents and Mara—Magda's sister—tried to convince her to stay in Italy and raise the baby. She refused. Said it would be too confining."

Sadie lifted her head, yawned on a high-pitched note, then settled herself back on the carpet, nose between her paws. Lara absently dropped her hand to stroke the thick fur, her attention on Nick. "California does have more freedom for a single woman than a lot of places do."

"The family seemed to have this idea that California was a bad place for children. Hollywood's reputation was…well…"

"Pretty much the same as it is today," Lara said. "Sin and scandal amid movies and moguls."

"In the end, Magda went back to work as a single woman, an 'aunt' raising her sickly sister's child. My grandparents insisted that I be told my mother had her hands full with three children and couldn't raise a fourth child. Heaven forbid there should be a bastard child in the family."

"That must have been rough on you," Lara said.

"I don't consider myself deprived. Magda was very good to me. I have dual citizenship and spent my summers in Italy with family, but I've always considered San Diego my home."

"And you never knew any of this until just this week?"

"No. The family kept quiet when I was a young child, and out here there was no family to tell me otherwise."

Lara thought of her own heritage. "I can't imagine what you must be feeling. It's like hearing you were switched in the hospital nursery."

"Surely not that bad," Nick said. "My family is still my family, no matter their correct biological titles. Dad and Mom will still be Dad and Mom. And Magda… Magda. What bothers me is knowing that Julio might still have been alive if I'd known the truth about my parents."

"Don't overreach," Lara said firmly. "Those kinds of mind games will drive you crazy. Your poor family, living with those lies all your life."

"Dad sounded more relieved than upset. I thanked him for what he did for Magda. Magda was only his sister-in-law. Neither of them had to cover for her. And my grandparents did threaten to disown Magda at first. My…aunt and uncle gave my grandparents peace of mind. And they gave us both respectability. It was important to them…to me. How could I do any less for our child?"

Lara's lips parted at the abrupt change of subject. "Nick…we don't even know if I'm pregnant."

"If you are and you want to keep the child, I want us to get married," Nick said.

"Married?" she echoed.

"Yes. For the child's sake—and for yours. I don't want you to go through what Magda did."

"This isn't the old days, and I'm not going to pretend to be a maiden aunt," Lara scoffed.

"There's still a stigma. And before you argue, think what your parents' reaction could be."

"Okay, so being single and pregnant isn't on my top-ten list of things to do. But, Nick, listen." She settled back on the love seat. "I'm not Magda. You don't have to worry about me."

"I do worry."

"Don't. Let me be honest. I fell in love with and moved in with Jim after knowing him for three days. Three days," she repeated. "My family wasn't very supportive. My father went ballistic. Nothing like having your own father call you a…well, never mind what he called me. When I met Jim, I knew he was the guy for me. I don't regret anything—except Jim's dying."

She lifted her chin. Her eyes remained dry. "Please understand, I make my own choices. If I'm pregnant, I'll go from there. I don't regret the other night, and I don't base my actions on family approval. I won't get married to make them—or you—feel better."

"That's not what I meant."

"Doesn't matter. I'm lucky enough to know what love is. The real deal. It didn't last as long as I wanted, but I'm glad for the time I had."

"Seems like you're right in character," Nick said. "Look what you've shared with me in just a few days. Maybe history's repeating itself."

"I…I…" She actually stammered. That wasn't true, was it? She regrouped and started again. "What if you met someone? What if you fell in love while tied down to me? Single parenting beats the alternative—custody fights and lawsuits. You'd be free to find your perfect mate. And I wouldn't be with a man who married me out of obligation. I'm not a helpless charity case."

"I'd never consider you one. You'd be the mother of my child, and treated with the love and respect that position holds."

"You're a nice man, Nick, but I'm not changing my mind. One cop in a family is hard enough for children. Two is terrible. My sisters and I grew up fearing every day that our parents could die. It's not an easy thing for an adult to handle, let alone children. Besides, this may be all academic—I may not be pregnant. And it's too late for serious discussions, anyway." Lara stood up, Sadie immediately following suit. Nick made no motion to move.

"You staying up?" Lara asked.

"No. I'll turn out the lights."

# CHAPTER TWELVE

*Sunday morning*

LARA SAT with her parents in their kitchen, drinking coffee and eating sweet rolls, while Nick packed his clothes and other possessions.

"I can't believe Nick's leaving for Italy," Sandra said worriedly. "How are you supposed to protect him there? You can't take Sadie or your gun overseas on a moment's notice."

"Yesterday I asked for permission to accompany him," Lara said. "It was denied."

"It's just as well." Ed reached for a cinnamon roll. "The case is on track now, he'll be met by Italian security and as long as he's gone, you're no longer needed. He probably won't need you around when he gets back, either."

Lara bristled at her father's satisfied tone. "He needs someone, and I want it to be me. He just buried his partner, the Valdez family won't leave Mexico, he learned his aunt was his mother, uncovered the family skeleton, and a day later his grandmother has a heart attack. I wish I could go with him."

The news about his grandmother had hit Nick hard, and when Nick's grandfather begged him to come to the hospital, Nick had been torn between duty and family. With the greater involvement of staff on the murder case, and after talking to Lilia, Nick finally decided that he could be spared, at least until his grandmother's crisis had been resolved.

"You've come a long way since your visit to Mexico," Sandra quietly said, playing peacemaker.

Saturday had been a day filled with chaos—and satisfaction. Both Nick and Lara had spent the whole day in the kennel office. Nick had damned protocol and proper channels to go ahead with his new plan— hard pressure involving arm-twisting and outright threats. At his direction, Lara had faxed a tersely worded summary of Julio's murder and the single set of copies to the State Attorney's Office first, the head of law enforcement in the State of California. Nick had then followed up with a personal phone call. The process was repeated with SDPD's Internal Affairs office, and then again with Homeland Security.

Nick had ended all three phone calls the same way: "If this case doesn't receive the proper attention in the next twenty-four hours, I will post this on every Internet media site in California—and let the general public question the death of my partner and the threat of depleted uranium to our civilian population." His voice wasn't that of a grief-stricken man, but a law-enforcement officer who meant business and didn't care what the consequences were. Lara saw a new side of Nick, a side that inspired both goose bumps and admiration.

Nick hadn't had to wait twenty-four hours for results. Within the next two, Girard, Lansky and Knox had been released from desk duty and were suspended until further notice. His cell and hers were kept ringing with sudden developments. The county coroner moved Magda Palmer's exhumed body to the top of their priority list. A full contingent of national, state and SDPD were assigned to all facets of the investigation, and a Colonel Doyle from Homeland Security took over Girard's office personally to handle the case. With Nick and Lilia's cooperation, Doyle now had possession of the laptop.

Lara felt her overall spirits lift, although Nick wasn't celebrating.

"They took long enough," he maintained. "And we haven't found the killer yet." Saturday evening, another phone call from Doyle himself showed the case was far from solved.

"The coroner's office reports that Magda's aged remains might not provide the best of samples for DNA testing," Doyle had said. "There are more complex tests that can be used to get results, but those tests will take considerably longer. As it stands now, we can't get a court order forcing our three suspects to provide a DNA sample. We can only show a connection to the death of Valdez, not to Magda Palmer."

"I hope those overseas police know what they're doing," Lara said. "I still wish I could go with him."

"There haven't been any more attempts on his life,"

Sandra pointed out. "And with Homeland Security taking over the case, your killer will probably want to lie low, not attract any attention to himself."

"True. Whatever Girard, Lansky or Knox know about Julio or Magda's death, they aren't talking—although Knox Sr. has agreed to DNA testing. Like Nick said, I doubt he has any connection with Magda if he agreed to the testing." At present, those results were still pending. "Nick still has no idea who his biological father was...or who killed his partner."

"It'll come," Ed said. "Homeland Security's been a big help."

"At least they're on the ball," Lara muttered. Federal sources did trace the weapon and ammunition—including depleted uranium—to Camp Pendleton Marine Corps Base, but all leads to who had actually taken the military ammo off base were dead ends. "I'm going to check on Nick."

"Let him be," Ed said. "He's a big boy."

Lara ignored him. She'd already arranged to follow Nick in her insurance-replaced Mercedes to return the rental car. From there she'd drive him to his apartment to pick up his passport and then drop him at the airport. She wasn't looking forward to the task. Saying goodbye to Nick bothered her almost as much as leaving the case unsolved. But as she pushed her chair away from the table, he walked into the kitchen.

"My bags are in the rental car," Nick said without preamble. "Mr. and Mrs. Nelson, thank you for your hospitality."

"You're welcome, Detective." Ed didn't rise from his chair or politely shake hands, his lack of manners embarrassing Lara.

Sandra rose, however. "Goodbye, Detective. I hope your grandmother feels better soon."

"Thanks."

"I'll see you later, Mom," said Lara. "I'm leaving Sadie here."

FROM KENNELS TO CAR RENTAL to apartment, the couple rode in relative silence. They left Nick's apartment with passport in hand, Nick's luggage on the back seat.

"You have everything?" she asked, turning the ignition key.

"Yep. My cleaning lady will get my mail and take care of the cat. I appreciate the ride, and all."

Words fell awkwardly between them.

"I guess you'll need a new car when you get back," Lara said, getting into the lane for the freeway to San Diego's airport.

Nick nodded. "Glad you got yours replaced." He rapped once on the glass of the passenger window. "Bulletproof?"

"Not this time." Lara concentrated on merging into the heavy traffic. Once safely in the desired lane, she said, "How are Lilia and the boys?"

"Okay, she says. She plans to stay in Mexico for a while. It's summer. The boys aren't in school. She's not ready to come back yet."

"Can't blame her."

"What about you?" Nick asked. "Where will you be staying?"

"Back at my house, since I'll be working La Jolla K-9 again. I'll keep in touch with Colonel Doyle, though."

"*I* sure as hell will."

Lara took the Sassafras Street exit, which led to the Port of San Diego and the San Diego Airport.

"When will you be back?" Lara asked.

"Within the week, I hope."

"Maybe I can pick you up?"

"If you're not working…yeah, thanks."

"You have my number. Just give me enough notice and I'll make certain I'm there."

Lara started forward as the light changed to green. "What terminal is your airline? The old or the new?" she asked, for San Diego's airport split into two halves.

"The old one."

Lara moved into that lane of traffic. "Shall I park?"

"Thanks, but just drop me off at the curb," he said. "It'll be easier. I'm not carrying my badge. It's lines and security checks for me."

She threaded the car through the five lanes of traffic at the drop-off point. Lara found the heavily armed security—military, police and private—depressing.

"When will you know if you're pregnant?" Nick asked as she inched the car forward.

"A few weeks, I guess." Traffic drifted away from the drop-off curb, leaving an opening for Lara to squeeze through.

"I plan on being gone only a few days." He paused. "I also want you to leave this case alone while I'm not here. You've been assigned back to K-9. Keep your focus on K-9 business."

Lara couldn't believe her ears. "Even if something new comes up?"

"Even then. Understand?"

"I'm not a quitter," she said quietly.

"Neither was Julio. You and Sadie already have a job. Stick to it."

She didn't promise, nor did she argue. Lara stopped at the curb and put the car in park. She left it running as she climbed out. Nick did the same, grabbing his bag and jacket from the back seat. Outside, the loudspeaker blared parking warnings, while security patrolled up and down the loading curb, hustling pedestrian and vehicle traffic along. One guard stared at Lara's running vehicle, gesturing for her to move it. Lara flashed her badge and the guard nodded his agreement.

"If you're pregnant, you should look into desk duty."

"God, no," Lara said.

"I don't want you or our child—"

"If there is one…"

"—hurt. You could do drug and evidence searches."

A driver waiting to drop off a passenger beeped his horn with impatience.

"I'll cross that bridge if I come to it. Safe journey, Nick."

Nick ignored the motorist. "I'll miss you, Lara. I'll miss saying your name."

Lara smiled. "The Spanish version of *Lara* means *protection*. Mom thought it would be lucky."

To her surprise, Nick kissed her lips and hugged her, his cheek against her hair. Then, with a final nod, he picked up his bags and headed for the terminal.

*Tuesday morning*

LARA HAD HAD MONDAY OFF. But today she went back to life as usual—at least as usual as it could be for a woman with her job. She put on her uniform, gun and badge, and she and Sadie went back to patrol work. There was always plenty of action for the pair, but for the first time in her career Lara found it singularly unsatisfying. Her pleasure at being part of the law-enforcement system didn't fill her with the normal sense of a job well done at the end of each day. It couldn't, not while Julio's slayer remained free.

Lara came home to the empty house above the La Jolla cliffs, feeling the unfairness of life. The notion of a killer walking free was disturbing, but uppermost in her mind was her possible pregnancy. Both subjects led to thoughts of Nick. She admired him as a man and a detective, but she wasn't ready to commit to marriage if she was pregnant. She even wondered if she should tell him if she was when he had so much on his plate already. Lara learned with real joy that she was to pick up her sister and housemate, Kate, at the airport, home from her conference.

With her supervisor's blessing, Lara finished her shift early and drove her K-9 unit to the airport. Sadie and Kate's dog, Lexi, shared the same house and had no

problems sharing a car. Lara and Sadie quickly passed
through the terminal and checkpoints to the disembark-
ing gate to wait for the plane. Due to Kate's job, Lexi had
special clearance to ride passenger instead of in the animal luggage area where jet engines screamed next to a
dog's sensitive ears—a place no Nelson animal ever
rode.

The crowds in the terminal parted as Lara and Sadie
moved through the throng. Behind her, long lines of
people slowly inched forward, accepting the earlier
check-in times, the searches and the delayed depar-
tures and arrivals as part of their safety. The days of
farewell parties at airport bars and greeting arrivals
with flowers and balloons as they stepped off the plane
were gone. Since the World Trade Towers attack, airports resembled military bases. Professionals carried
out the strictest searches and identification checks, and
casual security was a thing of the past.

Sadie alertly at her side, Lara watched through the
high glass windows as her sister's plane taxied in. The
connecting tunnel in place, security opened the entrance
at Lara's end. Kate and Lexi were the first ones off. Lara
lifted one hand in greeting, and Kate nodded and smiled.
There were no hugs or kisses, for Kate was also in uniform, Lexi wearing a customs K-9 identification badge.

"Kate, it's good to see you. Hey, Lexi. Sadie, *nein!*"
Lara restrained Sadie from a joyful reunion with Kate
and her fellow canine. Even the well-trained Sadie
broke ranks with Kate, a beloved family member. "How
was the flight?"

The taller woman adjusted her carry-on backpack. "A pain in the ass. People get nervous about flying, then when they see a working dog, they think the worst. They should have their doctor prescribe a tranquilizer or take a bus next time," Kate said in her no-nonsense way. "Thank God I was in first class. Even then, some fool asked why I didn't crate Lexi with the luggage. I almost asked her why she didn't try it herself…but for the sake of the uniform, I restrained myself."

Lara grinned. "You need a pit stop?"

"No, but Lexi does. And she's thirsty, too. I cut her water back this morning before the flight." As she dropped a hand to pet her dog, Kate's brown eyes warmed, adding an attractive light to a face as composed, as cool, as one working with explosives could be. "Let's get out of here."

The two sisters strode briskly down the long concourse, their dogs trotting along beside them. Kate traveled light with a backpack, and hadn't checked any baggage. Once outside, the women tended to their animals, then happily left in Lara's squad unit.

"Glad to be home?" Lara asked, turning on the air-conditioning.

"Oh, yeah. San Francisco weather has nothing on San Diego. Fog, rain and more fog. Interesting conference, though. Customs is considering having K-9 units ride along with federal air marshals on civilian flights. The military does it all the time. They sent us a speaker."

"That's different."

"Interested?"

"Only professionally. Personally, I like my own bed every night, no hotel, and Sadie's used to cars, not planes."

Kate nodded, and unbuttoned the neck of her uniform blouse. "How are the folks?"

"Good."

"And you?"

"Not good. I've been working a homicide case."

"What?" The unflappable Kate actually sounded surprised.

"You missed a lot while you were gone." Lara related events of the past week until they reached the driveway of their shared residence.

"My God. Antitank rounds with depleted uranium."

"Yeah. Too bad dogs can't smell radioactivity," Lara said.

Kate opened her car door and climbed out. "You have to go back to work?"

"No, I'm done for the day," Lara said. "I've got clearance to keep the unit overnight." Both women stripped off the dogs' ID and turned them loose in the backyard.

"Good. You change and order a pizza, I'll take care of Lexi, then I've got to hear the rest of this story," Kate said.

ONLY ONE SLICE and the crusts both sisters refused to eat were left in the pizza box. Outside on the patio next to the pool, Lara had finished her iced tea. Kate, who never drank because she, like others in her profession, remained on permanent standby during off-hours, sipped at a soda. She remained a firm believer in the maxim "Bombs and booze never mix." She hadn't had a drink since she started working the bomb squad.

"Split the last piece?" Kate asked.

"You have it," Lara said, knowing Kate refused to eat airport food. "I'm done."

"You twisted my arm."

Kate reached for the pizza slice and remarked, "You out of beer? I've never seen you eat pizza without one."

Lara flinched. Trust Kate not to miss a trick. "We're not out. I'm just on the wagon for a while."

Kate lifted an eyebrow as Lara took in a deep breath.

"Here goes." Lara launched into her tale of the funeral, how she and Nick hadn't come home to the kennels that night, how they'd shared a bed, and how Sandra had suspected their liaison.

"I'll bet Mom has a few more gray hairs," Kate said when Lara finally finished. "I hope she hasn't told Dad. I swear, he's the original prude."

"It gets worse," Lara sighed. "We had unprotected sex. That's why I'm off the beer—until I know for sure."

Kate's hand with the half-eaten slice actually paused in midair. Lara held her breath as she watched Kate struggle with her emotions. Finally she spoke.

"I hope you didn't share *that* news with the folks."

"Mom gave me the third degree there, too. I didn't admit anything, but that didn't work, either. She may be retired, but she's still a bloodhound."

"I would have told her to mind her own damn business."

"I did."

Kate put down her pizza to reach for Lara's hand. "How are you doing?"

The kindness in her big sister's voice, the touch of her hand, caused Lara's voice to tremble just a bit. "I'm a nervous wreck," she said. "I can't believe my stupidity. But at least he's HIV free. We swapped blood tests from our last police physicals."

"Thank God for that," Kate breathed, squeezing her sister's hand even harder, showing the softer side that only family ever saw.

"Glad you're not going to disown me. After what I went through when I moved in with Jim… And get this—Nick wants to marry me if I'm pregnant, because of his own past. I swear, Kate, it's like a bad plot from some old movie."

"How do you feel?" Kate asked.

"Me?" Lara exhaled. "A little scared."

"Yeah."

"Nervous."

"Uh-huh."

"And angry," Lara finally confessed. "I don't want anyone marrying me just because I'm pregnant. It's old-fashioned at best, and insulting at worst!"

"So what you're saying is, pregnant or not, no marriage."

"That's right. And if I'm pregnant, I'm keeping this baby."

"Ah." Kate passed Lara an unused napkin. "Wipe your face," she said with big-sister familiarity. "You've got sauce on your chin."

Lara obeyed.

"So you want this child?" Kate asked.

"Yes. It's not like I'm a rape victim. My health won't be compromised. And I can't see giving up my own child for adoption just because I'm single."

"That's not what I asked. If you're pregnant, do you *want* the baby? Or are you merely planning to *keep* the baby?"

Lara paused, then said slowly, "Yeah, I guess I do want it. I've always wanted children. Jim and I had hoped to start a family someday. This isn't how I dreamed of becoming a mother, but now that the opportunity may be here, I won't turn my back on it."

"It's good you know that much."

Lara sighed. "It's not like I'm gonna find another Jim."

Kate gave her a sharp look, then reached for her soda.

"What?" Lara asked.

"Nothing."

"Don't tell me nothing, Kate. I know you. Spill," she ordered. From her sister, she could expect honesty without any parental hysterics.

Kate shrugged. "When you met Jim, it was instant romance. You moved so fast. In fact, you quit your job and moved in with him less than a week after you'd met."

"Three days. So what's your point?" Lara said defensively.

"Well, looks like it's happening again, that's all."

"I wish everyone would stop saying that!"

"Everyone?" A pause. "So I'm not the first who's noticed?"

Lara didn't answer, but Nick had made the same comment to her.

"Lara, you're an all-or-nothing woman when it comes to men. You never had a serious steady until Jim came along, then wham—he was the one. You haven't dated since he died, yet then Nick comes along, and all of a sudden you're talking babies, he's talking marriage. Maybe there's more to this than pity sex."

"I never said we had pity sex!"

"Then it must have been pretty damn passionate for a sensible woman to forget all about contraception and protection," Kate retorted.

"Was it ever!" Lara blurted out. "We—" She stopped self-consciously. There were topics that even close sisters didn't share.

"Your life's never boring, Lara. After listening to your latest escapades, I could use a beer myself. This waiting until retirement sucks. I remember my college days…." Kate broke off, then smiled. "But, Lara, you should pick yourself up a home pregnancy kit. Or I could pick one up for you," Kate offered. "I remember when you first started your periods and were too embarrassed to go to the drugstore. Mom or I always had to do your shopping."

"Thanks, but I'm not a little girl anymore. I'll pick up the kit myself later this evening."

"Some condoms for yourself, too. Can't always rely on the guys." Kate finished the last of her soda. "Would you grab me some Milky Ways? I want the one-pound bag of full-size bars. None of those insulting minibites."

"Chocolates, condoms and a pregnancy kit. I can't wait to see the cashier's face," Lara groaned.

Kate lifted an eyebrow. "Armed criminals don't scare you, but cashiers do?"

"This is different!"

"And you said you weren't a little girl anymore." Kate grinned. "Tell you what. You can have one of my Milky Ways when you get home for being a brave girl."

"Yeah, thanks. Anything else?"

"Since you asked…a word of advice. Get the flesh-colored condoms. The colored ones look cheap. Although the glow-in-the-dark ones are kinda fun…."

"I don't wanna hear this!"

"I *am* the oldest sister." Kate nonchalantly picked up the empty pizza box, crusts, iced tea glass and soda can. "I'm gonna go unpack and shower," she said.

LARA CHANGED out of her uniform into jeans and a T-shirt. She left Sadie at home with Kate and Lexi for company, then took a drive in the Mercedes to the closest drugstore. The cashier was blessedly nonchalant, the trip home mercifully free of traffic clogs. Best of all, Nick called on her cell before she reached the house. She didn't even try to keep the enthusiasm from her voice, the questions bubbling from her lips.

"Nick! I'm so glad to hear from you! How's your grandmother? And how was the flight?"

"Much better. I'm on my way back to my parents' house. I just left the hospital." He sounded tired, but his voice was still strong—still Nick. "Thought I'd give you a ring. I'm hoping to fly home soon, but not sure when. I'll call you tomorrow, okay?"

"Yes. Please do. I'll say some prayers for your grandmother."

"Thanks. I've got to go, Lara. Take care."

"Bye…"

Lara smiled, then dropped her cell on the passenger seat beside her drugstore bag and drove on. She returned to see Kate sitting in the living room with bare feet, fresh clothes, combed wet hair and the two dogs at her feet.

"That didn't take long," her sister said.

"Nick called while I was gone."

"How's his grandmother?"

"Out of danger, he said. He was on his way back from the hospital and sounded exhausted."

Lara dropped her purse and bag of purchases on the coffee table, and joined her sister on the couch. Kate leaned forward to draw out her package of candy bars. She opened the plastic, tossed Lara one and kept one for herself. "I guess he's missing you already."

"Or maybe he just called to update me on his grandmother. But he did say he's hoping to fly home soon." Lara opened the candy bar, took a bite and grimaced.

"What?"

"This tastes strange."

"Really? Mine's okay."

Without words, the sisters immediately traded bars of chocolate. Kate took a bite of her sister's chocolate.

Lara did the same and swallowed. "This tastes off, too."

"Tastes fine to me—they both do." Kate paused. "You coming down with something?"

"Not at all. I feel fine. You don't think…" Lara swallowed. "Hormonal? Already?"

Kate shrugged and held out Lara's sampled candy bar. "Hey, I'm a rookie when it comes to pregnancy."

"I don't want the candy," Lara said. "You finish it."

Kate didn't argue. "Okay. While I do, maybe you should try that pregnancy test."

"I thought I'd wait another week."

"Why?" Kate said around a mouthful of candy. "Supposedly these new pregnancy kits are supersensitive. Almost as good as the lab's."

Lara reached for the pregnancy kit, opened the box and pulled out the instructions. "Really?"

"Couldn't hurt. *Something's* up for you to pass on chocolate. Next you'll be wanting—"

"I swear, Kate, if you say pickles or ice cream—"

"—raw potatoes. Mom ate them unwashed with the dirt still on the skin. She'd send them back if Dad rinsed them."

"That's sick! Didn't she take prenatal vitamins?"

"Yes, but she still had potato pica. I remember one of my co-workers had this cooked-cereal craving," Kate recollected. "Ordinarily she hated the stuff, but suddenly she craved oatmeal three times a day."

"That makes more sense for nourishing a pregnant body than pickles," Lara said, unfolding the white sheet of paper.

"If you *are* pregnant, promise me you won't eat dirty vegetables," Kate teased.

"Would you hush up? I'm trying to read this. It might be too early to test. I could be wasting a whole kit."

"Don't be a coward. Give it a whirl. If it comes back negative, I'll buy another in a few weeks. Come on, aren't you dying to know? *I* am!"

Lara picked up the drugstore bag with trembling fingers and stood. "Stay, Sadie." She didn't want canine company in the bathroom.

"Run warm tap water," Kate suggested, reaching into the candy bar bag for a third Milky Way and opening it.

"I can manage. You're eating *another*?" Lara asked.

"Hey, I'm behind on my calorie count. That rubber-chicken conference food was terrible. Besides, Lexi and I work it off. We always do."

"Try not to go into a sugar coma while I'm in the bathroom."

"So we'll know in…what…?"

"The box says anywhere from thirty seconds to twenty minutes. I'll wait for ten minutes."

"Ten minutes it is. I won't move an inch."

THE TESTING STICK LAY flat on the back of the toilet. Lara finished washing her hands. She dried, checked her hair in the mirror, then checked her watch. Eight more minutes to go. She refused to look at the stick until then, afraid of an early, and possibly false, result.

"This is stupid," she said out loud, rearranging her cosmetics in the medicine cabinet. She should leave and come back in eight minutes. But she felt nervous—awkward—and unwilling to wait with her sister.

"It was just one night," she said to herself. "And it's probably too soon to tell, anyway. I should have waited another week." But she didn't leave the bathroom. Instead, she hung up two fresh hand towels, debated on whether she needed a new shower curtain, rechecked her watch, and at the appropriate time, dared to pick up the stick.

The blue color and plus symbol stated, "Pregnant."

With trembling fingers, Lara slid the used stick into the empty box and quickly scanned the instructions until she found that part that said, "Percentage of error: false positives and false negatives." The percentage was listed, complete with the usual mumbo-jumbo advising the purchaser of the product to consult a doctor, etc.

Lara read that once, twice, then carefully refolded the white sheet and shoved it into the box with the testing stick. She took the stick out of the box again, stared at it one more time, then not knowing what else to do, carefully placed the box into the bathroom trash can. She opened the bathroom door to see Sadie patiently waiting. For once she didn't even think to correct her dog for disobeying a "stay" command.

Kate sat up straighter on the couch as Lara reentered the room. "What's the verdict?"

"Looks like…"

"Well?"

"I'm pregnant."

## CHAPTER THIRTEEN

*Thursday morning*

LARA SAT in the OB-GYN clinic of San Diego's Women's Hospital, waiting for her name to be called again by the doctor she'd just seen. Earlier, when the pelvic exam had been inconclusive, Dr. Evans had said, "Ordinarily I'd do routine labs, and call you back when the results were in. But considering your occupation...I put a rush on this. You'll know the results within the hour."

While waiting, Lara had tried to read the newspaper she'd brought along, but found her attention distracted by some of the obviously pregnant women in the room. Most had someone with them. Lara had turned down Kate's offer to accompany her.

"You just got back from the conference," she'd said, "and this was the earliest appointment I could get. They didn't have anything free on your day off. I'll be okay."

"You sure?" Kate had asked, unconvinced. "Maybe Mom could come along for moral support."

"It's just a blood test and a pelvic. If that home test

kit is correct, I'd rather tell Mom in private. In fact, I'd rather she didn't hear about this visit for now."

"You know I wouldn't say anything without your permission. I do wish you didn't have to go alone."

"It's okay, Kate. I'll be fine."

Only now, waiting for the lab results to come back, Lara didn't feel fine. She felt nervous—and alone.

Lara defiantly picked up a waiting room magazine. If she were pregnant, she wouldn't really be alone, she told herself. Kate would certainly be a hands-on aunt. Lindsey would be a happy relative, as well. Her mother, and hopefully her father, would give up their traditional dream for her—marriage, and *then* baby. And there was Nick. He'd claimed he wanted to be active in the child's life. She decided to take the same tack with Nick she'd used with her parents: until she knew for sure, no point in going public. It was her body, her responsibility. Her call.

She did find herself longing for Nick. She'd rather he were here to lean on, instead of Kate, because she and her sister were opposites. Kate, as the oldest, tended to be somewhat traditional herself, though much more tolerant than either of her parents. Unlike them, Kate rarely offered her opinion unless asked, and she didn't judge, only advised. Kate had always been "the sensible sister" and Lara had often taken advantage of her advice. But this was one time Kate couldn't offer the experience of an older sister.

"Lara Nelson?"

It was the nurse. Lara rose and followed her back into the doctor's office. Dr. Evans delivered the information as soon as the nurse left and closed the door behind her.

"Your suspicions were correct, Lara," she said. "You're definitely pregnant."

"My God!" Lara gasped. "This is great! I can't believe it!" She felt like dancing for joy. Instead, she settled for the age-old gesture of protectively placing her hand over her belly.

"So, we're talking prenatal appointments, then?"

"Yes. I want my baby." *My baby.* How possessive she sounded!

"All right. I'll prescribe some vitamins with extra iron, provide you with literature and since this is your first pregnancy, set you up with the nurse practitioner for counseling on nutrition and what you can expect in the upcoming months. That will help in determining how long you want to keep working in your present position. Toward your last trimester, you'll probably want to switch to something less strenuous."

"I can't believe it," Lara repeated.

"You want to update your next of kin?"

"Next of kin?"

"Yes, someone local. It's usually the baby's father, but doesn't have to be. Check with the front desk."

"Oh." Lara hesitated only a moment as she thought of Nick, then said, "My sister's down as my next of kin. Let's keep it that way." She'd add Nick's name later—if he hadn't changed his mind about fatherhood. Suddenly she found herself silently praying he hadn't.

The rest of the visit passed quickly, information exchanged, and all went well except for one moment, when the doctor asked, "Do you have an idea when you conceived? A ballpark figure would help me calculate your due date, since you don't have regular cycles."

"Actually, I can give you the exact date of conception. It was a week ago yesterday."

"Ah," Dr. Evans said, then punched some numbers into her calculator. "Ms. Nelson, your baby is due around the middle of next February."

Lara received her due date with awe. That sense of awe continued as she arranged new appointments, provided insurance data to billing, and picked up her prenatal pills at the hospital pharmacy. She felt euphoric all the way home, humming along with the radio and picking out names in her head, both boys' and girls'. She wished even more that Nick was back; she couldn't wait to share her good news with him. But when Kate finished work, maybe she and Lara could celebrate by strolling through the mall, shopping for children's things. Baby furniture and clothing and toys and...

Lara blinked. A parked motorcycle stood in her driveway—*Julio's* motorcycle. At its side stood a travel-weary Nick Cantello.

She quickly parked. In her joy to see him, she left her purse, pamphlets and prescriptions in the car and hurried to his side. It seemed the most natural thing in the world to hug him and let him hug her back.

"I thought you were still in Italy," she said when they parted.

"I got back this morning," he said simply. "Thought

I'd swing by and see if you were home. I tried your cell."

"Oh, I had to turn it off at the—" She stopped and reached into her pocket to turn her cell back on as she said, truly meaning it, "It's good to see you again! Come on in and sit down." She wanted to share her news with him.

"I can't stay," he warned. "I only have a few minutes."

"Only a few?" Lara echoed.

"Yeah. I called Colonel Doyle and told him I was back in town. He wants to see me."

"I'll go with y…" She remembered she was back on K-9, even as Nick shook his head.

"Doyle's got everything back according to protocol, at least for now."

"I see." Lara walked to the kitchen and quickly provided him with a tall glass of soda, then they moved into the fenced yard. "Tell me about your visit home."

Sadie was busy growling and stalking a stray duck. The defiant bird paddled around the pool as Lara listened to Nick's brief story. He didn't take long, nor did he go into details. Reading between the lines, Lara suspected the visit hadn't been pleasant for all concerned.

"It was awkward at first," Nick admitted. "Relatives explaining why I should or shouldn't have been told. My grandfather blamed the whole mess for my grandmother's heart attack—apparently it was triggered more by anxiety than cardiac dysfunction. The doctors say it was mild. She won't need surgery."

"I'm glad. And, Nick, her illness isn't your fault.

Things will get easier with everything out in the open."
She thought of the pharmacy bag she'd left in her car,
waiting for the opportunity to tell him of her pregnancy.

"Don't worry about me," Nick said. Lara realized he
meant it. The grieving man of earlier was gone. In his
place was a confident man with no trace of vulnerabil-
ity, a detective who had his emotions firmly under
wraps—and who could easily handle her news.

"My visit home didn't help with Julio's case," Nick
said. "However, Doyle called while I was gone. He
wants to discuss the results of Knox's DNA test with
me later today. Who knows? I may have T. J. Knox as
a half brother."

"I wish he'd told you over the phone."

"So do I, but I promise to keep you posted, just like
I'll be doing with Lilia," he said, seeming to read her
mind. "So how're you doing?"

"No bullets, no broken windows," she said. "Just
me and Sadie keeping our piece of the streets safe for
San Diego's good citizens."

"And your health? Although I suppose it's too early
to tell if you're…"

Lara smiled at his oblique reference, glad for the
heaven-sent opening. She hadn't wanted to blurt out the
news. "It's not, and I am."

"You are? You're really…?" For a moment Lara
couldn't read his face. It seemed wiped of all emotion.
Then joyous warmth sparked in his eyes and spread to
his lips. He smiled hugely.

"I really am," Lara replied. For a moment, she forgot who and what they were—law-enforcement members...ships who'd passed in one grief-stricken night. For that moment, they were man and woman caught up in the wondrous miracle of creation.

That moment started to fade—as all times of pure emotion must—until Nick wrapped his strong arms about her, drew her close, and held her in a protective embrace as old as time. Lara felt herself a part of Nick and he a part of her, in a way she'd never experienced—not even with Jim, the man she'd planned to marry.

She felt conscious of the new life inside her, and Nick's protective body around them both. It seemed natural, right. And when Nick shifted to kiss her, it seemed like a whole new experience to her. She'd never felt anything like it. She could feel them both trembling from shared, positive emotions, and wished it could go on forever. It seemed as if it could—until the rest of the world intruded.

Sadie barked and launched herself into the pool, her frustration at the duck finally conquering her aversion to water. The duck flew off, and a satisfied Sadie swam to the steps of the pool to exit and contentedly shake herself.

Nick's cell rang. He reluctantly dropped his arms, pulled out his phone, and checked first the caller ID number, then the time on his phone. "Damn. It's Doyle's office wondering where I am. I'll call them back, tell them I'll be in later."

"No, Nick, don't. Not on my account. Go. You won't find Julio's killer sitting at home, and you don't want to antagonize your new boss."

The intimacy of earlier faded. Nick shoved his phone back in his pocket.

"Well, then, I guess I should be going," he said.

Lara ignored her disappointment as she rose to walk him back to her driveway and the motorcycle. "You be careful," she said as he climbed on. "Call me, okay? No wait, come back here in person. I don't want you at your apartment alone. Plan on spending the night here."

Nick nodded. "Count on it."

She watched him leave, then faced her wet dog. "Come on, you. Let's go find a towel."

WHEN KATE ARRIVED HOME, Sadie's fur was only slightly damp but still glistened.

"Bathtime again?" Kate asked as she came through the garage to release Lexi for exercise, food and water.

"Ducks," Lara announced. She'd had to blurt out the news of her pregnancy to a time-pressed Nick. With her sister, she could enjoy a more leisurely sharing.

"Sadie and her ducks..." Kate needed no further explanation. Inside the high-fenced private backyard, she stripped down to her underwear, tossed her clothes on a patio lounger, turned on the spa jets and then sank into the hot tub with a weary sigh. Lexi relaxed on the grass, and Sadie followed suit.

"Rough day?" Lara asked with sympathy, recognizing the signs.

"A retired gentleman didn't clean his shoes before packing. His hobby is gardening. Guess what was on his shoes."

"Don't tell me…"

"You got it. Large trace elements of chemical fertilizer." Kate dunked her head under the water, then came up again. "You'd think they'd never heard of the Oklahoma City bombing. Everyone knows fertilizer can be made into explosives. Lexi signaled when we were spot-checking the carousels. I called for backup. We held up all three flights using that carousel. I'm just thankful it was a happy ending."

"So am I. What about your gardener?" Lara asked curiously.

"A nice guy, very cooperative, but he did hate giving up, and I quote, his 'most comfortable pair of shoes for vacation.' But we had no choice."

"Makes sense. A Seattle bomb dog would know the smell."

"And we'd have the same false alarm all over again." Kate smiled. "He kept his cool. His wife, however, was a bit upset when they missed the last direct flight to Seattle. They'll have to connect through LAX."

Lara groaned at the mention of Los Angeles International, the nightmarish, congested behemoth of an airport that plagued both travelers and security alike. "That'll be the last time he gardens before a flight."

Kate chuckled. "His wife said she'd make certain of it."

Lara kicked off the sandals she'd worn to the hospital and dangled her legs in the spa as Kate continued.

"I need a cushy job with an air-conditioned car. My feet are tired. And I'm sure Lexi's are, too, from the concrete." Lexi lifted her head at the sound of her name, then flopped back down onto the grass. "Extra treats for you at dinner, I promise." Kate lifted a leg out of the water to rub first one sore foot, then the other. "That feels good. So, enough about my day. How was yours?"

"I came home and found Nick Cantello in the driveway."

Kate sat up straighter in the spa. "He's back already? I'm surprised."

"I sure was."

"Well, well, well. Rushed right to your doorstep. Did he give you any notice?"

"He couldn't. I had to turn my cell off in the hospital. He just happened to catch me coming home."

"Ah." Kate paused. "And?"

"I told him the results of my test. So, you wanna know what the doctor said?"

"I'm dying to know! *Are* you pregnant?"

"Yes."

Normally calm Kate squealed like a little girl and stood straight up in the water. "Congratulations! You're gonna be a mom!"

"Yep." Lara backed away from the shower of spa water.

"And I'm gonna be an aunt! If I wasn't so wet, I'd hug you!" Kate lowered herself back into the spa. "So when's the due date? Have you decided on any names? What did Nick say?"

"The middle of February, not really, and he's pleased."

"Wow. What else did the doctor say?"

"I have some vitamins and iron, and more appointments. Plus, I go to see the nutritionist. Not much else to do this early…"

"Except spread the good news," Kate said enthusiastically.

"I'm going to wait a bit. Not even tell Lindsey. It's so early yet…."

The spa timer expired, the jets stopped, and the backyard became quieter.

"There's plenty of time later," Kate said with the tact and sympathy Lara had always admired. She sat a while longer, then stared at her hands. "My fingers look like prunes. I should do laundry. I'm out of uniform shirts."

"Or…we could go to the mall…check out baby stores…maybe do some shopping tonight."

"I wish I could, Lara, but I'm beat. If I didn't have to work tomorrow…"

"Okay, the Internet mall it is."

Kate paused a moment. "We have plenty of time to shop. Why not wait for when we can both do the mall?"

"Now you sound like Nick," Lara sighed. "Can't we be a little impulsive?"

"What do you mean?"

"Oh…you're both so traditional. He wants to marry me if I'm pregnant. You want me to go slow on the preparations."

"I'm not trying to be a wet blanket, truly," Kate protested. "And I'm not all that traditional trying to push a marriage you obviously don't want."

"I'm not against marriage to anyone. It just looks like I'm going to have the child first."

"Whatever happens, I have room in my heart for a healthy Baby Nelson, whatever the gender."

Lara murmured her agreement, swinging her legs back and forth in the warm water.

"What about work?" Kate asked, making no move to get out and tackle her waiting laundry. "You're not gonna stay on patrol for long, are you?"

"As long as I can. Until I'm too big to run, I guess."

Kate's lips thinned with disapproval. "I wouldn't worry about running, Lara. I'd worry about bullets. It's not just you and Sadie putting your life on the line. There's three of you now."

"Most police officers go their whole lives without firing their weapon or being fired upon."

"Yeah, most. *You* can't say that."

"Well, lightning rarely strikes twice," she said, trying to make light of the matter, though deep down, both sisters knew otherwise. "Besides, I'm off Julio's murder case for good. And sooner or later Nick will be getting a new partner."

"You sound disappointed. Is it because you're not playing detective or because you'll be missing Nick?"

"Naturally I want Julio's killer found."

"Talk about noncommittal. Doesn't sound like you're off this case at all to me." Carefully, so as not to drip on Lara, Kate exited the hot tub and walked over to the clothesline. She shed her underwear, draped it over the line, retrieved an oversize beach towel and wrapped it around herself sarong-style. "Your baby's no safer in a cruiser on patrol than on a murder case where the suspect is still at large. Skipping K-9 patrol would be safer still. You could do searches. Drug sweeps. Friday-night drug and alcohol traffic stops. Sadie's cross-trained. She does patrol duty and narcotics."

"I know," Lara said irritably. "I don't plan on being reckless."

"That doesn't mean the perps aren't." Kate studied her sister's face and relented. "Sorry. I'm really happy for you, Lara. I trust your decisions. Anything I can do to help, just let me know." Now dry, Kate finally gave Lara a hug.

"Thanks."

"Hey, any time." Kate pulled away and picked up her uniform from the lounger.

"Actually, there is one thing. Do you mind if Nick stays here with us? That is, if I can get a police patrol to swing by and keep an eye on the place, especially at night. What with Colonel Doyle working the case, I don't think we need to go back to Mom and Dad's. I'd prefer to stay, if you don't mind."

"Not at all, and I won't mind the extra security. You've got to eat and sleep sometime," Kate said. "Speaking of which, I bought us a case of juice and some white chocolate. They're in the kitchen."

"White chocolate and juice?" Lara was confused

"Just in case you were pregnant, I bought something healthy for the baby and something sinful for you. The white chocolate might taste better than the dark. I also bought a paperback for expectant mothers. You know, health and delivery options and stuff. I want to read it after you're done."

Lara smiled. "What would you have done if I wasn't pregnant?"

"I saved the receipt. The juice wouldn't go to waste. And neither would the chocolate," Kate said, slinging her arm around Lara's waist. "Give it a taste and check out the book. Then as soon as I put my shirts in the washer, you and I will hit the Internet malls for Baby Nelson."

# CHAPTER FOURTEEN

*Thursday afternoon*

"GLAD YOU'RE BACK," Doyle said, gesturing Nick to a chair. The muscles of a career marine rippled beneath his shirtsleeve. "Homeland Security's placed me in charge of investigating the depleted uranium and any connection it has with your partner's death. My regrets."

"Thanks."

Nick studied Girard's replacement. Colonel Doyle wore a military uniform of the Provost Marshall's Office, the marine corps equivalent of a civilian police captain. Like Girard, the man was tall. There the similarity ended.

"Right now, I'm busy kicking butt," Doyle said. "Supposedly much of Homeland Security's resources are tied up with Amtrak."

Nick nodded, one jerk of his chin. California's coastal train network had become Homeland Security's present local danger. Bombings of trains in Europe had alerted them to threats and problems with Amtrak, as well as other commuter trains and their many passengers. A sudden increase of derailments and crashes had drawn attention away from a few DU bullets.

"I will *not*, however, take that as an excuse," Doyle said.

*I*, not *we*. Nick appreciated the man's involvement. It seemed as if he and Lara alone had been shouldering the caseload. Perhaps that was changing.

"I've done some probing," Doyle said. "The Department of Energy has five nuclear-weapons production sites in this country."

"You pinpoint any particular DOE site?"

"Not yet. They're all in the Midwest or South. I have people back there working on it." Doyle glanced at a single notepad in front of him, a big difference from Girard's confusing piles of scattered papers. "Next topic—DNA results. I did manage to light a bonfire there. You ready to hear?"

Nick appreciated the man's tact, but didn't need hand-holding. "Go for it."

"Magda Palmer, aka Palameri, is your biological mother."

"My family admitted it."

Doyle shoved him a copy. "That's for your personal records. Knox's voluntary DNA samples conclusively shows him no relation to you."

"I suspected as much. Have Girard or Lansky changed their minds? What about getting that court order?"

"Negative on both. Girard politely says he's still discussing it with his wife—who's back in town—and lawyer. Lansky has flat-out refused, and with a fair amount of hostility." Doyle's jaw hardened. "I'm not impressed by either emotion. Nor am I impressed that no cohesive financial studies of these three men have been completed. I've ordered my own—and not through the banks, but through the Internal Revenue Service. I have those results—on-the-surface results, anyway. They intend to dig deeper."

Nick grinned. Some of the most notorious criminals had literally gotten away with murder, only to be thrown into jail for nonpayment of taxes on their ill-gotten gains. A good lawyer might be able to prove them innocent, or at least lessen the punishment in a court of justice. The IRS was far less flexible, and it wasn't part of the justice system.

"Girard looks clean. Knox's records are a mess—his taxes often paid late and with penalties, but nothing to put him in jail."

"He's a self-admitted gambler," Nick inserted.

Doyle's chin jerked up. "I didn't know that. I should." Doyle jotted himself a note.

"Lansky?"

"Red flags a-plenty. Lots of smoke, lots of mirrors, to quote the local office. In other words, his records are too neat, too exact, yet he filed the taxes without assistance. It looks suspicious."

"Consistent with a blackmailer and money?"

Doyle's eyes narrowed shrewdly. "Perhaps. If your partner's notes are to be trusted."

"He was a good worker. A damn good worker. He…" Nick broke off awkwardly. His intercontinental round trip in so short a period must be taking its toll on him.

"Speaking of working, I want you up in grief counseling—now. They've got a two-hour block set aside."

Nick temporarily shoved aside his weariness. "I'd rather work this case."

"Then prove you're fit. Get evaluated. Do the two-hour block, arrange for whatever else they say, and we work on this until it's solved."

"All right. We should keep Officer Lara Nelson, as well," Nick added.

"As long as I hear that from her personally," the colonel qualified.

"She's a damn good cop, too. With your permission, I'll call her right now."

"No," Doyle said. "I'll do it myself later. And, based on the progress so far, I'd prefer her to stay on board. Assuming she feels the same, or even if she doesn't, I want to know where you two will be staying so I can monitor your security. I won't lose another soldier under my watch."

"We're both at Officer Nelson's home."

Doyle raised one thick eyebrow, but merely said, "Got it. I expect semi-daily debriefs from both of you."

"You can count on those, too."

Doyle nodded with military briskness. "Counseling first. Seventh floor. Dismissed, Detective."

Nick felt hope rise again. "Yes, sir. I'm on my way."


"I WONDER WHERE HE IS?" Lara asked Kate. "He's been gone hours."

"Be patient," Kate replied, browning the hamburger and precooked rice in a frying pan for the dogs. "Not to be nosy," she said, "but which room are you planning for Nick? I mean, strictly from a security point of view."

"He'll have his own room, of course. Finding Julio's killer is our first priority."

"Actually, that's *Nick's* first priority. Yours should be your heath and safety, and the baby's."

"I know. But I can't just forget about Julio Valdez."

Kate didn't argue. "Hopefully you'll get routine assignments now that you're pregnant. Maybe volunteer for routine searches tomorrow. Definitely talk to your police doctor."

Kate's parental tone irritated Lara. She didn't need another parent. "I only just found out I'm pregnant, you know."

"It's never too soon to plan. Call tomorrow."

"I won't have time. Sadie and I hit the agility course for conditioning, then a K-9 refresher test." Monthly tests were required to monitor and maintain K-9 team efficiency. "After lunch we get the test for recertification. I'm not worried. Sadie always passes with flying colors."

Kate nodded, flicking a piece of rice off her wrist. "Speaking of work, I'm back on swing shift tomorrow. As it is, I'm going in late today."

"I gathered that." Usually Lara missed her sister's company when their shifts didn't coincide. It also made sleeping harder on both them and their dogs. In this instance, Lara didn't feel disappointed at all. She'd have more time—and privacy—with Nick, even if they had separate bedrooms. The thought quickened her pulse.

She hid her feelings by asking, "Is it shift change time already?"

"Actually, it's not, but we've got people going out on vacation. I tried to get graveyard…."

Lara instantly understood. In the heat of the summer, graveyard shifts were the easiest on the dogs. Day shifts weren't too bad with the cool seaside mornings. However, canines and handlers working swing shifts suffered the hottest part of both the afternoon and the evening, and the greatest number of civilians out in public. Temperatures remained high long after sunset.

"Lexi and I will be sweating it out during the vacation shuffle. You have no idea how hot runway concrete can get in the summer. I melted a pair of soles last year. Had to boot Lexi's paws."

"Lexi tolerates heat well. You'll be rotating inside with carousels and passenger lines before either of you break a sweat," Lara consoled.

"Fingers crossed." Kate checked her watch. "Gotta run. Love you."

"Love you, too," Lara replied. "Be safe."

"Always. Even though we haven't met, tell Nick I said hi."

THE EVENING NEWS BLARED from her big-screen television in the background. In her bedroom, Lara readied her working jumpsuit and uniform trimmings for the following morning. Rush-hour traffic reports droned on, then the weather—always the same this time of year—and the pollution reports, which tended to vary with the sea breezes. Colonel Doyle had called and made an appointment for Lara to meet with him after her K-9 shift the next day. Soon after, Nick had called to say he was on his way, his voice and manner on the phone hopeful.

But the California sun was almost at the briny horizon, low and tangerine-orange, before Sadie's barks alerted Lara to Nick's return. She showed him in, jet-lag circles under his eyes, fingers clenched around a broiled garlic whole chicken, fries, pasta salad and plastic bottle of soda in a grocery store "take-home combo-dinner" bag.

"My God, Nick, sit down," she said, taking the bag from him. "You look beat."

"A good night's sleep and I'll be fine." He didn't protest when, instead of showing him to the kitchen, she sat him down on the nearest piece of furniture—the living-room couch—and set his dinner on the glass coffee table in front of him. Sadie sniffed appreciatively, positioning herself close enough to be at the ready, far enough away not to be scolded.

"I bought enough for two," he said. "Join me."

"Gladly. Let me grab some silverware and glasses."

Minutes later they'd tucked into the meal, carrying on a conversation between mouthfuls, Nick doing most of the talking, filling Lara in on his visit to Doyle.

"So basically Magda's your mother, Knox isn't your father, and the other two men are question marks," Lara said. "And the IRS is doing an in-depth financial check on Lansky. And you've had some grief counseling. Good."

"Plus, you get to stay on the case," Nick said.

Lara smiled. "I didn't forget. I have an appointment to meet Doyle late afternoon tomorrow, right after Sadie and I are done testing."

"We can hook up afterward," Nick suggested. "I've got grief counseling in the afternoon, and I'm sleeping in tomorrow morning."

"Can't do Julio's case any good if you're sleep-deprived." Lara gathered up the trash and leftover food, much to Sadie's disappointment. "I'll be with you in a minute. Let me deal with this and lock up the rest of the house. It's dark out. Unless you want to turn in now."

"Not yet. In a bit. I'll wait."

"Okay." Lara wasn't gone for long, but when she returned, he was asleep, slumped on the couch, head on the cushions, feet still on the floor. Lara removed his shoes and gently lifted his legs onto the other half of the sofa. Nick didn't awake. She placed a light blanket over him, gazing down at the still face with an unexpected rush of tenderness. Then, she placed a soft kiss on his forehead and left the room.

*Friday morning*

NICK WAS STILL ASLEEP on the couch when Lara got up. Kate, who'd returned from work sometime during the night, was asleep in her own bed; Lexi roused herself to check on Lara and Sadie, who were now in the kitchen for breakfast, but then left for Kate again.

Lara had hoped Nick would be awake. She was slightly disappointed to be leaving without a word exchanged. However, it would be selfish to wake him. In official garb, she and Sadie slipped outside to her car.

Soon after, Lara and Sadie waited their turn on the agility course, both glad the morning breeze continued to blow cool from the ocean and not the desert. Dogs were trained to work in all weather, and handlers in the Sunbelt were taught how to prevent canine heat exhaustion and the more serious heatstroke. But mornings were best for strenuous exercise and testing. There was no sense risking their health needlessly; they risked much more on the job, as did their handlers.

All dogs had to prove that they could perform in the important areas of searching, apprehending, assisting and protecting. Lara and Sadie's turn came up. Sadie easily tackled the various hurdles both on-leash and off. The A-frames, tunnels, jumps up to six feet high, fences, water hazards, bridges and overhead beams presented no problem. Sadie maintained her focus on Lara and the tasks at hand. The other three dogs being tested did well, too. While tackling a pile of rubber tires to test the dog's footing on shifting surfaces, only one K-9 team tripped, but it quickly recovered.

After a water break for handlers and dogs, the refresher testing began again. The dogs were tested against escaping "suspects," handlers dressed in protective suits and padded arm slings. Lara held tightly to the excited Sadie's leash. This was pure fun, a delightful game to all canines, and deliberately taught as such. Lara watched a black-and-orange shepherd's handler yell to the fleeing "suspect" the standard warning sentences.

"Drop to the ground or I'll release the dog! Stop now!" The decoy purposely didn't stop. "I'm releasing the dog!" he yelled.

The handler released his dog, who didn't need the command to attack, even though it was given. The dog knew what to do. Lara watched the black-and-orange easily catch the running suspect and grab the padded sling. Dogs were deliberately trained to strike the arm first, preventing the more instinctive, possibly deadly, aim for a human throat. Their job was to apprehend, not kill. However, this particular dog didn't "sink," or lower, his teeth into the target hard enough to hold on. This was mandatory. The decoy shook off the dog, his arm free.

Lara felt bad for the team. Sinking was extremely important. One arm restrained meant one less hand to use a weapon against dog or handler. The decoy suspect should be able to lift the dog off his feet after biting. The animal shouldn't release his hold until commanded or the decoy dropped to the ground, motionless. Lara watched the black-and-orange team go to the back of the line to be given another test. Another team did the exercise, only this time the male canine refused to release the subject when ordered. He had to be ordered to release a second time, which was a strike against him.

Lara was up next. She approached the start line, both her voice and leash tightly restraining Sadie. Her devoted pet had disappeared, replaced by a working police canine. The furred ears twitched forward with anticipated attack adrenaline, the muscled haunches tightly coiled for an immediate racehorse-type start as the keen eyes watched the soon-to-be-moving target. Sadie strained against the leash as the decoy took off.

"Stop or I'll release the dog!" Lara yelled. "Drop or I release the dog!"

Lara released Sadie from the leash. There was no need to yell, "Attack!" in German. Sadie knew the drill. Lara followed on foot as Sadie bolted at top speed. Ears pinned back, running at top speed, her body extended over the grass, the dog reached the target. All four paws left the ground in her attack lunge, and she hit the padded arm target on the first strike, hit it hard enough to knock the decoy's legs out from under him. He thudded on the ground hard, and Sadie held on tight while growling and worrying—but not releasing—the arm.

"Stop fighting the dog!" Lara ordered. "Stop fighting the dog!" The decoy froze, and then deliberately moved again. Again Lara's dog responded correctly with a renewed full-body attack.

Sadie halted at Lara's command. "No! Leave it!" Sadie released her grip but continued to growl, her lips curled, the hair on her neck and between the shoulders straight up. *"Watch him!"* Lara ordered, the command to guard only, which meant no biting as long as the decoy remained motionless.

Sadie allowed Lara to restrain her and resnap the leash, but Lara knew she hated giving up the attack. No K-9 could go from full attack to complete docility in seconds. Instinct and adrenaline prevented it, but the dogs were still required to respond immediately to commands in the interests of both team and public safety.

The examiner called off the exercise as Lara gave her canine partner the praise she deserved. "*Ist brav,* Sadie!" You're brave.

When the dog was safely leashed, the decoy stood up. Lara returned back to the "start" where the examiner nodded his head in satisfaction. "Nelson and Sadie, right? Nice grip for a female," the examiner said. "She's fast, too."

Sadie continued growling her triumph for everyone to hear, ancient instincts challenging anyone to deny her "the kill." Lara smiled her own satisfaction. As "pack leader," Lara had shown her dominance by ordering Sadie to attack, catch and release her "kill." The results required split-second coordination and trust; otherwise the safety of team and decoy was compromised.

The rest of the group went through their paces, then the examiner spoke.

"Officers, you're required to stay here on the premises until testing is complete. Kennel your dogs until we resume. We'll meet again after lunch." He checked his watch, announced a time, told them where catered deli lunches would be served outside and dismissed them all.

Lara watered Sadie and left her happily curled up in the air-conditioned kennels. After a quick stop in the ladies' room, she headed outside toward the parking lot, instead of the picnic tables. Her packed lunch was in her little cooler in the K-9 unit. To her surprise, she saw Nick leaning against her car. He continued to wear the plain clothes from earlier, with his gun and shield visible, the motorcycle parked beside her cruiser.

"Hey, stranger," she said with pleasure. "You're looking better."

"I feel better. You've got a soft couch—though you should have gotten me up."

"You looked so tired I didn't have the heart. What's up?"

"I've only just left the counselor's office—thought I'd swing by. By the way, your lunch is over there," he said, jerking his chin toward the picnic tables and the cluster of people.

"I usually pack my own. If you're hungry, you can have mine," she offered, "unless you want to share this." Lara retrieved her cooler. "Though I have to warn you, I'm not a meat-and-potatoes gal."

"You're eating for two."

"Barely," she said with a laugh, although she allowed him to carry her cooler over to the picnic tables. They soon sat down at a table all their own, Lara with her cooler lunch, and Nick with the catered lunch.

"Anything new from Doyle?" Lara asked, then popped a grape into her mouth.

"Not yet. But he gives the impression he won't stop until there is."

"Strange…a military officer in charge of a police investigation. It's a world gone wild," she quipped.

"At least Girard's gone. I'm impressed with Doyle," Nick said. "You'll like him."

"I'm not worried about liking him. Just as long as we can work with him."

"If not, we have each other," Nick said.

Lara didn't know how to respond to that. The instructor blew his whistle and ordered everyone to retrieve his or her canine from the kennel and report to the "housing" area for the search exercise.

"That's me. I've gotta go." Lara rose.

Nick flashed her a thumbs-up. "Mind if I watch?"

"Not at all." She gathered Sadie's leash and the two trotted over to begin the exercise.

The four K-9 teams gathered at the small, specially built units that simulated houses, apartments and narrow alleys. The exercise was divided into two parts. The first required searching empty buildings for drugs, weapons and other contraband, which tested the dog's ability more than it did the handler's. The second exercise did just the opposite. The team must search buildings that might or might not have people hidden, and might or might not be safe to send in dogs or handlers.

Lara didn't mind being last in line for the empty-building drug search. The satisfaction she'd felt at Nick's appearance was still on her mind. A working lunch had turned into a romantic interlude. She found it hard to shift back into work mode, and that disturbed her on a professional level. The old saying, "Your emotions travel down the leash to your dog" had much truth behind it. Daydreams had a way of creeping into your work. She took several slow, deep breaths in a conscious effort to calm herself and her dog.

By the time her turn arrived, she was ready. She and Sadie entered the exercise scenario: a previous police team had found the staff-planted narcotics. The premises were lighted and secured, as this was a narcotics-search mission only.

"*Revier,* Sadie." Lara ordered the building-and-blind search, as opposed to the specific-article search, such as tracking missing children using items of their clothing.

Sadie scored perfectly on finding contraband, as did the previous teams. All the teams had extensive on-the-job experience with the war on drugs. San Diego and its 1.2 million people bordered Mexico, and with Los Angeles and its 3.7 million people just beyond, both cities were prime targets of foreign illegal narcotics. Worse, Mexico often provided a conduit for South American drug traffic to the U.S.

Sadie had the best time of the teams for her search exercise. She found all five packets easily. When Lara emerged with her dog, the other teams and the few police spectators, including Nick, applauded. Lara praised her dog, proud of her work. Even the instructor nodded as he checked off her time and perfect score. "Like I said, one speedy dog."

"As long as she gets the job done." Lara refused to boast or take away from the other teams' accuracy. Speed was important, but thoroughness counted, too. Fortunately for Lara, Sadie consistently performed well in both areas. "*Ist brav,* Sadie," she praised again, rubbing the soft ears and stroking her forehead. Sadie wriggled her delight.

The teams and dogs waited upwind as human staff entered the buildings from the back, where neither canine nor human would see or smell how many people entered or where they hid themselves. More important, the dogs could not immediately identify scent. As before, Lara and Sadie went last. In this exercise, many of the rooms were purposely windowless. Most of the building was in shadow to heavy darkness, with built-in partitions, and cardboard, metal or wooden obstacles for decoy suspects to hide from sight. In this exercise, the handler would send in the dog first, follow the dog's lead and allow the dog to target hidden persons.

Lara hated this part of her job in real life. Going in blind could be deadly for the dogs. They were quite fearless. K-9 training made them unflinchingly familiar with the sound of gunfire. Training did not teach them that gunfire meant danger.

Killed K-9s were accorded a police member's funeral, the mourners as tearful as at any other funeral. A wounded K-9 usually had to be retired, for the dog would have made the connection between injury and a gun's sound. It would never again work fearlessly around gunfire. The dog was "ruined" for work, but never blamed. Those recovering dogs usually lived out their retirement as pets to the officers who'd handled them.

During the real searches, handlers didn't have time

to think about the potential negative endings to their dog's work. During the exercises, however, Lara found herself praying she'd never become a handler who lost her dog in the line of duty. She wanted Sadie to retire in the California sunshine and enjoy her golden years.

"All right, Nelson. You're up," the examiner called.

Lara drew in a deep breath, gave a leashless Sadie the go-ahead command in German and began. Slowly she approached the exercise houses, checking the few windows, the alleys and the sides of the building. At the first structure, Lara stopped outside the doorjamb, away from the line of fire, carefully watching the inside.

Sadie didn't alert, and after a moment Lara stepped inside for a more thorough search with flashlight and dog....

# CHAPTER FIFTEEN

"WATCH OUT, GIRL," Lara ordered. "Here we go."

Lara waited a moment by the door to let her eyes adjust to the dimness in the apartment mock-up. Sadie's eyes glowed green as rod-dominated retinas registered in the dark with the motion-oriented vision of a predator. However, suspects were rarely out in the open. A decoy suspect would be completely out of sight, deliberately downwind, up above in the rafters, hidden inside a mattress, inside a child's upside-down wading pool, hanging outside a window, wedged inside a chimney, hiding inside a sofa-sleeper, as quiet as possible. Even then, the canines weren't easily deceived.

Lara ruefully remembered one on-the-job search where Sadie had flushed a juvenile drug offender from inside a washing machine, curled around the inside agitator and covered by wet laundry. But Sadie, with her powerful sense of smell, hadn't been fooled. She'd immediately launched into repeated barking before Lara had even lifted the lid. Without Sadie's signal, she would have walked right on.

Sadie found nothing in the first room. Lara slowly

advanced, her flashlight peering into the depths, yet carefully up and away from Sadie's eyes so as not to shrink the dog's pupil. The second room was empty, as was the third. Lara continued to send Sadie ahead before she advanced. She halted her dog. Both paused before the darkened hallway, windowless and narrow. No cover for her—no cover for a suspect, either.

"Go on," she ordered. Muzzle lifted, ears perked, Sadie padded ahead to the first closed door in the hall. She sniffed under the door, around it and started scratching at the door. Lara pretended to draw her phantom gun, opened the door, and both entered the bedroom. Sadie took one step into the room and went ballistic, barking at the closed closet doors. Within seconds the first decoy exited the closet, his padded arm out and offering Sadie her reward. Lara let the dog lunge and bite, then quickly pulled her off and praised her.

"One down, Sadie," she murmured. The first decoy left, either to hide again or exit the area. She never knew how many decoys were hidden, but three to five had been the average number so far. Lara refused to become complacent. She still had half the complex to go. Two rooms down, underneath the floorboards, Sadie apprehended another decoy.

"They didn't have this crawl space last time we tested," Lara said to the decoy, pulling Sadie back.

"Surprise!" the female decoy replied. She crawled out on the floor and rested facedown, seeing if Sadie would attack her while in a "freeze" position. Sadie made one nip at the woman, but her teeth closed only on air—a warning. Lara releashed her dog, let the decoy leave and continued.

Ten minutes later yielded no more decoys or Sadie's signals. They were in the last building. Lara wondered if this exercise involved only two decoys, but she didn't assume anything. She also knew that decoys could move around and change positions, although in this exercise she wasn't required to retrace her steps to where she'd entered. In the interest of examination time, the "start," or entry, building and "finish" building were clearly defined. She had only a few more rooms to check before exiting into the fresh air. Lara rounded a corner and pointed toward the open, second-to-the-last door.

"Search, Sadie!"

Sadie's nose sniffed at the door frame. Then her eyes picked up motion. Her head jerked and she swung around with a warning growl. Lara immediately pivoted just as a shadowy figure emerged around the corner, barely a yard away.

"Drop or I'll release the dog!" she warned.

The decoy rushed her! This wasn't part of the exam—or was it? Automatically she reached for her nonexistent holster to draw her firearm as the figure raised an arm in an at-the-ready firing position. She didn't have a real gun. But the decoy, her assailant, did…and just out of leash range from her, fired from a very existent gun.

Totally surprised, Lara felt a red-hot impact to her

stomach. It knocked her to the ground, took her breath, and sent her flashlight rolling along the floor. At the decoy's lunge, Sadie immediately attacked the figure. Another shot rang out, and Sadie gave a loud *yip*. Lara's dominant hand slid down over the warm, bleeding hole just below her rib cage, as she reached for the radio on her shoulder with her other.

"Officer down." She didn't know if anyone heard her words, not over the noise of Sadie and her assailant fighting. The sounds of shouts from outside blended with the chaos inside. Lara tried to get up, desperately needing to see and assess the situation. The effort caused so much pain she almost blacked out. A third shot was fired. She heard nothing more from her assailant. Or her dog.

"Sadie? *Hier,* Sadie! Come!" she cried raggedly. In moments Sadie, whimpering in pain, flopped next to Lara. Lara threw her free arm around the dog's neck, despite her own agony, and felt blood in the dog's fur. Lara's eyes were still open, and she still had one hand on her radio, the other holding her dog's collar, as help arrived. She didn't recognize the footsteps racing toward her as someone switched on the master lights, illuminating the enclosed space. She blinked, and closed her eyes against the brightness until she felt Nick—the first one to reach her—cup her face with his hand.

"Nick…my dog's hurt," she moaned, not seeing Nick's blanched cheeks. "And the baby…what about my baby…"

"The entry wound is high," he said. "You'll be fine. All three of you." Nick rolled up the bottom of her police T-shirt to her wound, and applied pressure with the heel of his hand.

Lara gasped at the movement, but didn't pass out. From her personal experience, there were only two kinds of gunshot victims: those who fell unconscious and were seriously injured, and those who moaned or screamed in pain all the way to the hospital. Already the pain was becoming worse. If anyone moved her, she knew without a doubt that she'd be screaming, too. She started to shiver as shock set in and prayed Nick's words were true, not just bravado from a professional trained to control panic in others.

In the background, someone called out, "Where are the paramedics?"

One of the other dog team members arrived, knelt at Sadie's side and expertly muzzled her. "Hey, Nelson. I'm here to check out your dog."

"Put her in the ambulance with me."

"There're no vets at the hospital. Besides, your partner won't need your ambulance. I don't see any punctures. She only looks grazed."

Lara moved her head toward Nick for confirmation.

"The wound is long and shallow."

"You…sure?" Lara gasped. Suddenly it was harder to talk, the adrenaline rush fading fast.

"Yep. We'll get her to the vet and patch her up."

Another man came in with two emergency blankets, the kind carried in the back of police vehicles. They covered Lara's legs with one, Nick still pressing her wound. Lara's shaking fingers released their hold of Sadie's collar. She could only stroke the dog once before her hand fell to her side.

"You be a good girl."

Sadie was gently lifted onto the other blanket, ordered to stay, and the two men carried her from Lara's sight. The tears of pain in Lara's eyes spilled over from worry, and she started shaking harder and hyperventilating. The K-9 instructor joined Nick at her side.

"The baby…"

"Keep calm, Lara," Nick ordered, his face as unnaturally pale as hers. "Deep easy breaths."

"Where's that ambulance?" Lara heard someone ask in the background.

"I'll get a 20 on it," another replied, referring to the location. "You call the morgue. Our shooter's dead."

"Dead?"

"The dog took the second bullet, but the shooter took the third."

Lara thought of the first bullet and her child.

"Looks like a suicide. The gun arm doesn't have the bite marks, and the weapon's still in his hand."

"Sadie…didn't stop him?"

The instructor said, "Your dog is fast, Nelson, but she can't outrun a bullet," he joked.

Lara didn't—couldn't—smile. *She and Sadie had both failed.* She heard the sound of multiple sirens.

"Nick…" She grabbed at his wrists above the makeshift pressure bandage. "This has to do with Julio. It has to… Oh, my God!"

"What?" the instructor asked as Nick ordered, "Hang on, love."

"Call my sister," she blurted out.

"What's her number?" The instructor whipped out a notebook and pen.

"Kate Nelson," Nick replied. "Airport customs." He rattled off Kate's cell and work phone number.

"How did you know…?" Lara asked.

"Hey, I'm a detective." Nick's voice regained some of its composure. "Parents are Ed and Sandra."

"Don't call them," Lara whispered. "Let Kate. Mom will take it better from her. Kate's got my doctor's number."

"Save your breath, Lara," Nick urged.

"Kate knows my OB doc. Wait…the number's in my cell."

"Got it."

"I can't reach my phone…."

"I'll get it," he repeated. "You're hurt," Nick's voice cracked slightly on the last word.

"Nelson's a micromanager." The instructor tried to keep the mood lighthearted. "I'll go make those calls."

"Hey, boss, you'd better make one to IA," someone said as he stood up. "Our DOA here is Lieutenant Lansky."

Lara actually turned her head, the grit of the concrete floor crunching against her hair. *One of the three men suspected of killing Julio? I knew it! But why would he do this, instead of laying low?* She tried to see him, unable to believe it, but she could only view a pair of legs around the corner of the hall. She gazed up at Nick.

"My God. What's going on?" she asked. Only, her words came out slurred and faint, and she didn't receive an answer. She tried to ask again and quickly gave up. Talking took too much effort. Nick yielded his place to the paramedics as they slipped an oxygen mask on her face and started an IV.

"Nick?"

"I'm right here." He wiped his bloody hands on his pants, and then she felt one of them grasp one of hers.

"I'll be riding in the front of the ambulance," he said. "I'll see you at the hospital, okay?"

"We're going to move you now, Lara. Ready?" an EMT asked.

"What about my baby? I'm only a week along…."

"We'll check everything out at the hospital," the EMT promised. The men strapped her to a board, transferred her to the stretcher. She didn't think it possible, but the movement hurt her even more. Her nails dug into Nick's hand until her stretcher reached the ambulance doors. Nick gave her hand one more squeeze, a quick, "I'll be up front, Lara. Hang on," and released her.

The EMTs lifted the stretcher, set it down inside and collapsed the wheels. Despite their careful attempts, the action jarred Lara enough to cause one last gasp, and then unconsciousness.

*Late Friday afternoon*

KATE NELSON, still in uniform but minus her dog, rushed into the waiting room outside the O.R. of the Trauma

Center at Women's Hospital. Nick rose to his feet to greet her, and the two immediately hugged each other.

"I got here as quickly as I could," Kate said. "How is she?"

"They took her into surgery about a half hour ago."

"How's she doing?"

"Dunno yet." Nick gestured Kate to the empty seat next to his. "The X rays are encouraging. The bullet went through the abdomen, hit the stomach just below the rib cage and exited in soft tissue—there's no spinal involvement, major arteries or bone splinters to be concerned about. The uterus definitely isn't involved. It's a small target this early, they said. No miscarriage so far."

"Lara told me this was a training exercise!"

"It was. She wasn't wearing her gun."

"It must have scared the hell out of her. Was she…" Kate swallowed hard. "Was she in a lot of pain?"

"The ambulance got there pretty quick, and she passed out when they loaded her up."

Kate saw through Nick's words. "So she was. Oh, God." Kate's eyes welled with tears, but her voice remained composed. "Thank heavens you were with her. To think of my sister going through that alone…" Her gaze met Nick's, her brown eyes suddenly cold. "Did they catch the bastard?"

"He's dead. His body's been taken to the morgue." Nick explained the strange circumstances of the shooting, concluding, "No one knows how Lansky got on the scene. And Lansky's not about to give anyone any answers."

"Too bad. I would've liked five minutes alone with him."

"Sorry, there wouldn't be anything left. I'd have been there first."

Both smiled at their mutual loyalty to Lara, then the smiles faded.

"Have you contacted your parents?" Nick asked.

Kate nodded. "Dad's at the vet with Sadie."

"How is Sadie?"

"Actually, not bad. She didn't need surgery or stitches, just wound treatment. The bullet took a strip out of her skin and just grazed muscle. The vet'll keep her overnight for antibiotics. Dad'll bring her home to the kennels tomorrow."

"And your mother?" Nick asked.

"On her way…but it's rush hour. Don't know when she'll get here."

"Do they know Lara's pregnant?"

"No. I promised Lara to keep quiet about that." A pause, then Kate said, "I guess congratulations are in order. I know Lara's happy about it. My parents…"

"I'll tell your parents myself when I see them."

"I can do it if you want." Kate ran her fingers through her hair. "I should call Lindsey, but I'd rather wait until Lara's out of surgery. I hate this. You said the doctor's not worried about her?"

"She's holding her own," Nick said more firmly than he felt. "Kate, you know this isn't the first time Lara's been shot at. Until I find out who's behind this, we don't dare leave her alone."

"Don't you worry," Kate said. "She won't be. I'll see to that."

"So will I," Nick said. "Shifts, I figure?"

"With weapons. I'll take nights."

The two settled down to wait. And pray.

IN THE RECOVERY ROOM, Lara moaned and opened her eyes. Her mouth and throat were dry, her stomach on fire. A scrub-clad nurse bent over her.

"How are you feeling?"

"My baby?"

"Fine. How are you feeling?" the nurse repeated.

"Ugh," she croaked. "Thirsty…"

The nurse reached for a glycerine-soaked swab and held it in Lara's mouth. "I'll get you a pain shot. Suck on this first. You're in the recovery room and you've just had surgery. Do you remember what happened?"

Lara sucked the swab dry. "God, yes."

"I'll find the doctor when I get your pain shot, and he'll talk to you," she said with a reassuring smile. "Be right back." The nurse carefully tucked the warmed blankets around Lara's shoulders.

The nurse was as good as her word. As soon as she returned and administered a painkiller, the surgeon arrived at Lara's bedside to answer her question.

"Your baby's still with you," he assured her. "We didn't see any problems…the fetus is very immature…no uterine cramping so far."

Lara slowly exhaled with relief. She hadn't realized just how attached to her child she'd become.

"We repaired the hole in your stomach. I'm afraid you'll be off solid foods until it heals. Your parents are on their way. Your sister and the child's father are here," he said. "And I'm supposed to tell you your dog is just fine."

"The child's father" sounded strange and comforting at the same time. She was relieved to hear that Sadie was okay. The surgeon went on to explain that Lara would be in a regular room in a little while, where she'd be able to see her family.

"How's the pain?" he asked.

"Better." Her pain was down to a less-than-dull ache.

"Good. You take it easy," he said, "and I'll be back to check on you soon."

Lara tried to relax, knowing her immediate concerns were not a problem. She fleetingly thought of Lieutenant Lansky and wondered why he'd lain in wait for her, but it was too much to puzzle over. She'd think about it later…much later. She shivered, brought the arm without the IV protectively over the new life budding within, and closed her eyes.

# CHAPTER SIXTEEN

*Four days later*

LARA DIDN'T REMEMBER MUCH of the first couple of days in hospital, but each time she woke up, she remembered Nick being there. She sought his presence first, before her family. He alone seemed a sea of tranquility among lab tests and repeated visits from the surgeon, the gastric specialist, as well as the staff and her own obstetrician.

Even now, feeling much better, she couldn't relax and drop her guard unless he was around. Memories of being shot were too fresh. Lara studied Nick half dozing in a too-small chair beside the bed, while her mother fussed and fluffed. Sandra raised the head of the bed for her daughter, adjusted the covers and stroked her forehead. Yet Lara found herself turning away from her and toward Nick. She had to force herself to concentrate on Sandra's words.

"...should be discharged by the end of the week. The doctors said you're doing great."

Lara managed a nod. "I do feel better. Not great

enough to go back to work, though. At least Sadie didn't need surgery."

"Don't worry about your job right now. Or Sadie. Perhaps with the baby coming it's all for the best."

She'd lost her health, her job for who-knew-how-long, and her K-9 partner—and her mother thought it all for the best? If it weren't for Sandra's obvious fear, Lara would definitely have spoken her mind. As it was, she was getting a headache. Finally she could take it no longer.

"Mom, would you mind leaving?"

Sandra looked hurt. "You want me to go?"

Lara made an excuse. "Only because I'd feel so much better knowing you were home with Sadie. And Dad needs help at the kennels."

"Dad dropped me off. He was going to come get me later."

"You can take my car," Nick suddenly volunteered. He'd purchased a new vehicle upon his return from Italy.

"Nick…you're awake?" Sandra asked.

"Uh-huh. I'll keep an eye on Lara. You take the car."

"Oh. Okay, if you're sure." Sandra reluctantly stood and kissed her daughter's cheek. "I can come back later and get you, Nick."

"You don't have to," Lara said.

"I'll catch a cab. Or ride home with Kate when she gets here," Nick said, following Lara's lead. "Either way."

Sandra frowned. "I should call Kate and let her know."

"I can do that, Mom."

"No, it's okay. I'll tell her to pick you up, Nick."

Sandra fussed some more, accepted Nick's keys and finally left.

Lara breathed a sigh of relief. "Thanks."

"Too much mother hen?"

"That, and she hates hospitals. Bad things happen here."

"That's the cop's point of view. Think of saving lives, high-tech cancer treatments, fixing broken bones…new births."

"There is that," Lara said, her mood lifting.

"You wanna watch TV?"

"No, thanks."

"Call your father, check on Sadie?"

"Later."

Nick shifted in the plastic chair, crossed his legs. "What *do* you want?"

"To get myself and this baby well…to help you find Julio's killer…and get rid of this headache so we can talk about it."

"Ring the nurse. She'll bring you something—at least an ice pack."

Nick handed her the call button, and Lara exchanged a short dialogue over the intercom with the desk nurse. Nick poured her some water and passed her the glass.

"Thanks." She gratefully took a swallow, washing away only the hoarseness. She finished up the rest when the nurse entered the room with an ice pack and a mild painkiller for her headache.

"You should lean back, close your eyes," Nick suggested after the nurse left. "Take a nap while the pill does its thing."

"I will." Lara held on to her ice pack as Nick reached for the bed controls and began lowering her head. "As soon as you tell me what's going on with the case."

"Say when."

"That's good. Now quit stalling." Lara adjusted the ice pack. She asked the question that had been burning in her mind since the shooting. "No, wait. I'll start. I never got a chance to thank you for everything."

"No thanks needed," Nick said.

"It is. It can't have been easy."

"Who knew Lansky would go off the deep end?"

Lara shivered at the memory. "Sadie saved me, you know." She wished Sadie were there to stroke, then realized even if she were, Lara had too many staples outside and too many stitches inside to move easily.

"If Sadie hadn't heard Lansky behind us…gone after him…I'd be dead. God, did he catch me by surprise."

"She's one hell of a dog." Nick took her hand in his and held it. "And you're one hell of an officer."

"I am." Lara lifted her head. "That's why I want you to tell me about Lansky. It's been over a week since the shooting. Why did Lansky target me? What have you learned?"

Nick took a deep breath and slowly exhaled. "You sure you're ready for this?"

"I'm ready."

"For starters, ballistics says Lansky's gun didn't kill Julio. Which doesn't mean he didn't have a second gun.

However, Doyle said the IRS found major tax discrepancies. When we went to Lansky's home to inform Helen Lansky of her husband's death, she cooperated fully. After the first shock, she said Lansky had been blackmailing the real killer for years. She discovered the blackmailing a few years after their marriage."

"Who? Girard or Knox?"

"She swore she didn't know, but I'm leaning toward Girard. Anyway, she claimed she was a victim of blackmail herself. Every time she threatened to go out and report Lansky's crimes, he threatened to divorce her. The police have arrested her."

"Do you believe her story?" Lara asked.

"I do. Her medical bills and frequent surgeries were more than they could afford. She's been in a wheelchair since Magda's death. Helen loses Lansky's HMO if they split."

"Oh." Lara understood. In a country without national health care, Lansky's basic medical plan didn't cover catastrophic illness or injury. "Enough about Helen. Tell me what went wrong with Lansky. Was it Julio?"

"Probably." Nick sighed. "It was in the best interests of the killer and the blackmailer to keep things status quo. Once Julio discovered the same information the blackmailer Lansky knew, all bets were off."

"So who killed Julio? Lansky the blackmailer or the person being blackmailed? And why were we targeted?"

"Helen Lansky said whoever her husband was blackmailing turned the tables. Said unless we were scared off the case, he'd report Lansky's blackmailing, frame Lansky for the crime of killing Julio and tell the police Helen Lansky killed Magda. That's why he fired at your Mercedes. He didn't want to kill us. Just scare us—and an antitank round would do it."

"But…the training course?" Lara shook her head in dismay. "I don't understand. We weren't using firearms on that exercise. Surely a loaded gun would give him away?"

"Lansky didn't plan on being arrested for anything, Lara. I didn't tell you this before—you were too ill— but Lansky left a suicide note. He intended to kill himself. The federal courts had filed for an arrest warrant for tax evasion. More charges would have surely been filed. You and baby and Sadie got caught in the fallout of the last frantic thoughts of a desperate man."

"It could just as easily have been you, Nick," Lara said, horrified.

"He left a copy for the police and for Helen."

"His poor wife," Lara murmured. "Is she in jail?"

"No. House arrest with an electronic bracelet around her ankle. She's been charged with being an accessory after the fact. She knew about her husband's blackmailing. I'm more worried about you than her," Nick said, his lips forming a thin line. "Helen Lansky knew what kind of man her husband was. I don't see her as an innocent victim."

"No, I suppose she isn't." Lara paused. "So we think…Girard is Julio's killer?"

"Yes, damn him to hell." The venom in Nick's voice sent a chill down Lara's spine.

"But we're not sure."

"Doyle doesn't have enough to charge him yet, but he's watching him. It's only a matter of time. He'll become desperate. Then he's going down."

"Why not Knox?" Lara asked in an attempt to defuse Nick's anger.

"T.J. and his father have both been extremely cooperative. Girard's the one with the lawyer who's waiting for court." Nick checked his watch. "I should check in with Doyle. He wants to see me in person."

"Then get going."

"He said it wasn't urgent. Just to touch base. I thought I'd wait for Kate and that ride."

"Call a cab. I'll be napping." Lara glanced at the clock on the wall. "And you should get something to eat, too. I'm all set." She gestured at her IV line. "Peppermint today."

"Right." He smiled, the avenging angel gone, the kind, tender man she admired in his place. He bent and kissed her cheek. "How about if I grab something downstairs and check on you before I go?"

"You take care of business. And take care of yourself, too. Be safe, Nick."

Nick paused at the door. "Don't you worry. I'll be back."

Lara kept up her composure until he left the room. Then she closed her eyes, thinking how lucky she'd been. Despite her wound and being out of work, she still had family and friends. And Nick and his child. Especially Nick and the baby. If she lost either of them... With deep breaths she kept herself calm, readjusted her ice pack and settled back onto the pillows. She said a silent prayer for her baby and added one for Julio's children. Thank God they all had Nick. She could stand anything knowing that. She sighed and concentrated on healing. Ten minutes later with merely a soda under his belt, Nick found her fast asleep.

LARA AWOKE to find Kate sitting in her room. She blinked, then remembered where she was. "Hey, Kate."

"Hi," Kate said. "How ya feeling, sis?"

"Parched. But my headache's gone. How's Sadie?"

Kate poured her a drink from the green plastic hospital pitcher and passed her the glass. "Sadie's doing fine. Nick caught a cab about an hour ago."

"But...I thought he left earlier."

"He stayed until I came. Hope you didn't snore," Kate teased.

"What time is it?"

"After eight."

"But what about your boss...and the vacation schedule?"

"Relax. I traded time with someone else." Kate took the glass back from her. "Someone bought you a present," she said, opening the nightstand drawer to pull out a clear cellophane bag. "Ta da!"

Lara stared longingly at the bag of individually wrapped hard candy. "I can't have anything to eat."

"But you can have these. We checked with your doctor. What flavor do you want? Red?"

"Please."

Kate unwrapped a red candy for her and Lara popped it in her mouth.

"Thanks."

"Thank Nick. It was his idea. He bought them."

"My hero," Lara sighed, meaning every word.

Kate took a red one herself, then put the rest in the nightstand drawer. "Dad's going to stop by later if he can get away."

"Dad? This late?"

"Everyone here knows you're a cop. You do remember us telling you that Doyle arranged full-time security outside your door, don't you? No one's going to say anything if we don't keep to visiting hours. If Dad can't get away, he said to tell you he'll be by tomorrow morning." Kate paused to suck on her candy. "You know," she said after a few minutes, "you hurt Mom's feelings earlier."

"Huh?"

"When you asked her to go home."

"Sadie needed her. And I needed Nick. I guess Mom didn't understand that."

"More than family? Is it that serious between you two?"

"I don't know. But somehow, when he's around, I feel better. I don't seem to need parents as much as I need Nick."

"You mean, when you're hurt."

Lara sat up more, her expression serious. "Maybe when I'm all better, too."

"Well, you're a big girl."

"I'm also going to be a mother. I want this child. Maybe Nick, too. I just…I can sleep when he's around, Kate. He makes me feel safe. Maybe more than safe."

"You should tell Mom that," Kate quietly suggested. "Or let me. I'd already figured it out. The way you look at him when you think he isn't watching…"

"What do you think of him?" Lara asked curiously.

"He's a good man. I wouldn't let just anyone move in with us, would I? If Nick makes you happy, I'm happy. Mom and Dad, too. The shooting not only scared them, it opened their eyes."

"Thanks for telling me." Lara lay back on her pillows, her eyes open.

Kate studied her. "You always did know what you wanted. Even as a kid." Kate reached into the candy drawer and drew out two more pieces. Lara held out her hand as Kate spoke.

"I guess Nick has taken over my role as candy supplier. I'll have to get you flowers and a card, instead. You want a funny one or a mushy one?"

"I'd rather have a taco with guacamole."

"Don't know if I can find one on a card. But I'll look."

"Very funny."

"If you're hungry, you must be feeling better." Kate stood and reached for her purse, then leaned down and gave Lara a hug. "You do what the doc says. Keep that baby safe. Get well soon."

"You be careful."

"Always. Good night."

THE NEXT MORNING Lara's father visited her. He brought her a bouquet of roses, prearranged in a vase, and set them on the nightstand.

"These are beautiful…and they smell so good, too. Thanks, Dad."

Ed nodded and handed her an envelope. "It's not a card," he said as she opened it. "It's a photo of Sadie I took this morning on my digital camera. You can see where the vet had to shave the fur, but the wound's closed and scabbed over."

Lara blinked back tears. The picture meant more to her than the flowers. "Thanks, Dad," she repeated. "And for taking such good care of Sadie." She carefully laid the photo on her covered lap.

Ed sat down. "I know you want to see her. Figured this is the next best thing. She's doing fine. How about you?"

"Okay."

"And the baby?" Ed asked.

"The doc says good."

"That Nick…seems like a decent man. I heard he was the first one to reach you when you were shot. Knows his first aid. Did a great job until the ambulance arrived."

Lara nodded.

Ed shifted on the chair. "Nick's welcome in my house any time, Lara. If you two wanna share a room, that's fine, too. Either way, I'll be there for you and my grandchild. Just wanted you to know. I wasn't supportive of you and Jim, not even when you decided to get married. I apologize, Lara. I was wrong. I won't make that mistake again. When I heard you'd been shot..." Ed stopped, tears filling his eyes.

"Oh, Dad..."

Lara reached for him, but an embarrassed Ed held up a restraining hand. "Here. It's not very good, but thought you might want this one, too." Ed passed her another photo.

"It's Nick!"

"Yeah. Figured I'd practice a bit before the baby comes." Ed stood up. His eyes were bright. "I—uh— need to use the men's room," he said awkwardly. "I'll be back."

Lara studied the two pictures, wishing she and the subjects were together—far away from the hospital. Soon, she told herself. *Soon.*

BY THE END OF THE WEEK, the doctor talked about discharging her, as the stomach hole was almost closed, the bleeding stopped. She certainly wasn't a hundred percent, but with a special diet and medication, she should eventually recover. Nick was in the room when she received the good news. She would leave the next morning for home, with follow-up appointments, and still be on full sick leave from work.

"Congratulations," Nick said. "By tomorrow morning you'll be a free woman. I'll be here to pick you up."

All agreed Lara would return to the safety of her parents' home for the duration of her recuperation. Kate had already moved back home to help out, and Nick planned on staying in the guest room. The day of her discharge, Lara voiced a token protest against uprooting them.

"Are you two sure?" she asked Kate and Nick.

"Yep," Kate replied.

"You were my protector earlier," Nick said. "It's my turn now."

She didn't argue, for she felt weak, shaky and sore all over. Once home, Lara was reunited with Sadie and she settled in, getting daily visits from the nurse, plus prescriptions and bland-diet instructions, all as pregnancy-friendly as possible. She also had a calendar full of future checkups. After the first few days home, when she rested a great deal, Lara knew it was time for a serious talk with Nick—a talk about their child, not the investigation, which seemed to have stalled again, especially where Girard was concerned.

NICK USUALLY FINISHED his shift to arrive at the kennels in time for dinner. On her fourth day home, after they'd eaten, she asked him to sit with her out on the front porch bench. Now they were seated side by side on the soft pillows that covered the redwood bench. Sadie lay at their feet, along with a couple of the house dogs.

Nick saw her fingers reach for his arm, saw the small bruise where her IV had been, a dark reminder of the horror she—and he—had survived. He'd been a desperate man at that time, as well. If anything had happened to Lara…if she had died, cheating all three of them of a future… During that bleak time waiting for the ambulance, Nick could truly understand how Lansky had chosen to end his suffering. Understood…but never considered it for himself.

"So, what did you want to talk about?"

"Nothing new on the case?"

Nick noted she always asked about the case first, always. "Girard's still stonewalling everyone. The grand jury is set for next week. You're not missing anything."

"In that case, I want to talk about our child."

"It *is* our child, isn't it," Nick said. "I don't want to see anything happen to you or it."

"Not it. He. Or she. We should name him or her. I think the baby's survived the worst part."

A pause. "You thought of any names?"

"Lots. But I keep changing my mind." Lara grinned. "I'll definitely need your help. Most of the good names I've used on puppies."

"Please don't name the baby Spot or Rover," he said lightly.

"There's always Abby, Daisy, Ginger, Lady, Lucy, Maggie, Missy, Molly and Princess," she rattled off from memory in alphabetical order.

"Huh?"

"The top ten names for female dogs. Dad made us memorize the new list every year when we were kids so we'd avoid them. Be original, Dad said. He named the dogs—the males—in the litters, but we girls named the bitches, especially call names for pups. Without those, every other dog would answer to Castor and Pollux."

"After the stars?"

"Originally. Castor and Pollux are two of the foundation canines used for Alsatians. All registered German shepherds alive today can trace their ancestry to them."

"So what did your father name the males?"

"'Crab' is his all-time favorite."

Nick frowned. "As in shellfish?"

"No, as in the only dog ever used as a character in Shakespeare."

"Sorry, you got me there."

*"The Two Gentlemen of Verona."*

Nick thought for a moment. "Okay, if Crab's original, you only gave me nine common names. What's the tenth?"

"You're very observant, Detective. Sadie, of course." Sadie pricked her ears and thumped her tail twice.

"I should have guessed. You obviously didn't listen to your father."

"Sadie's a perfectly good name! In fact…" She hesitated. "I know it's early. I mean, really early…but I thought maybe I could pick the name if it's a girl, and you could pick the name if it's a boy. For the baby, that is."

Nick felt his chest expand at her generosity, and felt the strong affection he'd felt for Lara Nelson turning into a powerful love, one that cried for a lifelong commitment with this woman. "You're sure?" he asked, his voice raspy with emotion. "I mean, you're the mother."

*This woman is my child's mother.*

"And you're the father."

*My God. I really am, aren't I?*

Lara leaned even closer to him. "I haven't told anyone, but I kinda like Molly for a girl's name. I know it's a top-ten puppy name…but…what do you think? Do you like it?" she asked hesitantly.

"Very much." *But not as much as your name, Lara.*

Lara's smile melted him. If she weren't injured, he would have drawn her into his arms and held her close to his heart.

"What about you? Any favorites for a boy's name?"

"I…don't know. Not yet."

Lara settled herself against his shoulder, and he lifted his arm and gently encircled her.

"You have plenty of time to think about it—and to decide if you want to be in the labor room with me."

"You'd want me there?" Again she impressed him with her generosity. "What about Kate? Or your mother?"

"I'm asking you first. And I'd really like Kate there, too, if you don't mind."

"Just us two?"

"Well, you said you wanted to play a part in raising the child. Unless you're too squeamish…" she teased.

"I'm not," he said. But there's been one exception. After Lara had been wheeled into surgery, he'd gone to the men's room to wash her blood from his hands before her parents arrived—and been violently ill.

At least the bastard who'd hurt Lara was dead. Nick was fiercely glad. As for the person who killed Julio and made Lilia a widow and her children fatherless, that person would pay. Nick vowed it by all he held sacred and dear.

"Anyway, I thought…" Lara faltered. "You okay, Nick?"

Nick forced himself to smile, to damp down the fierce wish for justice. "Of course I am. You thought…?" he prompted.

"Should we hyphenate the baby's last name on the birth certificate? Nelson-Cantello? Cantello-Nelson? Or maybe forget the hyphen and make one the baby's middle name and the other the last? I'm not Emily Post, you know. This is all very confusing."

Nick couldn't help himself. "You could marry me, and we could all have the same last name."

Lara didn't answer. He watched her stroke Sadie's ears with her foot and felt renewed anger, this time with Lansky for robbing her, however temporarily, of physical agility and strength.

Then his anger was replaced by anguish. Had he come on too strong for marriage?

"You mean Nelson or Cantello?" she finally parried.

Nick relaxed a bit. At least that wasn't a firm refusal. He replied in kind. "Nelson's easier to spell, but Cantello comes earlier in the phone book."

"We'll have to think about it some more. I have another question."

"Go for it." Nick continued to enjoy her presence in the quiet evening air.

"Would you like to go with me to my doctor's appointments?" Lara asked. "Not the surgical ones, the prenatal appointments."

"I want to go to both. There's no problem with my

schedule." That much was true. Doyle still had him in counseling and on desk duty, ever since Girard had been suspended.

His watch beeped the hour. Nick checked the time. "Damn. I need to call in to Doyle—just an end-of-shift call," he said truthfully, seeing true concern in her eyes. "You want to come back inside?"

"I'm fine here, thanks. You go on in."

Nick brushed her cheek with a kiss and went in.

AS THE DOOR CLOSED behind him, Lara found herself somewhat disappointed. Yes, he'd repeated his proposal of marriage. She wasn't foolish enough to believe a child was the only basis to build a stable relationship upon. She thought, however, she'd be entitled to a kiss on the lips at least.

"Stop looking at me like that, Sadie," she complained. "What do I expect, wearing my old sweatpants, my hair a mess and a Frankenstein stomach, complete with staples?" Sadie opened her mouth and happily panted. "Next you'll say I have doggie breath."

"You're not in a fashion contest," Sandra said with parental crispness. She'd come out onto the porch carrying a glass of juice. "Dose time. It's your antibiotics that give you the tart breath, and you're almost done with them."

"Thanks." Lara took her pills, then finished off the juice.

"Ready to come inside?"

"Sadie and I are comfy."

Sandra sat down next to her daughter. "I saw Nick go inside. You two okay?"

"Uh-huh. We were talking about the birth certificate and baby names."

"Not marriage?"

"Marriage is not a solution to every pregnancy, Mom," Lara hedged.

"Jim would have done the right thing."

"Jim isn't here. Nick is. He and I are compatible. He lets me be me. You know, Mom, you're not this way with Kate or even Lindsey, and she's younger than I am."

To her credit, Sandra didn't disagree. "True. Kate's always been mature. She's a sensible woman who makes sensible decisions. I don't worry about her. Even as a child she thought things through."

"And I don't?" Lara challenged.

"Not like Kate. Or even Lindsey. On the job or off, Lindsey has good instincts. Her intuition and reactions are usually right on the money. As long as she follows them, she's okay. Lindsey's just as sensible about keeping herself safe as Kate is."

"So am I!"

"Neither of your sisters have moved in with or became pregnant by men they barely knew."

"I trusted my instincts with Jim, and I trust them now with Nick."

"Lara, your being shot nearly scared us to death! And being pregnant by a man who has both personal and professional problems worries me."

"Let me be the one to worry, Mom."

"But I hate seeing you like this. All shot up, moving like an old woman and grimacing with every step." Sandra's eyes filled with tears.

"Mom, when it comes to this baby, I'm *not* suffering. I'm happy. I want this child. I want Nick in the baby's life."

"But not in yours?"

"I didn't say that."

The tears spilled over. "Who's going to help you when your father and I are gone?"

"Don't be silly. You taught us all how to take care of ourselves. Be happy for me," Lara said softly, taking her mother's hand. "And if you stop crying, I'll tell you a secret."

"Lord." Sandra wiped at her eyes. "I don't know if I can take another shock."

"This isn't a shock. Ready? I like Molly for a girl's name."

Sandra blinked back tears. "Molly Nelson. It's a good name."

"Molly Nelson-Cantello."

"That's quite a mouthful.... But it's up to you," Sandra quickly added.

"Unless it's a boy. If it is, Nick will name him."

"A boy, huh? I never seriously shopped for a baby boy before."

Lara smiled. "I know." Mother and daughter sat quietly for a moment at the thought.

"What about your job? What will you do?" Sandra asked.

"I'm not giving it up."

"You may have to for a while. What if Sadie can't be recertified? If she's made the association between gunshot and pain…"

"She might be able to be reconditioned not to balk. I can't retest her until she and I heal, Mom. You know that."

"What does Nick say?"

"When it comes to my job, it's what *I* say."

"At least you and Jim were in love. Jim would have…" Sandra halted. "I'm sorry, Lara."

"It's okay. Nick's not Jim. We both know that."

*I wouldn't want Nick to be a copy of any man, and my heart could be in it if I thought he cared about me for myself, instead of as the mother of his child.* Lara pictured the two men in her mind. Nick outweighed the now shadowy figure of Jim. The past didn't hurt anymore, nor did she want it back. But Nick's past had hurt him, and wanting to prevent that for his child didn't make her anything more than the baby's mother. If only she could know her future—*their* future—the three of them.

"You look tired."

"I am. Perhaps I did too much today."

"Come on. I'll settle you in bed. I bought you some DVDs. Tom Cruise, for one," Sandra tempted.

"Tom Cruise?" Lara echoed as they stepped inside, her steps slow and careful. She'd always liked the actor, but now she realized that his Hollywood looks couldn't eclipse Nick Cantello's in her mind.

"When Tom Cruise became big in *Top Gun,* I used to fantasize about him," Sandra revealed.

"Mom, please!"

Sandra's voice lowered even more. "Sometimes I still do."

"I'm not listening!" Lara put her hands over her ears.

Sandra snorted. "I'm not over the hill yet."

"I don't care. Enough details."

"Fine. I'll fix myself some popcorn and get you some pudding. Vanilla or banana?"

SHORTLY AFTER, Sandra settled herself next to her daughter in bed to view Tom Cruise in heroic leading-man glory. Lara had, of course, seen *Mission Impossible 2* before. The happy ending had Tom save the world, get the girl and make love to her in a tropical paradise. After the movie finished and her mother left her room, Lara found herself thinking that Tom's sexy female lover wasn't pregnant.

No matter how hard a parent tried to keep violence at bay in the real world, families like Julio's sometimes paid a tragic price. She didn't want that for her child. She already loved the unborn baby, and she cared for Nick. He seemed to care about them both. Should she stay a single mother or not?

# CHAPTER SEVENTEEN

*Two weeks later*

LARA SAT PATIENTLY as Colonel Doyle studied her medical file. Nick waited outside Doyle's office. They'd gone together to all the civilian-doctor visits, but he wasn't allowed in for this interview, postponed by the shooting. The vivid redness of her surgical scar minus staples would fade with time. She hoped the return of her strength wouldn't take nearly as long.

"I understand you're better," Doyle said with a crispness Lara instinctively liked.

"Another month or so and I'll be good as new," Lara assured him.

"If you don't have any setbacks. A month might not be enough for your type of injury. What about your dog?"

"Sadie's wound is completely healed."

"But she hasn't been retested around gunfire."

"No, sir."

"That'll come later, too. Keep up with your doctors' appointments and counseling. Come back in a month. For now, you're still on full sick leave. And, Nelson?"

"Yes, sir?"

"We'll solve this mess."

"Thank you, Colonel."

"THAT DIDN'T TAKE LONG," Nick said when Lara emerged from Doyle's office.

"Just more paperwork saying I'm not ready to work, and to continue with police-ordered trauma counseling. I mean, how long do I have to go? There's such a thing as overanalyzing," she said with irritation. "I want to solve our case."

Soon after the shooting, the investigation had openly become "our case," although Lara had always considered it such. By mutual agreement they stopped for a quick snack at a nearby coffee shop.

The waitress arrived to pass them menus. Nick waved his away. "Just coffee and a Danish for me, please."

"I'll have milk and an apple muffin," Lara ordered.

After the waitress left, Nick asked, "No more gelatin and weak tea?"

"I've had enough of that to last a lifetime. And so has the baby."

"Can't say I'm surprised." Nick sipped his coffee. "You and I need to pack up, leave your parents and set up shop again at your place. If you have no objections."

"None. I like having you around."

"Good. Plan on me being around for a long time." He leaned across the table, as much as his broad chest would let him. "I can't concentrate on making you my wife with Julio's killer still free. But once that's settled…" His body suffused with a heat totally unrelated to his coffee. "I want us married before the baby is born."

Lara found his intensity both disturbing and exciting. "I can't say yes yet, Nick. It's too soon."

"We're good together, personally and professionally. Especially personally."

"I…you've been very good to me." Lara unexpectedly reached for his hand, his fingers curling a welcome around hers. "Don't think I've forgotten how you pulled double duty, taking care of me and still working on Julio's investigation. I hope you won't come to regret it."

"I used my phone, Doyle kept me posted, and I won't regret a thing."

"But Lilia and the kids…"

"I keep in touch with Lilia daily. They know I haven't abandoned them." Nick exhaled heavily. "Since Lansky's death and Girard's suspension, the case has ground to a halt, anyway. Even with Colonel Doyle cracking the whip, nothing new has happened in the past few weeks, save the retirement."

Girard and Knox had both unofficially retired, pending results of the investigation, although with far less pomp and circumstance than originally planned. Everyone in the police department knew that if anything else happened to Nick or Lara, those two were the number-one suspects. No new threats had materialized against the couple, nor were they expected to do so. Lansky's funeral had come and gone, with only a handful of law-enforcement officers present. Knox and Girard had been conspicuously absent.

"About the baby…" Lara took a breath, her fingers still in his.

Nick was all attention. "Yes?"

"I didn't bring this up, it being this early in the pregnancy, and then I was so sick… But maybe you wouldn't mind being my Lamaze partner? If Julio's case is solved by then," she qualified.

"It will be, and you're on," Nick said immediately.

"Thanks, Nick." Lara lowered her voice. "I feel kind of guilty, but I don't want my parents in the delivery room. I love them dearly, but…"

"Don't feel guilty. This is *our* child, not theirs." Nick lifted her hand and kissed it, making her feel especially cherished.

Lara smiled. "Have you thought of any boys' names yet?"

"I like Marcus—Marc for short."

"Marc—I like it. If it's a boy. We've got months before we find out."

Nick nodded. "Until then, let's get packed. We should be home by lunch."

NICK WAS as good as his word. Kate also moved back to the La Jolla home with Lexi. As Nick emptied out their bags from the car, Kate said to Lara, "I know two's company and three's a crowd, but I'm still on swing shift, so you'll have lots of privacy."

"Don't be silly," Lara replied in her best offhand

manner. "I'm in no shape for mad, passionate bedroom sessions, and it's your house, too."

Kate grinned. "It is, but you don't fool me. Nick can stay forever if you want. Just so he knows I'm not moving out, I'm fine with it. And I meant privacy to work your case, Lara, not having mad, passionate…"

"Shh, he'll hear you! Just…get the door," Lara ordered.

WITH KATE GONE and everyone's bags safely in their rooms, Nick settled Lara into the music room on the couch, his cat sleeping on top of the piano, Sadie comfortably beneath the piano bench. He'd insisted she relax while he unpacked for them both.

"You look tired."

"Just a little," she admitted. "I'll be glad when I'm back to full strength. I need to get recertified on the firing range and pass my physical. I've got a long list."

"You can't heal overnight. Both will have to wait, Lara."

"I know." She sneezed. "But the dusting can't. I've been gone too long."

"Then dust later. Or I will. Do what you can and leave the rest to me. What else is on your list?" he asked curiously.

"One—I'm going to look into Lamaze class schedules for us."

"Plenty of time for that. When you're ready, I'm there." The classes would educate them both. He hoped Lara wouldn't commit to a drug-free delivery. Birthing pain was no walk in the park, and every delivery was different. After being hit by a bullet, he didn't want Lara to *bite* the bullet until she knew what she was personally dealing with.

"Two—I need to get Sadie to the vet one last time. And get her working again. Kate will help."

Nick's lips thinned. Sadie was a serious subject. He suspected Lara'd been afraid to retest her dog. Even though she wasn't up to it, she could easily ask her family to retest her. Nick couldn't help there. He knew that Lara hoped Sadie's "vacation" would dull her memory of the gunshot and accompanying wound. The team's law-enforcement career would immediately end if Sadie failed her test. Lara would need to start out with a new dog. Nick had talked to Lara's peers while she was hospitalized. Apparently a very low percentage of previously hurt dogs ever returned to work. What would happen to Lara emotionally if Sadie never worked again? She had enough drama on her hands already.

"Three—we need to get back on the case," Lara said.

"Right this second? You're pale enough as it is." He looped an arm around her shoulders.

"Most cops are adrenaline junkies. You know that. As exciting as dusting is, I need more."

Nick couldn't help himself. "How about this?" He leaned over and kissed her cheek, then her lips, ever so softly.

"Nice," she sighed. "But I think I need more adrenaline."

He didn't even get the chance to follow up on her invitation for another kiss, if that's what it was. His cell phone rang. Much to his chagrin, Lara leaned closer—not to snuggle—but to overhear the conversation.

"It's T. J. Knox, Nick. I need to see you."

"What's this about, Detective?" Nick asked.

"Just want to talk. No guns or sirens needed. How about…" He named a nearby Mexican restaurant. "Shall we say a half hour?"

"I'll be there." Nick beeped off the cell, his forehead furrowed.

"I'm coming, too," Lara said.

"No, you're not."

"Yes, I am. If it's something that he couldn't talk to you about at work, it's something I want to hear. Sadie will be fine here alone."

"Then promise you'll just sit and listen."

"Done."

T.J. WAS WAITING outside to meet them. "Hope you're feeling better, Nelson. Hey, Nicky," T.J. said without preamble.

"What do you want, Knox?"

"Doyle's out the rest of the day with Homeland Security. He wanted me to deliver this." T.J. pulled out an envelope from his windbreaker pocket.

"What is it?" Nick asked as the envelope changed hands.

"He ordered a DNA check during Lansky's autopsy and asked the lab to compare it with your DNA and Magda's." T.J. passed the file to Nick. "Take a look."

Nick did, the news almost as shocking as hearing Magda was his mother.

"What's it say?" Lara asked.

T.J. answered for him. "Seems Lansky was Cantello's biological father. Doyle told me ahead of time—just in case you went off the deep end."

Nick found his voice. "Doyle doesn't know me very well."

"Or my father. He's a lot of things, but he's no killer. You're not the only person who has family—or friends—" T.J. glanced at Lara "—involved in this. For my money, Girard's our man. You can investigate Dad all you want. You'll be wasting your time. It won't bring you any closer to Julio's murderer."

"I already figured that out. Thanks for the info, Knox," Nick said.

"No problem. Doyle didn't want to tell you over the phone. I volunteered to play messenger boy. Not my usual style, but between Julio and Nelson and her partner, it's for a good cause. Later." Knox pivoted on the ball of his foot to leave.

"Hey, Knox," Nick called.

"Yeah?"

"About your father. I'll keep my options open. Just make certain he doesn't take any sudden trip to Mexico," Nick said.

Knox smiled. "Dad's not going anywhere. Neither am I. Glad you're out of the hospital, Officer Nelson," T.J. said. "I gotta go."

Nick watched him leave, the envelope with the DNA results burning in his hand.

"Nick?" Lara's concern snapped him back to his police persona.

"I need to see Lansky's wife. She's out on personal recognizance until her court date. This is one piece of information she didn't bother to tell us." His police attitude slipped back as he studied Lara. He should have insisted she stay home. "You don't look so good."

"Neither do you," she said frankly. "Lansky's your biological father? I wish we knew how this ties into Julio's death."

"I intend to find out. I should drop you off first, though."

"Sure."

Nick stared at her. "No argument? You okay?"

"I need a nap and I'm getting a headache," she admitted.

"I'm definitely dropping you off. You want me to call anyone?"

"No. Just check in with me later."


"YOU DON'T LOOK SO GOOD," Kate said as Lara sprawled on the couch. Dressed in her uniform and ready for her swing shift, Kate stood in a rare pose of uneasiness and indecision. "Morning sickness?"

"I haven't had that yet. Joe Lansky is Nick's biological father."

"You're kidding."

"I'm not. We just found out. Knox's son just gave us

the DNA results. What this has to do with depleted ura-nium and Julio Valdez is beyond me. I keep going over and over it."

"Your cheeks are pale."

"That's because I've been stuck inside since I got shot."

Kate reached over and laid her hand on Lara's fore-head, then frowned. "You feel a bit warm. Everything fine down below?"

"What am I, a submarine?" Lara asked irritably.

"No cramps or spotting?"

"Nope."

"You sure?"

"I *think* I would know. I just have a headache."

"When's Nick coming back?"

"He wanted to track down Lansky's wife. That's one interview I wouldn't want to conduct. Give me K-9 in-stead of his job any day."

"So he'll be home late. If there was something to worry about, you'd tell me, right?"

"Before you went to work sniffing explosives?" Lara replied. "No way."

"But if it was a real emergency, I wouldn't go to work. I'd call in."

"Kate, you're very sweet. But it's just a stress headache."

"If you're sure… Want me to call Mom?"

"Nope." Lara stared pointedly at her watch. "Good-*bye,* Kate. Love you."

"Love you, too."

Lara waited a good five minutes after Kate drove away before she picked up the house phone and dialed her doctor's office. She left a message for a callback consult, something she'd planned to do before her sister even left. Kate was right. She *did* feel lousy, as if she was coming down with a cold, even though she didn't consider it an emergency. Lara wasn't worried, and she refused to send Kate to work worrying. She hadn't been waiting twenty minutes when the phone rang, Dr. Evans herself on the line.

"What's going on?" she asked Lara.

"I woke up this morning with a headache. I did have a busy morning, but this afternoon I started running a fever."

"What's your temp?"

"Not very high." Kate's fussing had prompted Lara to check herself, after all. "Just 99.6, but it's only a drugstore thermometer. Anyway, I thought I'd check with you. It's probably just a virus...."

"Could be, but in view of your recent health..." Dr. Evans refused to commit herself. She went through a line of gynecological questions, then said, "I think you should pop in for a quick checkup today. Don't worry about an appointment. Just come and I'll work you in."

"I'll be there. Thanks, Dr. Evans."

Lara lay back down on the couch, Sadie curled on the floor. She'd wait until she felt good enough to drive, or wait for Nick to return to give her a ride. Her first day back in her own house, and now this...

NICK STUDIED Mrs. Lansky as they sat in her living room. A black, looped ribbon was pinned to her collar, and she had an air of defeat about her, but also defiance. She also wore an ankle bracelet, which he found ironic for a woman in a wheelchair.

"Yes, I knew my husband was probably your father. He was having an affair with Magda. But he's dead. What does it matter now?"

"It matters to me as Julio's partner," Nick replied.

Helen shrugged. "I can't help you there. He made mistakes—he was a blackmailer who'd had the tables turned on him. But then, I told the police that. Just like I told them I don't know who killed Julio."

"How did your husband obtain the hush money?"

"I didn't say he was blackmailed for money."

Nick sat up straighter. "Then…"

"He was forced into smuggling."

"Drugs?"

"No, he was a cop. He'd never touch drugs. He brought exotic birds into the country from Mexico for private collectors."

Something bothered Nick, nagged at the back of his mind. "Even after Magda died?"

"Yes."

"Then what did the blackmailer use against your husband when I reached adulthood?"

Helen's eyes filled with tears, which overflowed down her cheeks. "I killed Magda."

"You?" Nick said. "Tell me, please."

Helen Lansky wiped her eyes with a tissue that had been tucked in her sleeve. She straightened her dress, feet motionless on the wheelchair footrests. "I'd gone to confront Magda. She smiled and denied everything. I knew she was lying, so when she said she had to go to the mall, I climbed into her car with her. She told me to get out, but I wouldn't, so she started the car and drove, anyway. The nerve. She always had nerve, your mother."

Nick remained silent.

"I started arguing. Crying. Begging. Please leave my husband alone, I asked. Please. Magda turned the radio on and blared it loud—like I was nobody—so she didn't have to listen. Nobody! I went crazy. I grabbed the steering wheel and jerked it. The car flipped and rolled."

Nick stared at her, taking in the horror of the story.

"My seat belt broke. Magda's held. She and the car ended up in the ocean. I was thrown onto the pavement and broke my back. Joe tried to cover it up—told everyone Magda's death was an accident. Some suspected that Joe and Magda had been an item and wondered if there'd been foul play. Someone did more than wonder, however. This person accused me of trying to kill Magda. That's how it all started."

"Did this person have proof?"

"A picture of them together at a munitions cleanup camp."

*The same picture Julio had found.*

"Joe started making trips to Mexico. He said he was forced to bring illegal parrots into the country as a police officer. That's what he told me. He got a cut of the action, you know. He didn't want to take it, but I had a lot of medical bills. I still do."

Nick kept a tight rein on his shaken emotions. His father's wife had killed his mother. "What changed? Why did he try to kill Lara Nelson and then kill himself?"

"I don't know."

Something bothered him about Helen's words. "But if Joe had been smuggling parrots in for years and refused to smuggle narcotics, why the sudden attack of conscience? Why the suicide? There had to be a reason."

*Maybe parrots weren't the only things being smuggled. Maybe depleted uranium was being smuggled out.*

Nick rose. "Thank you for your time, Mrs. Lansky."

"It doesn't matter. I'm going to jail, anyway."

Nick already on his way out, didn't hear her. He had to call the Homeland Security office. Then he had to call Lara and explain what he'd learned.

She called him first.

*San Diego Women's Hospital Office Complex*

NICK BRIEFED HER on the way to the doctor's office.

"Let me see if I've got this straight," Lara said. "Girard or Knox allegedly blackmailed Lansky because Lansky was having an affair with Magda and fathered a child. Lansky was forced to take parrots *out* of Mexico to San Diego. Helen Lansky killed Magda, so Girard or Knox began to blackmail him, forcing him to smuggle DU bullets *into* Mexico from San Diego?"

"Julio could have been killed for knowing about the

smuggling, not about Magda or how she died. I find out who's smuggling depleted uranium ammo into Mexico, I find out who killed Julio. I've called Doyle. He's got Homeland Security rechecking any connections between our three suspects and the five DU manufacturers."

"And you were on your way to interview Girard again," Lara said. "I wish I hadn't called you. But thanks for picking me up."

Nick trolled the parking lot to find a shady spot to park, Sadie along in the back of his car.

"No problem. You're wise not to drive when you aren't feeling well."

"It's nothing major. If I wasn't pregnant, I wouldn't have even bothered. Oh, look, there's some shade over there." Lara pointed to a lone spot at the far end of the parking lot near trees and the junction of office complex and the actual hospital building.

"I see it. Where do I drop you?" he asked.

"That's okay, I can walk. Hurry or we'll lose the parking spot."

Sadie settled down with a bowl of water, shade, and windows half down as the couple crossed the asphalt to the doctor's office. Before they reached the office the dog had stretched out for a snooze.

"Fingers crossed, Dr. Evans didn't have a sudden delivery," Lara said as she checked in and found seats in the waiting room. "One thing about this place. The wait's really short or really long, no in-between. There's always one pregnant patient who throws the schedule out of whack." She grinned.

"The babies do that, not the women," Nick said.

Lara politely sneaked a look at one very large woman in her last trimester. "I've never had to deliver one on the job," she whispered. "You?"

"I came close once. Thank heavens for our fire department paramedics. Back seat car births…those poor ladies. Trust me, you don't want to be one of *them*."

"I have no intention of having Molly or Marcus anywhere but a hospital."

The nurse called her name to get her weight and blood pressure. "That was fast," Lara said, standing just as Nick's phone rang again.

"Take it," Lara insisted. "I'll go alone this time."

Lara hurried after the nurse. She had her vital signs taken, then entered the exam room. Dr. Evans asked questions, performed the exam and ordered lab tests, all while frowning. When she pressed on either side of Lara's healed surgical wound, Lara winced.

"Where's the pain? At the incision site or deeper?"

"Definitely deeper."

"Hmm. Why don't you get dressed and step into my office?"

"I don't want to wait. Please tell me now." Panic set in and must have shown on her expression.

"I didn't palpate anything abnormal in the uterus," Dr. Evans quickly reassured her. "But you may have a post-op infection going on. You've followed the diet? No heavy roughage, spices, acids, alcohol…"

"No, no, no. I've done everything right."

"You're running a slight fever, but I don't think it's a virus. I'm sending you over to the hospital lab and the on-duty internist. After your surgery, the team put you on a milder form of antibiotics because of your pregnancy. Maybe they didn't fully address the problems of your initial injury. I think an ultrasound is in order, too. You might have an abscess."

"But I don't feel terrible. Just lousy."

"The majority of pregnant woman can and should be just as healthy as the next person. You're only a month or so into your pregnancy."

"So now what? Stronger antibiotics?"

"I'll talk to the internist as soon as your tests are done. I want to get a white blood count. If there's an infection, we can clear it up. I want to make sure whatever medication we prescribe doesn't adversely affect your pregnancy."

Lara nodded, relieved. She relaxed her death grip on the disposable paper gown.

"A post-operative infection during a pregnancy is a serious matter, Lara. You may not feel that bad, but we can't let infection spread." The doctor hesitated only a moment. "You may have to be admitted again if you need intravenous therapy."

"What?"

"Be prepared for the possibility. We'll do your labs, talk to gastroenterology."

She swallowed hard, wishing Nick's call hadn't prevented him from coming in with her. "I see."

Dr. Evans smiled and patted her shoulder. "Chin up. You did the right thing, calling in. Don't forget to stop at the front desk."

Lara dressed, picked up her paperwork and rejoined Nick.

"What's wrong?" he asked immediately.

She barely shook her head, indicating she wanted to wait until they were outside, away from the listening public. He took her arm when they stepped outside.

"What's going on?" he asked as soon as they had privacy.

"The doctor thinks I've got a post-operative infection."

"Damn. What are they going to do?"

"I need to go to the hospital for more labs. Right now. I'm sorry, Nick," Lara sighed. "I didn't think this would take so long. I should have left Sadie at home."

"We'll check on her, then take care of business."

She appreciated his briskness, the no-nonsense approach to handling the situation, Nick.

"No problem.

She smiled. "You always say that. You're not afraid I'll go all hormonal, are you?"

"I just keep a positive attitude, ma'am. All part of the job." He dropped his pretend TV law officer voice and spoke as Nick again. "Besides, I can't picture you on a crying jag. But if you have one, how should I respond? Tissues, a glass of water? Pat your shoulder? Call for a relative?"

Lara smiled. "Pretend it never happened afterward."

Her smiles didn't last once the two of them were inside again. By the time she'd finished the procedures, the internist delivered the news, finishing up with, "To be on the safe side, I think you should be admitted for 48 hours of intravenous therapy."

"Now?"

"Yes. I've already talked to the radiologist about your ultrasound and to your OB. Both feel it's the wisest choice. Your surgeon's on call tonight. He'll see you then."

Stunned, Lara nodded, listened, showed her heath insurance card, signed more papers and received her room number. When she returned to Nick in the public waiting area, she didn't even wait until they were outside to deliver the bad news.

"My stomach wound isn't healing correctly," she said. Not only was it infected, but a small section of the sutured hole made by Lansky's shot had reopened. Antibiotics and IV were the least-invasive hope of curing the problem. She couldn't risk eating and causing peritonitis or damage to the baby. If the IV diet and medication didn't allow the hole to reseal itself, she might be up for more surgery. "I'm being admitted," she concluded in the calmest voice she could manage.

Nick's eyes widened only slightly. "I can notify Doyle and the police doctor. What else can I do to help?"

"I…" For a moment, Lara felt overwhelmed. Nick took her hand.

"Do you want Sadie at your mother's or with Kate?"

"My house is closer. Kate can take her to my parents' later. I should go tell her."

"Kate?"

"No, Sadie. If you drive away without me, she'll be confused. Maybe aggressive. And don't say I shouldn't walk," Lara said as Nick started to speak.

Nick didn't press the point. At the car, Sadie got to her feet in greeting. Lara let her out onto the small patch of green beneath the shady tree. She sat on the grass and took her insurance card out of her purse to slide it into her pocket, man and dog watching. She unbuckled her watch and dropped it in, along with her earrings.

"Would you please take my purse into the house when you drop off my dog? It has my gun and badge inside." Even while on sick leave, she carried them. She handed her purse to Nick, who locked it in the trunk of his car.

"Will do. Lara, listen to me, it'll be all right."

Lara never had a chance to answer. An older car drove by, smoking from the rear. As it accelerated past them, it backfired. Nick and Lara both jumped, as did Sadie. Unlike the humans, Sadie didn't settle down after her initial start. She yelped and cringed, and curled herself around Lara, shivering in fear. Lara threw her arms around her dog, hands and voice gentle, reassuring. It took a long time before Sadie's brave heart stopped racing and she stopped shaking. Lara lifted her face from the soft fur, her arms tight around the dog's body.

She looked into Sadie's deep brown eyes, and despite the tears in her own, managed a smile. "It's okay, Sadie. You won't be hurt ever again, I promise." Lara's voice broke. She cleared her throat.

"Nick, would you please call my parents? I can't wait for Kate. I need someone to meet me here and pick Sadie up."

Nick's voice sounded as hoarse as hers did. "What should I tell them?"

"Just say Sadie's retired. For good."

## CHAPTER EIGHTEEN

*One day later, Women's Hospital*

LARA STARED morosely at the IV dripping into her arm, the clear bag of saline and dextrose hydrating and nourishing, the piggyback yellow antibiotic bag hopefully curing infection. Or so the doctors told her. The insertion spot in her vein seemed particularly tender, and her head ached from fever.

Even her parents, who had raised Sadie from puppyhood, couldn't coax the nervous dog into their van. Lara had to do it. It took all her concentration not to break into sobs at the sound of Sadie's high-pitched yips as she closed the van doors.

When Lara told her parents that she was being admitted to the hospital and why, Sandra had insisted on staying with Lara and announced she wouldn't go home. Ed had said he'd drive Sadie home and keep an eye on her. Sandra wanted to know all the medical details. She even suggested calling in another doctor.

Nick didn't join in the discussion of who would do what. He took in Lara's pale face and silently offered her his arm. She gratefully accepted and let him walk her through the parking lot to the admission desk, leaving the parental commotion behind. Once again, Nick showed himself to be good partner material on or off the job.

HALF AN HOUR LATER, after Lara had convinced her mother to go home with her father and Sadie, and she, Lara, was settled in her room, Nick looked at her and said, "I'm sorry about Sadie. Very sorry."

Lara thought of Nick's partner, Julio, and refused to give in to sadness around Nick. "So am I. But she's alive and thanks to her, I am, too. She'll live out the rest of her life in comfort. And I'll see her often. We just won't work together anymore." Lara lifted her eyes. "Listen, Nick. I don't want you to stay," she said bluntly.

He lifted his head, obviously confused.

"Julio's case needs you more. The first time I was admitted I needed you, desperately so. But lying around with an IV running and Sadie safe—I can handle it."

"You're sure?"

"You bet. I want you to solve this case. I want it over and done for Julio's family. You concentrate on that, and only that. Understand? No flowers, no cards, no hand-holding permitted—not until this is finished. I'm cutting you loose. You're a good detective, Nick. Go *be* one. Now."

Nick stood. He lifted her hand and drew her fingers

to his lips. He held them there for a brief moment, his eyes meeting hers. Then he slowly released her hand, turned and left.

Nick and Doyle sat facing each other, Girard's old desk between them.

"What do you mean, the arraignment's been postponed?" Nick asked.

"We got a continuance and another week to finish submitting our evidence. Despite the Homeland Security Act, the D.A.'s office feels what we have could be stronger."

"That's bull. We have Lansky's suicide note and his wife's confession," Nick argued.

"The death penalty applies in this case, and the courts in this county say strong evidence is needed for sentencing."

"Yet Girard's out on bail, still sitting at home in front of his TV. What does that say about our justice system?"

"Look, we're going to court a week later, that's all. Quit wasting our time. You want to know what the D.A.'s office said or not?"

"Fine. Bring me up to speed."

"My problem—and theirs—is establishing a solid link between Girard and depleted uranium. Is it DU smuggling? We might get away with old photos and circumstantial evidence with Mrs. Lansky testifying against Girard. Then again, with charges pending against *her,* she's not the most credible witness. Girard might walk—especially since DU is stockpiled up and down the California coast. I want a concrete tie to Girard and the ammunition."

"It's there," Nick insisted. "Julio found it—either the DU itself or a supply line."

"I've worked that theory at other Department of Energy nuclear weapons production sites. Those sites are all east of the Mississippi River."

Nick's forehead furrowed as he tried to remember. "There's one in South Carolina. One in Tennessee, too."

"The other three are in Kentucky. Plus two more factories in Ohio—one in Aiken and one near Cincinnati."

Nick said, "Girard's wife has a sister in Ohio."

"We checked that angle."

"When? And why didn't you tell me?"

"None of the immediate family had any connection to ammunition purchases or work history. And that's the week Nelson was hospitalized. I figured you had enough on your hands."

"She's there again," Nick tersely informed him. "But that's no excuse for not briefing me."

"I don't make excuses. And why wasn't I informed about Nelson?" Doyle asked angrily.

"She'll be out after a few days of intravenous therapy. Not a good feeling being out of the loop, is it?"

The two men glared at each other. Doyle finally said, "We're on the same side, Cantello. I'm as frustrated as you. I can't find a solid connection to ammunition purchases. Girard's the logical choice. *Someone* shot at

Julio with a DU bullet, and you can't buy those at Wal-Mart. And yes, Girard's sister-in-law and husband live near a nuclear-weapons factory. We've had security watching the couple—no kids—but the wife has cancer, and the husband's busy taking care of her. The male Knoxes have no connection back East save the ex-wife in Florida. We're watching them all."

"Including…Nell Girard, the captain's wife?"

"What are you saying, Cantello?"

"It's *her* sister. She visited her earlier this year—Girard even told us."

"So…Girard's wife is bringing DU to San Diego and blackmailing Lansky, forcing him to smuggle it across the Mexican border to South America? With parrots as the red herring?"

"Yes and no. I think the plan changed from smuggling endangered parrots to transporting a single parrot—one legitimately bred and big enough to swallow a DU pellet."

Doyle immediately caught on. "A doctored pet with proper papers. Lansky could drive through customs with a cage on the front seat."

Nick nodded. "Border officials wouldn't suspect a thing."

"That's a treasonable offense. Gets the death penalty in this country. I think you're reaching. Why would this police officer's wife risk it?"

"Because," Nick said slowly, "we've been looking at this from the wrong perspective. This isn't about three men. It's about three *women*. Lansky's wife killed

Magda because Lansky had an affair with her. They were blackmailed by maybe not Girard, but *Mrs.* Girard. The captain had a close professional relationship with Magda. He admits he owes his career to her. It isn't sex, but it's time—a lot of time a husband spent with a woman who wasn't his wife. Jealousy is more than a motive, it's a deadly emotion—and Girard still misses Magda, stills talks about her."

"Until he got a lawyer. Let me play devil's advocate." Doyle leaned back in his chair and rubbed his chin. "Even a policeman's wife couldn't get through the security at a nuclear weapons plant. For argument's sake, if she did manage to steal some, she couldn't get the stuff back here on a plane. The dogs would smell the powder in the cartridge. It's even tougher at the borders. They have radiation detectors set up there and at all freeway weigh stations. It's iffy."

"The woman has geographic proximity to a supply and is familiar with the area," Nick insisted. "Unlike Girard."

"The ammo's strictly controlled. The U.S. is the major producer of DU rounds. Homeland Security—and I—would have found concrete evidence before now."

"Julio found it. He had to. That's why he's dead. He concentrated on the women when he wrote up the retirement speech and researched old photos for the display. It's there. It's—"

Nick broke off. Suddenly, he knew where the evidence was…where the ammo was stored. Julio had left it with Nick, after all. Right under his nose.

"What?"

"I think I know where the DU is."

"Where?"

Nick told him.

"Are you sure?"

"No. But it doesn't matter. Either way, we'll find out which Girard—or whoever the hell it is—killed Julio. Here's how we're going to do it." Nick told him the plan.

"Not by the book. Deceptive. And very dangerous."

"This is war, Colonel. We've only got a week left. I can do this, with your permission. Three days to set it up, tops."

"Done." The men stood, and Doyle shook his hand. "Gook luck, Cantello. Save me more paperwork and try not to get yourself killed," Doyle said with his usual bluntness.

Nick responded in kind. "Don't worry. I've got too damn much to live for."

He left to see Lara—and to get her help.

NICK FOUND LARA RELAXING in the hospital chair, looking stronger, and some of her normal color was back. He smiled and kissed her cheek.

"You look pleased with yourself," she said.

"Good news." He glanced over his shoulder at her bed, freshly made. "Mind if I park myself here?"

"Of course not."

"I just came from Doyle's," Nick said without preamble. "I think Julio found the DU, and I think I know where it is."

"My God, Nick! Where?"

"In Julio's motorcycle. That's why he traded it with me that night. I was going out of town, and he knew one of the retirees was involved. Knowing Julio, he decided to share the info with me after the weekend. Start fresh on Monday. Because if he'd told me Friday..."

"You wouldn't have gone boating."

"No. Then, it started to rain...and his wife needed ice for the broken refrigerator and I ended up with the bike. That's where the DU has to be. He found it, and he hid it. He couldn't trust the evidence room."

"Are you positive it's in the motorcycle?"

"The bike was the only thing Lilia released to me. She always trusted me with it because Julio did. I moved it from Impound to my storage shed while you were in the hospital the first time."

"But, Nick, it would have been searched by dogs at Impound. They would have found any ammo hidden in it. Any dog would. They'd smell the gunpowder in the cartridges."

"Not projectiles that hadn't been in contact with gunpowder. I'm talking pure DU metal projectiles. Pre-cartridge slugs."

Lara nodded. "Sadie wouldn't signal a find on just metal, radioactive or not. No dog would."

Nick edged closer to the side of the bed in his excitement. "No one ran a radioactive scan on the bike. Why would they?"

"Uranium in a motorcycle…"

"If there are DU projectiles hidden in the bike, they're still there. And I've got Julio's motorcycle locked up in private storage under my name."

"Only one way to find out. And I know Kate could get you a Geiger counter superquick—probably quicker than Doyle." She reached for her room phone.

"No." Nick's hand on hers stopped her call.

"Why not?"

"We don't want one from your sister. We're going to requisition one through the police station."

"But that will take a lot longer. Plus everyone will know what you want to do."

Suddenly she followed Nick's train of thought. "You're going to use Julio's bike as bait? Even if you don't know the ammo's there?"

"That's right. And Doyle's gonna let me."

"He'll be backing you up, right?"

"No, I'm going alone—with his blessing."

"Alone."

"Yes. My partner was killed because he found the DU projectiles. He knew the suspect was onto him, so he stored the evidence in the one place it would be safe. With me. Doyle will pretend this case is ready for court—except for one last check. He'll order the Geiger counter tomorrow, and let it be known it should arrive in two days and will be used on the motorcycle. I'll stake out the storage shed to see who turns up the day after tomorrow. Doyle won't post the address of the shed until the Geiger counter actually comes in. Right now, we three are the only ones who know where the bike is located."

"You'll need backup!" Lara said immediately. "I'll be out of here tomorrow night."

"No. Not you. It's too risky. If there *is* any depleted uranium, it's still radioactive. It's strong enough to cause health problems with nonpregnant people, never mind pregnant women and their fetuses. Just ask the military."

"We don't know if there's DU in the shed," Lara argued. "That's just the story you're telling. If it's true—*if*—I don't have to sit on the bike to watch your back. I'm a police officer licensed to carry a gun."

"Did you even requalify at the shooting range?" Nick answered his own question. "No, because you're still on sick leave. You're recovering from stomach wounds. You're not even off your medication yet—certainly not at your peak physically."

"I'm no danger to you or the stakeout," Lara said firmly.

"You run a risk to yourself and our child. It's against all rules and regulations for you to take part. I wish I'd never mentioned the place to you."

"You're right. And this will be the last time I don't toe the line," Lara said, meaning every word. "But I started with the case, and I'm going to finish up this case. Including watching your back. Who else are you going to trust?"

"I'll call for backup if and when I need it."

"You need it, and you've already got me."

Nick sighed in exasperation. "Promise you'll stay away."

Lara defiantly crossed her arms.

"Don't make me pull rank on you," Nick said. "And don't you dare interfere. I have Julio's wife and children to consider. And you and our child, Officer Nelson. If I have to report you to police or your family to keep you safe, I will."

Lara didn't flinch an inch. "You play dictator with my life, you'll never be a part of it again."

Nick blanched.

"Understand, I won't keep you from your child, Nick. I won't use the baby as a pawn. But nobody decides what's right or wrong for me. I firmly believe you need backup. You need someone! That's me. If you insist on being my conscience, whatever we have is over. We're through."

"What *do* we have, Lara?" Nick asked, his voice as low and as serious as she'd heard it since Julio's death.

"We mesh—mentally, physically, emotionally. We have from the first moment we met. You know it. So do I."

"You're willing to throw it away."

"I'm not willing to throw *anything* away—especially when it comes to us! But I'm a sworn woman of law enforcement. I have to be willing to take risks."

Nick lifted his head. "I believe that. And if you had a working K-9, I'd even consider it. But without one…"

Lara ignored the pang at the thought of Sadie.

"Fine," he said, changing tactics. "You're willing to take risks for yourself. You swear you'd protect the baby. But listen to me. With your health, without a working canine, you're a liability—to *me*."

Lara froze.

"Aren't you."

"I…" She hesitated, reality fighting with decision. "You're a liability."

For the first time in his presence, her eyes filled with tears. "Oh, but I wouldn't be, Nick!"

"You told me to solve this case so we could have our future. I'm doing exactly that. Stay home, love."

"That's the second time you've call me 'love.'"

The expression in Nick's eyes softened. "So you've noticed."

"The first time was when I was shot."

"I want to hear it back from your lips when this is over. Until then I'm on my own."

# CHAPTER NINETEEN

*Late afternoon, two days later*

LARA LISTLESSLY SCOOPED dry food from the plastic, insect-proof bins and filled bowl after bowl. She'd been released from the hospital with more pills and appointments. Her father had driven her home to Nelson Kennels, but when he had to hurry to the office to take a delivery, Lara refused to rest. She joined Sandra in tending the young dogs in the first row of kennels. Ordinarily the friendly antics of the big pups would have brought a smile to her face. Worry about Nick and her inability to help him had robbed her of the ability to relax. Sandra stood beside her, opening cans of wet dog food to add to the dry. The two women worked in silence, Lara silent and withdrawn, Sandra worried, Sadie at their heels. The older woman had almost given up trying to draw out her daughter. She made one last attempt.

"Maybe you need to go rest, Lara. You just left the hospital this morning."

"I can scoop dry food out of a bag, Mom."

Sandra let the electric can opener run its course, then release the open can. "What's wrong, honey?"

"I'm fine."

"You're not. Talk to me. What can I do?"

"You can't do anything." Lara savagely scooped up more dry nuggets. "Nick needs me—tonight's the storage-facility stakeout—but I'm a liability. Without Sadie, he's right. Still, he shouldn't be there alone."

Sandra reached for another can. "You're healing," she gently reminded Lara. "And Nick chose to do it this way. Colonel Doyle agreed."

Lara dumped more dry onto Sandra's wet. "If only Sadie were her old self, I could help. If anything happens to Nick, anything at all, I don't know if I could stand it." Lara dropped the scooper and gripped the metal counter with both hands. "I have to go after him."

"Lara, get someone else! You're sick…and…and you barely know him."

"That's no consolation if Nick gets killed. He's going to do this alone because he doesn't want anyone else. I can't let him set a trap, then wait there and see who bites without me."

"He'll have backup."

"That still takes a radio call and transport time. I know something will go wrong. I just know it!"

"Aren't you being a bit melodramatic?" Sandra suggested.

"No." Lara picked up the plastic scooper again and continued scooping dry nuggets for multiple bowls. "I'm not hysterical—or hormonal. I have instincts—damn good instincts. Nick needs me." She stopped and faced her mother. "I need a dog from you. With an advanced-class guard dog, I'm as good as back to full strength."

"Lara." Sandra carefully put down the can. "You can't pick a dog out of training class just like that—" Sandra snapped her fingers "—and know he's the best match for a handler."

"*You* can, Mom. You always could. Just like I could always pick a man out of a crowd and know he's good for me, and I for him. We're not that different!"

"You're on sick leave! Tagging along would be breaking police regs and protocols. Even if you weren't, I won't stand by and see you risk your life."

"I did it for you—every single day when you put on your uniform and went to work. I deserve the same. Please, Mom, give me a dog!"

"Give her the dog, Sandra." Ed stood at the end of the corridor, ignoring the dogs' welcoming yips.

Sandra closed her eyes. "No."

"Yes," Ed said. "Look at her—she's you all over again. Stubborn, determined and full of courage—the same courage you've always had and Lara's inherited."

Ed walked down the hall. "We have a dog for you," he announced.

Lara's eyes opened wide. "Where? Who?"

Sandra reached down and rested her hand on Sadie's furry head. "Right here."

"*Sadie?*"

"We reconditioned her while you were in the hospital. She's not gun-shy anymore, is she, Sandra?"

"No. Your father fired round after round of blanks

under all testing conditions. After the first few times, Sadie straightened right out."

"She works like a champ, Lara," Ed said. "A true champ. Just like you. She'll pass any test given, I'd bet my reputation on it."

"Just like *you'd* pass," Sandra said tearfully.

Lara was stunned. "I...can't believe it." She smiled with joy. "You're the best."

Ed and Sandra both hugged their daughter. "If we were," Ed said, "I wouldn't have given you such a hard time with Nick. Or Jim."

"And I would have told you about Sadie if you hadn't been readmitted...and just released."

"This was your mother's idea," Ed said proudly. "Even Kate didn't know."

Lara's voice broke as she whispered. "Thank you, both of you." Lara kissed her father's cheek, then her mother's. Her hand dropped to Sadie's head as she thanked God for her parents and the way fate had given her another chance with Nick. She'd been denying her feelings for Nick—because of Nick's job. She'd been left alone once before and had been too afraid to take another chance. But she'd crossed that barrier when she had taken Nick into her home, when she'd become pregnant and knew she wanted his child. Nick had suffered a terrible loss, but hadn't given up on life. It was time to take the final step—tell him she loved him. She wanted a future, a family, with him.

She was untying her work smock as Sandra said, "You're leaving...now?"

"Soon as I change and get my badge and gun. Love you."

"Be careful," Ed ordered.

"Love you, too," Sandra whispered, but Lara, hurrying toward the door with Sadie, didn't hear.

"Oh, Ed... I hope we did the right thing."

Ed kissed his wife. "Let's finish feeding the dogs."

AT LARA'S HOUSE in La Jolla, Nick changed into dark pants and a dark T-shirt with SDPD in yellow on the back. He holstered his gun, attached his badge to his belt, and covered his T-shirt and weapon with the matching dark windbreaker. His unmarked vehicle waited outside in the driveway. The two-story storage facility closed at 7:00 p.m. Nick planned on waiting inside the facility, out of sight, within view of his own personal storage unit holding Julio's bike. The barbed wire atop the surrounding chain-link fence with its electronic security cameras wouldn't prevent a truly determined person from getting in. A pair of wire cutters and some black tape for the camera lens usually did the trick. Many storage-facility owners didn't use dogs anymore, trusting high-tech gear and alarm companies instead. Nick thought longingly of Lara and Sadie.

Memories of the way they'd last parted, the look on her face, made his chest and throat tighten. He trusted her as a cop, but without her usual robust health and K-9 partner, she didn't belong on the job, especially a risky stakeout. The sound of a car interrupted his thoughts. He hurried to the front door in time to see

Lara park behind him in the driveway. She exited, dressed like him, Sadie at her side, complete with collar and badge.

"I see you're ready to go," Lara said without preamble. "Unlock your unit so I can put Sadie in the back."

Nick ignored his joy at the sight of her to concentrate on business. "What are you doing?"

"Sadie's her old self again, thanks to Mom and Dad. I'm past the walking-wounded stage. We're going with you. And before you start arguing, I've blocked your car in. I don't go, you don't go." She leaned against the front of her vehicle. "I'll hook my keys to Sadie's collar. You'll be needing a taxi to get to your stakeout."

Fear for her safety warred with admiration for her courage—and the love he felt, had felt almost from the beginning, for Lara Nelson. He couldn't stop her from coming. Suddenly it didn't feel right to leave her behind.

"You'll go, if you'll play it safe until our baby's born."

"Please," she said, almost insulted. "I'd already planned on it."

"Promise you'll follow my orders, not go running off on your own. You'll be backup, I'll take point."

"Done."

"I mean it."

"So do I."

The two continued to stare at each other, neither willing to give an inch. Finally Nick nodded. "Move your car and load Sadie in mine." He tossed her his keys to drive. "I've got shotgun."

THE SILENCE OF THE DRIVE unnerved Lara enough to break it. "So who are we going after? Mr. or Mrs. Girard?"

"Could be either one. Hell, for all I know, it could be both—like the Lanskys."

A car swerved in front of them, changing lanes without signaling. Lara hit the brakes, not violently, but enough to make the seat belt she wore tighten around her hips. She immediately dropped her hand, protecting her child.

Nick swore. "I'd pull that young fool over in a second if—"

"It's Mrs. Girard," Lara interrupted.

"Huh?"

"It's Nell Girard. She started all this."

"I don't understand."

"The Knoxes had T.J. Magda had you. Nell Girard had no one! You told me—Doyle said her sister had cancer and no children. Both sisters grew up around DU stockpiles. Neither could have children. That's why she hated Magda so!"

"But Magda had the affair with Lansky. Helen knew."

"But Nell Girard didn't! She thought her husband had the affair! That's how all this started! Everything else spun off from it."

"Because she couldn't have children?"

"No. Because the wrong person did."

*Dusk, Sunshine Storage*

THE COUPLE WAITED inside the shadows of the doorless outbuilding that held handcarts, brooms and dustbins, and sheltered the soda machine. With the doorless shed's front and back openings, and position at the end of the row, it provided both cover and access for retreat or advance among the grid: rows and rows of parallel storage units and alleys between them. Nick waited on his feet, out of sight back from the opening, as did Lara. After the first few hours of watching and waiting, Lara had chosen to sit on one of the larger handcarts. Sadie quietly lay down on the concrete beside her.

"Want to trade and rest your feet?" Lara whispered to Nick. "She might show up late…if at all."

"I'm fine," Nick replied quietly. "And it'll be tonight."

Lara looked out into the softly lit alley where Nick's ground-level storage unit held Julio's bike. "What makes you so sure?"

"Requisitions filled my request for a Geiger counter today, but when I went to pick it up, it couldn't be located."

"You didn't tell me that!" Lara whispered.

"You were sick."

"Who took it?"

"Don't know. We'll find out sooner or later," Nick murmured.

A few minutes later Sadie's ears pricked, her head high as she listened and sniffed the air.

*There!* Nick gestured toward the end of the long corridor of storage sheds, first- and second-story doors facing each other. Lara nodded acknowledgment as she tightened her grip on Sadie's leash and gently held her hand over Sadie's muzzle for silence. Lara squinted, trying to make out who was quietly making their way down the dimly lit corridor. Sadie tensed, as did Lara, but Nick held up his hand. They continued to watch as the intruder studied the unit ID numbers, coming closer and closer to Nick's until finally stopping.

The intruder didn't bother with bolt cutters, just used a tool that easily opened most standard locks. The lock soon rested, unlocked, on the floor of the concrete alley. The intruder bent to grasp the bottom edge of the aluminum roll-up door. In seconds the door had been pushed up and back, exposing the gaping entryway. The person didn't bother with the light switch, instead pulled out a tiny penlight and flicked it on, then entered. Nick signaled for Lara to wait, and she nodded agreement. They would apprehend the suspect when he or she exited the storage unit. Two officers and a canine against one suspect were good odds.

But then Sadie's nostrils quivered, and her mouth dropped open to better allow scent to activate glands in her mouth and throat, as well. Her ears perked, then her head swung upward. Lara tapped Nick's shoulder. He stared at the dog, obviously confused, until a few seconds later they heard and realized what Sadie already knew: someone was moving across the second-story tar-and-gravel roof. Nick grabbed his night-vision binoculars, but inside, he had the wrong angle. He'd have to come right out of the shed, exposing his location, to see anything.

Nick swore silently. The stairs and elevators were locked at closing.

"How did someone get up there?" Lara whispered. "We would have seen them!"

"Must have climbed up before closing."

Lara carefully peered through the back of the shed, guarding the rear. She noticed the large boats and towing trucks parked at the ends of the alleys, and knew immediately how an athletic man or woman could use the vehicles as a launching pad to the roof. She also realized that the slippery fiberglass shells of the boats and smooth paint of the trucks would provide a problem for her and Sadie.

Nick realized it, too. He pointed to himself and the roof, then pointed to her and the storage unit. A second later the person above accidentally kicked gravel off the roof, instantly alarming the person in the storage unit. He began to sprint out of the alley, while the person above could be seen jumping to the nearest boat and noisily descending, jumping off the roof from the back.

Lara reacted immediately. As Nick drew his gun and called for backup, she yelled out, "Stop or I'll release the dog!"

The man from the storage unit hadn't gone far. He immediately stopped and shone his penlight on his face. "It's me—T. J. Knox! You're letting Girard get away!"

"Girard?" Nick asked as Lara and Sadie advanced, Nick with gun drawn.

"My father's been after that smuggler for years!"

"The smuggler's his wife," Lara said. "That's why she's never been caught."

"Nick? Is this true?" Knox asked.

"Maybe." Nick lowered his gun.

"Sadie and I can find her, Nick," Lara urged. "Just say the word!"

"I…" Nick hesitated.

"You know the drill! K-9 locates, you and T.J. provide backup. Sadie and I can do this. I swear, we can do this," Lara begged.

"Let her!" T.J. seconded. "If whoever the hell it is gets away before they arrive, if he gets to the border…"

Nick kept his guard on T.J., then nodded abruptly. "Be careful, love. We're right behind you."

Lara ran down the alley with Sadie straining ahead on the leash until they reached the end of the rows and the start of another alley. Carefully, she reeled Sadie out first to peer around the corner. Sadie didn't react.

"Nothing, girl?" Lara relayed Sadie's call to the men, and she and Sadie crossed the empty alley end to the new row. Before she could send Sadie into it, all the lights went dead at the facility.

"Damn!" she silently mouthed, not making a sound. She could see nothing, her vision blank, pupils still adjusted to the dim lighting of earlier. She ignored the flashlight on her belt, not wanting to target herself and the dog. The men behind would carefully use their own. She didn't need one.

Sadie pulled on the leash. Lara followed as they

crossed more empty alleys, Sadie confident in her direction. Sadie whined with eagerness, and started barking at the next alley, frantically pulling and dragging Lara on the leash. All three humans knew the dog had found the quarry. Lara carefully peered around the corner, searching for Sadie's target. She had no intention of exposing any of them to gunfire.

"Come out or I release the dog!" Lara yelled.

Nick and T.J. split up, each flanked her, T.J. on the radio for backup.

"We know you're here!" Nick yelled, gun in one hand and flashlight in the other. "Come out now!"

Sadie went into full bark mode at the sounds of someone climbing a fence. Hands on a fence meant no hands free for a weapon. Lara emerged from her safe position to see, made her decision and unleashed the dog. "*Fass,* Sadie!"

Sadie bolted down the alley at top speed, Lara running after her. Sadie lunged at the figure on the fence, fastening onto a limb. Lara heard a human yell as Sadie planted rear paws on the ground and pulled the suspect off the fence to fall backwards, flailing uselessly, onto the ground. Sadie continued to hang on to the suspect's leg.

Nick reached the suspect first. "Hands out to the side! Facedown!"

"Release, Sadie! Guard!" Lara ordered in German, hurrying to leash the dog once more. Sadie immediately let go of the leg and settled for stiff-legged growling, daring the suspect to move again.

Knox arrived to help Nick, but Nick had already cuffed the suspect, his knee in the back. Only then did Lara advance, leash in one hand, her flashlight in the other illuminating the suspect's face. She gasped—not at the sight of the teeth-torn pants leg, but at the fury on the face of the suspect. A woman. So this was Nell Girard.

BACKUP HAD ARRIVED at the storage shed. One team had found the Geiger counter still on the roof. Right now they were searching Julio's motorcycle. Doyle himself had advised Nell Girard of her rights. She sat handcuffed on the ground while paramedics checked her leg.

"Has anyone called Emil Girard?" Lara asked. Nick held her hand, and with her free hand, she held Sadie's leash. Her heart still hadn't stopped pounding.

"Doyle sent a car for him," Nick replied. "Seems to be in shock. Never suspected his wife."

"Neither did my father," T.J. said quietly.

Lara shivered. The elder Knox's detective skills had been less than perfect, as had Girard's. "How could Girard have been married to her for so long and not known?"

"Dad said he was always a lousy detective. Why do you think he needed Magda Palmer?"

"How did you know to show up?" Lara asked T.J.

"Lansky's dead. My dad said it was Girard. I believed him. Nick, we need you back at the storage shed to get Julio's bike."

"In a minute. Thanks for the assist," Nick said.

T.J. nodded and left, stopping to speak to Doyle as he did so.

Doyle rejoined them. "Nice work, you three. Knox, too."

"You need to stay here. You can't go near the bike," Nick warned. "In fact…"

"I'll stay with her," Doyle said. "You go to the shed." Doyle faced Lara. "Nelson, put your dog in your car, please. Nell Girard wants a word with you. She's been advised of her rights. You want to humor her? You don't have to. I know you're still on sick leave."

"Give me a minute," Lara said.

"I'll meet you at the cruiser."

Nell Girard sat in the back seat of the cruiser.

"How's your leg?" Lara asked, taking in bandages as she leaned near the cruiser.

"Hurts. That damn dog."

Lara leaned against the car. "You've got two minutes."

"That's all? Magda Palmer took every minute of my husband's life. She wanted my husband's job, my husband's life. She got her way, all right—through him. When she wasn't sleeping around and getting herself pregnant. Like you and Magda's son."

"You won't be a part of our lives anymore," Lara said quietly. "The courts will see to that. Anything else?"

"You don't understand," Nell said impatiently. "My point is that it's a man's world. I blackmailed Joe when she was sleeping with him. I did it to get back at my husband, because he had her days, and Joe had her nights. And when Magda died, I kept blackmailing him. I felt sorry for Helen. We were both Magda's victims. I never got the time I wanted with my husband. Or children. I don't even have nieces or nephews, thanks to those old DU stockpiles I grew up around." She paused. "At least Magda didn't put me in a wheelchair like she did with Helen. Lansky was a lousy husband."

"Magda died a long time ago," Lara reminded her.

"Yes. I didn't lose sleep when she drove into the ocean. That's when I started in with Lansky."

"But Magda was dead. You had your husband back."

"I didn't!" Nell protested. "Without Magda, he had to work twice as hard, twice as long on his caseload. I could still get back at Magda by hurting her lover. I didn't want his paycheck or benefits, because Helen needed it. So I made him a smuggler." She smiled.

"Exotic pets?"

"Only at first. It gave me extra spending money, too. He was so careful to be a good cop. I made Lansky smuggle for years. Nearly drove him crazy. But later, he didn't know *what* he was smuggling. When I started smuggling DU, he refused to do it anymore, no matter what threats I made."

"What happened?" Lara prompted. "Julio Valdez found out?"

"Julio was supposed to write these retirement speeches. Joe Lansky wasn't above giving out hints. Joe helped out with the right clippings. Julio found out I was raised in munitions country. He found some of my stock—I kept it in the police station. What safer place?"

"So you killed him?" Doyle asked, his voice harsh with emotion.

"Technically, Lansky did. He decided he couldn't let Julio go public. Joe and I would both go down, and not just for smuggling. For treason. We'd get the death penalty."

Lara stared at Nell.

"Joe got sneaky on me. Used a DU shell on Julio's car to give you all a heads-up. And used 25 mm rounds on your Mercedes…not DU, light rounds, but the same caliber. Another hint for you. I caught on."

"Where did he get the original weapon?" Doyle asked.

"From my smuggling connections, of course. Easily arranged over the Internet. They'd give me anything for DU. It's easy to get if you know where the old stockpiles are. That stuff's been lying around for decades. In my hometown kids played with the stuff—nice little pill-shaped pellets. I collected them, Lansky delivered them. But then Lansky got a conscience at the last minute."

"Conscience?" Lara echoed.

"At my urging, Lansky planned to kill you and Nick at the canine test field. But he couldn't do it."

Lara gasped.

"We've heard enough, Mrs. Girard," Doyle said. "Watch your feet." Doyle slammed shut the door of the cruiser.

"I'll be in my car," Lara said. With Sadie, safely away from the storage shed, she waited for Nick.

NICK GUIDED the radiation techs into the storage shed. Encumbered by Geiger counters, lead aprons and other gear, they moved too slowly for Nick.

He reached for his toolbox. "I'll take it apart."

"Sir, we don't want you exposed," said one of the technicians.

"I've ridden the Harley. I'm already exposed. A few minutes won't make any difference."

"It's our job, Detective."

"The bike belonged to my partner. It's my job."

Minutes later, Nick held a flashlight on the disassembled handlebars and the small packet within. Only then did Nick let the techs take over. With tweezers they removed the packet and carefully opened it.

Nick put away his tools with shaking fingers. He already knew what they'd unwrap. Small, powderless, pill-shaped pellets—slugs of depleted uranium.

# CHAPTER TWENTY

*Early the next morning*

THE COUPLE WITH the black-and-tan German shepherd sat on the sand atop the La Jolla cliffs overlooking the beach. Behind them, to the east, the orange rays crept above the foothills' foggy, dull horizon.

"You should be in bed," Nick said, his arm around Lara's shoulders. She had her arm around his waist, one hand resting on her dog's head. "We both should. Think you could sleep now?"

"I don't know. God, what a night. I still can't believe it."

"You did good," Nick said with approval.

"We all did." She felt proud of the work she, Sadie and Nick had done, but sad, nonetheless. "What's going to happen to Nell Girard?"

"Dunno. These are different times. Harsher rules."

Under the Homeland Security Act, the federal government had taken the woman into custody. She had a choice of being arraigned and tried for treason, or working undercover with them to expose the illegal connections she'd forged. Understandably, she'd chosen the latter, leaving her husband—who had no connection with his wife's activities—a broken man.

"Do you think she'll ever see him again?" Lara wondered.

"She's made enemies on both sides. If she cooperates, she'll be in protective custody for the rest of her life. If she doesn't, it could be the death sentence. She knew what she was getting into."

"I know…but I feel bad for the captain. And Helen Lansky. She was cheated on, put in a wheelchair, blackmailed, widowed and now faces jail. All from a desperate impulse years ago. It's no excuse for what she did to Magda, but I pity her."

"I talked to the D.A. at the station and asked for leniency," Nick said. "I don't want to testify against her."

Lara sat up straighter, surprised. "Her actions caused your mother's death."

"I had a weak case against Helen with few credible witnesses. Without strong testimony…" He shrugged. "And jail—if she were convicted—would probably kill her."

"It's very generous of you, Nick."

"Don't give me any halos. I talked to Girard, though. He's agreed to look in on Helen daily. She'll be on probation a long time."

"At least she'll have someone. I know Lilia's been glad to have you."

Behind them, the sun slowly flooded the eastern horizon with hints of orange in the far distance. Jagged shadows started on the faces of the rock and sand cliffs, while far below the frothy edges of ragged waves tore at the cliffside.

"I wish I could do more." Nick's phone call from the police station to the Valdez family hadn't been easy. He'd given them a very brief version, ending with identifying Joe Lansky and Nell Girard as Julio's killers. Lilia had thanked him, then hung up—more from overwhelming emotion than the lateness of the hour.

"She'll be all right," Lara assured him. She'd made a call to her family, as well, informing them of the successful conclusion of the case. And how she would stay home until fully well enough to return to work. Right now she needed to concentrate on Nick.

Nick met her gaze. "I talked to Doyle. Nell told you it's a man's world. Do you believe that?"

"It's a violent world at times," Lara said softly. "Women can be as guilty of violence as men. And women, with or without K-9s, can be as effective as men in stopping it. But I prefer my dog." She smiled. For the first time, she reached for his hand and placed it on her barely rounded belly, over his child. "We have a good reason to keep trying, don't you think?"

"For our child."

"For all children," she said.

"And for us." Then he kissed her, as slow, as leisurely, as the sun rising. "You *are* going to marry me," he murmured as they drew apart.

Lara stroked Sadie's head. "Only if you want me, too, not just the baby. I need to be sure."

"Lara, I love this baby, but I love you more. I have almost from the start—a start I never planned, but am thankful happened. Julio would be happy for us."

Joyful tears filled her eyes and, embarrassed, she buried her head in his shoulder.

"Aren't you gonna say you love me?" he asked.

She still kept her face covered.

"Don't tell me you're shy?" he asked in disbelief. He gently drew her back. "A policewoman, no less?"

"I'm not shy," she said, wiping her eyes. "I'm happy."

"And you love me," he prompted, "and will marry me."

"I love you." Lara's gaze sobered. "But before I agree to the other, we have to settle a few things first."

He waited.

"I'm proud of the Nelsons—what our family has done—and what we'll continue to do. I plan on keeping my job, Nick. And my last name. The baby will be Nelson-Cantello," she said to soften the blow. "But I've lived my life and career as a Nelson. I want to retire as one."

"I understand," Nick said.

Lara lifted her chin. "If this child wants to follow in the family footsteps, we need to prepare her for that, not stand in her way. Both of us. Can you agree to that?"

"Yes, unless…"

Lara held her breath.

"…it's a he." Nick smiled.

"Nick, I'm serious. Many marriages fail under the strain of having a spouse in law enforcement, let alone two of them. My parents may be an exception, but trust me, they had their bad times."

"We three will find sensible middle ground."

"Not three. Four," Lara corrected. She lovingly wound one arm around her dog's neck. "Canine handlers are with their dogs twenty-four hours a day, Nick. I'm her protector, just as she's mine. The public needs us. In some ways, you'll never share as much with me as Sadie will. Just as my parents shared much of their lives with their dogs instead of their children. It's the only way we can be so successful on the streets."

"I know you and Sadie can't work without each other."

"It's more that that. Much more, Nick. Not everyone can be married to a K-9 handler without some jealousy. You've seen us together. We're a team. We can't be separated."

"I learned that at the storage shed," Nick reminded her. "Nell Girard could have escaped. I'd never have found her."

"Yes, you would," Lara said loyally. "Just not as quickly."

"Either way, I won't resent your dog. How could I? I share memories with you Sadie will never have. Like when you gave me hope again after Julio died. Or both of us starting new life that night. Soon we'll have a child to raise. Trust me, love, I have more than enough to be happy." His one hand gently caressed her cheek, while his other rested on Sadie's neck.

"Oh, Nick…truly?"

"Yes. You and Sadie have nothing to fear from me."

Nick kissed her again. "I'd never want you living in fear about your job, like Magda. Now I have a question for you."

"It's not about Magda, is it? Because I do admire your mother, Nick. I think of all the good she did as Girard's unofficial partner, and I'll be proud to call her family."

"No, it's not that." Nick smiled. "I've never been ashamed of my roots, then or now. My question is, *when* will you marry me?"

"Soon." Lara kissed him to seal the promise.

Nick wasn't satisfied. "How soon?"

"I'm on sick leave, remember?" she reminded him. "There's nothing stopping us. And since this marriage is for love…"

"It is."

"I'd like to do it before the baby's born."

"How about in the next few weeks? You up to ring shopping?"

"Not now, I think." Despite her happiness, Lara yawned, and rested fingers atop her belly. "I wanna go to bed. *That's* what we should shop for—a king-size bed. Baby and I need more room if you're joining us. Starting now."

Nick gathered her close. "Definitely starting now."

*February 14*
*Birthing Room, Women's Hospital*

LARA MOANED as another contraction hit. Nick stroked her forehead as the pain rose, peaked and passed. The only other person in the room, the labor and delivery nurse, checked her progress.

"Soon," the nurse said cheerfully.

"How soon?" Lara asked. "I'm ready to have this baby."

"You're almost fully dilated," the nurse announced with satisfaction. "Past nine, and ten's the magic number. It won't be long now. I'll get your doctor."

Lara nodded, too breathless to answer with words. Her parents and her sisters sat anxiously in the waiting room. Lindsey's husband hadn't been able to make it, but would come see the baby as soon as he could. Lara only needed Nick at her side. Since the night at the storage facility, Lara realized his love made her complete in a way that her family, her job, even Jim in the long-ago past hadn't been able to accomplish.

She felt Nick's hand around hers as she gazed at her focal point, their wedding portrait. She wore a beautiful gown she and Kate had discovered in a local boutique. Nick wore a suit, and the couple had purchased matching gold bands. The police chaplain married them in a simple ceremony at a chapel by the sea, with close friends and family witnessing, including T. J. Knox, Nick's new partner. Sadie was there at Lara's side, with Nick's blessing. After the exchanging of the vows, she and Nick lived in the happiness of the moment. Her wedding portrait had captured it all. Lara smiled, gazing up at the photo, until another contraction gripped her. She left the photo and the past and concentrated on the baby in the present.

Nick watched as the baby's head crowned, and he helped the doctor catch his child as it emerged into the light. Seconds later the baby hiccuped and began to cry, then was placed on Lara's belly. Nick touched the new child first, his fingers resting on the child's cheek.

"It's a girl!" Nick gasped with all the amazement of a new father. "She's beautiful."

"Let me have her." Lara had an overwhelming urge to hold her child. Nick lifted the baby and placed her in Lara's arms. The infant immediately stopped crying. Lara kissed her naked daughter, and marveled at the perfection of new life.

"My God, Lara, she's amazing," Nick whispered.

"As soon as we've tidied up and baby's nursed, we'll get your family," the delivery nurse said.

A few minutes later Ed, Kate, Sandra and Lindsey entered the room.

"I'm a grandmother." Sandra squeezed Lara's shoulder. "You did good, sweetie."

"Congratulations," Ed said gruffly.

"She's gorgeous," Lindsey observed.

Kate was so moved she couldn't speak. She leaned forward and kissed Lara's forehead.

"She's a healthy six pounds, six ounces," the nurse cheerfully informed the newcomers.

Lara didn't hear a word. All her attention was for her daughter and husband. She whispered, "Hello, little Molly. It's Mom. And Daddy's here, too." She traced the baby's delicate mouth with a finger. Molly sighed contentedly and snuggled closer to her mother. She settled the baby closer, feeling a bond with Molly she knew would last a lifetime.

She met Nick's gaze, smiled, then closed her eyes.

"You okay?" he asked.

"A little tired," she told him, eyes opening again. "You?"

"My heart was racing there a while ago. I don't know how you did it."

"It was easy with you here," she said honestly. And truly, it had been. She hadn't needed modern technology as much as she'd needed Nick's presence. He'd been the best medicine for her, she realized. But then, she'd known that since the first time she'd met him. Like her strong maternal instincts, Lara's mating instincts had been just as healthy and powerful when she'd first met Nick. She'd trusted herself and trusted him.

*When it comes to important things, I've been so lucky,* she thought.

"You hold her, Nick," Lara said. Nick's hands looked so secure, so tender, so protective as he placed Molly over his shoulder that Lara's motherly side permitted her to pull up the blankets, settle her head deeply into the pillow and close her eyes again.

Despite the presence of her whole family, she immediately fell asleep.

Sandra gently stroked Lara's hair. "She's out cold."

"The baby, too," Lindsey whispered.

"They've had quite a day," Nick agreed.

Kate finally found her voice. "Oh, look! Molly's smiling! We should wake Lara up…."

LARA WAS DREAMING. She and her family had the whole beach beneath the beautiful cliffs of La Jolla to themselves. A German shepherd pup with floppy ears and gangly legs barked at the scurrying crabs. A giggling little girl in blue jean shorts and pink top joined the chase and ran barefoot through the shallows. The pup hesitated, deciding between catching a crab or herding his child away from the water.

A glint of sunlight flashed off the girl's favorite piece of jewelry, a toy sheriff's star pinned lopsidedly to her chest. The glint caught the pup's keen eyes, and he placed himself protectively between the girl and waterline just as the child caught her miniature quarry. She laughed and jumped and crowed her triumph to another of the child's protectors. A man joined the crab inspection. He shared in the child's joy while keeping watch on tiny toes near the prancing pup's clumsy paws, the dark bottle green of the waves' backwash and chubby fingers beneath maroon pinchers.

Lara smiled at father, daughter and puppy, content to watch the trio from her seat on drier sand. She smiled, and leaned into the mature black-and-tan bitch sharing her beach towel. The pair could relax for now. The family was safe and would always remain so. After she'd rested some more, just a little more, she'd get up and join the others. For now, seeing father and daughter and pup together was enough…a happiness she'd never imagined possible.

She thought she heard someone say, "Quick, get the camera! Lara's missing this!"

*Wrong.* Lara felt the warmth of family, two-legged and four, touching every part of her, inside and out. *I haven't missed a thing.*

In her dream, she felt rather than heard Nick's reply.

*That's right, love. We have it all.*

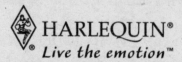

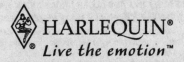

If you enjoyed what you just read,
then we've got an offer you can't resist!

# Take 2 bestselling love stories FREE!

# Plus get a FREE surprise gift!

**Clip this page and mail it to Harlequin Reader Service®**

**IN U.S.A.**
3010 Walden Ave.
P.O. Box 1867
Buffalo, N.Y. 14240-1867

**IN CANADA**
P.O. Box 609
Fort Erie, Ontario
L2A 5X3

**YES!** Please send me 2 free Harlequin Superromance® novels and my free surprise gift. After receiving them, if I don't wish to receive anymore, I can return the shipping statement marked cancel. If I don't cancel, I will receive 6 brand-new novels every month, before they're available in stores. In the U.S.A., bill me at the bargain price of $4.69 plus 25¢ shipping and handling per book and applicable sales tax, if any*. In Canada, bill me at the bargain price of $5.24 plus 25¢ shipping and handling per book and applicable taxes**. That's the complete price, and a savings of at least 10% off the cover prices—what a great deal! I understand that accepting the 2 free books and gift places me under no obligation ever to buy any books. I can always return a shipment and cancel at any time. Even if I never buy another book from Harlequin, the 2 free books and gift are mine to keep forever.

135 HDN DZ7W
336 HDN DZ7X

| Name | (PLEASE PRINT) | |
|------|----------------|--|
| Address | Apt.# | |
| City | State/Prov. | Zip/Postal Code |

*Not valid to current Harlequin Superromance® subscribers.*

*Want to try two free books from another series?*
*Call 1-800-873-8635 or visit www.morefreebooks.com.*

\* Terms and prices subject to change without notice. Sales tax applicable in N.Y.
\*\* Canadian residents will be charged applicable provincial taxes and GST.
All orders subject to approval. Offer limited to one per household.
® are registered trademarks owned and used by the trademark owner and or its licensee.

SUP04R

©2004 Harlequin Enterprises Limited

HARLEQUIN®

AMERICAN *Romance*®

is delighted to bring you four new books
in a miniseries by popular author

# Mary Anne Wilson

RETURN TO
*Silver Creek*

In this small town in the high mountain country of
Nevada, four lucky bachelors find love where they
least expect it. And learn you can go home again.

## DISCOVERING DUNCAN
### On sale April 2005

## JUDGING JOSHUA
### On sale August 2005

*Available wherever*
*Harlequin books are sold.*

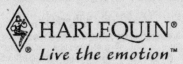

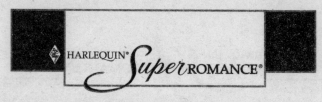

# COMING NEXT MONTH